Mums and Mayhem

Also available by Amanda Flower

Magic Garden Mysteries
Death and Daisies
Flowers and Foul Play

Magical Bookshop Mysteries
Verse and Vengeance
Murders and Metaphors
Prose and Cons
Crime and Poetry

India Hayes Mysteries
Murder in a Basket
Maid of Murder

Appleseed Creek Mysteries
A Plain Malice
A Plain Disappearance
A Plain Scandal
A Plain Death

Andi Boggs Mysteries
Andi Unexpected
Andi Under Pressure
Andi Unstoppable

Living History Museum Mysteries
The Final Vow
The Final Tap
The Final Reveille

Amish Candy Shop Mysteries
Marshmallow Malice
Botched Butterscotch
Toxic Toffee
Premeditated Peppermint
Criminally Cocoa
Lethal Licorice
Assaulted Caramel

Amish Matchmaker Mysteries
Matchmaking Can Be Murder

Piper and Porter Mysteries
Dead End Detective

Mums and
Mayhem

A MAGIC GARDEN
MYSTERY

Amanda Flower

**CROOKED
LANE**

NEW YORK

Published in the United States by Crooked Lane Books, an imprint of The Quick Brown Fox & Company LLC.

Crooked Lane Books and its logo are trademarks of The Quick Brown Fox & Company LLC.

Library of Congress Catalog-in-Publication data available upon request.

ISBN (hardcover): 978-1-64385-298-0
ISBN (ebook): 978-1-64385-319-2

Cover illustration by Ken Joudrey

Printed in the United States.

www.crookedlanebooks.com

Crooked Lane Books
34 West 27th St., 10th Floor
New York, NY 10001

First Edition: July 2020

10 9 8 7 6 5 4 3 2 1

In memory of my mother,
Rev. Pamela Flower, who taught
me the magic of gardens

Where you tend a rose, my lad, a thistle cannot grow.

—Frances Hodgson Burnett, *The Secret Garden*

Chapter One

Magic wasn't something in which I believed. It was for fairy tales and myths. At least that's what I thought until I found out I had inherited a magical garden, part of the estate of Duncreigan on the east coast of Scotland. That's when I learned I'd been wrong about magic, and a good many other things too.

I was walking through the garden, and everything was in bloom. Even though it was November and there was a bite in the air, the garden flourished. Asters and sunflowers pointed their bright faces toward the sun. Chrysanthemums filled up every corner of the garden, and behind the wide hedgerow in the middle of the garden, the menhir, or standing stone, stood with its yellow rose pointed at the sky.

But as I watched in horror, the yellow rose withered and fell to the ground. The garden shriveled up around me. I started to scream.

I jerked up in bed, wide awake. My long black hair covered my eyes, and I pushed it away. My gray-striped Scottish Fold cat, Ivanhoe, sat at the end of my narrow bed and hissed.

My hand was on my chest and my pajamas were soaked with sweat. I flopped back onto my pillow. "It was just a dream. Get a grip, Knox," I whispered to myself. I noted that my native Tennessee accent was a tad more pronounced because I was out of breath.

Ivanhoe walked the length of my body and stared down at me with the same morbid interest he had when spying a mole in the garden. It wasn't that comfortable being on the receiving end of his gaze.

"It was only a dream." This time I said it with far less confidence, because I didn't know that to be true. In May, when I came to Scotland and learned I'd inherited this cottage and magical garden from my late godfather, I'd begun to receive visions that predicted the future or what the future might be. The visions came in the form of dreams or happened when I touched the standing stone in the middle of the garden.

This might be a dream, but I would have to see the garden to be sure. I grabbed my phone from the nightstand. It was five in the morning. Hours before daylight. I groaned. I would have to check the garden in the dark. I had to go; I would never be able to rest until I knew the garden was all right.

I threw my legs over the side of the bed. I shuffled out of my bedroom with Ivanhoe on my heels. The cottage was a tiny building by any American measure. There was my bedroom that was just big enough for a double bed and a wardrobe, a small bathroom, and the main room that served as my living, dining, and kitchen space. Until a few weeks ago,

I had shared the cottage with my younger sister, Isla. She'd graduated from college and, wishing for adventure, followed me to Scotland. She had since moved out of the cottage and into a flat in the village with her new boyfriend. I winced to think of my parents' reaction when they learned of her living arrangement.

I pulled on my puddle boots, then grabbed my winter coat and stocking cap from the hook by the door and put those on too. While I finished donning my winter clothes, Ivanhoe sat expectantly by the door with his gray-striped tail swishing back and forth on the hardwood floor.

I grabbed a large flashlight from the pantry and shook my head. "No, Ivanhoe, you are not coming with me. It's dark and cold out. Stay here in the cottage."

His tail swished faster along the floor, and I could have sworn he understood every word I'd said. It wasn't too much of a stretch to believe it, I supposed. In for an inch and all that. And seeing as how I believed in magic, wasn't anything possible, really? Even a cat that understood English? I opened the front door just a crack large enough for me to slip out, but the cat was too quick for me and raced out the door.

"Ivanhoe, get back into the cottage," I ordered.

He stood a few feet away from me, just out of my reach.

"I mean it," I said.

The cat turned and started in the direction of the garden. He knew where we were headed. It was the only place we went on these walks.

I sighed and stood in the dim porch light for a moment. The cold wind cut through my coat. I almost turned around and went back into the cottage, but I couldn't do that. I would not be able to rest until I saw for myself that the garden was safe. I flicked on the flashlight and could see fifty yards in front of me. The light was bright and glaring, and I focused the beam on Ivanhoe's gray tail. I liked to know where the feline was at all times. The flashlight had been a gift from my boyfriend, Chief Inspector Neil Craig of the County Aberdeen police. At the time, I'd thought it was the most ridiculous flashlight, or torch as he would have called it, I had ever seen. Now, I was happy to have it.

I knew I could call Craig and he would be there as quickly as possible to check the garden for me, but I didn't want to be the type of woman who couldn't take care of her own magical responsibilities. And didn't that sound fanciful? Besides, if something was wrong, I would call Craig. If all was well, it was best not to wake him up; as a police officer, he had so few nights he could sleep through.

I turned up the collar on my coat and made my way over the moor behind the cat. The still-green grass was peppered with smooth boulders that poked just a few inches above the surface. It was important to keep an eye on things as I walked. It would be easy to turn an ankle on one of the smooth rocks or shallow divots beneath my feet.

The walled garden came into view, and the first thing I noticed was the waxy ivy still in place, clinging and all but obstructing the eight-foot wall, creating an impenetrable blanket of green. The heart-shaped leaves shimmered with early-morning dew beneath my light. From outside all seemed well, and I was comforted. Typically the ivy was the first sign something was amiss with the garden; it would lose its leaves and wither. Knowing this, I could have turned back then, but I had come this far, so I figured I should go all the way.

I came up to the place in the wall where I knew the door was from the hundreds of times I had been there before. I slid my hand through the tangle of ivy, found the keyhole, and slipped the old skeleton key inside. The door opened easily, and I went in.

Ivanhoe, who had been patiently waiting at my feet, also went inside.

I let out a breath. The garden was fine. The garden had been fine for the last three hundred years. The asters, sunflowers, and chrysanthemums were all there and in bloom. I stepped deeper into the garden and passed the weeping willow with its branches so long they brushed the ground. I moved around the hedgerow. The yellow rose around the stone bloomed in my flashlight beam. All was well. Why had I thought any different?

At times I didn't know what to expect from the garden, which I had inherited from my godfather, Uncle Ian, after his death seven months ago. He'd told me very little about my magical inheritance. There were only three rules he'd left me in the letter that Hamish, the garden's elderly caretaker, delivered to me after I moved to Scotland when I first learned I was the Keeper:

Rule #1: It's important that you and the garden stay connected.

Rule #2: The garden should be cared for and treated like any other garden.

Rule #3: The menhir and the rose are the heart of the garden and the source of the magic.

I had committed the three rules to memory. I also knew the magic was to be used to help. Each Keeper of the garden over the last three hundred years had been given a gift that he or she was meant to use to help the people of the village of Bellewick, just three miles from Duncreigan. My gift was visions. For other Keepers it had been the ability to heal or tell the future.

The magic had come to be when Uncle Ian's ancestor, Baird MacCallister, made a deal with the sea after his merchant vessel crashed on the craggy rocks near Duncreigan. As he was pitched into the water, he told the sea that if he was allowed to live, he would stay in Scotland and do good works. The sea spat him up near the menhir and its yellow rose.

When I first heard Baird's story, I hadn't believed it. My godfather had never shared the tale with me when he was alive; Hamish told me after Uncle Ian's death. But slowly over the last few months in Scotland, I had experienced the visions and found it all to be true.

I reached out and touched the stone, wondering if I would see my dream again in a vision, but nothing happened. The dream I'd had was a false alarm. The garden was blooming. It was safe. All was well.

I heard whistling behind me just as the sunrise was beginning to come up over the mountain. "We have much work to do today, Duncan. Lots of pruning."

I immediately recognized the voice of Hamish Mac-Gregor. Hamish had been the caretaker of Duncreigan when Uncle Ian's father had been the Keeper of the garden. He came every morning to work in the garden. I didn't know how I could have taken care of it all without him. Hamish helped with the day-to-day work around the garden, but he didn't have access to its magic like I did.

Ivanhoe flattened himself in the grass. He had heard Hamish as well.

"No, Ivanhoe," I said. "Don't even—"

But before I could finish the sentence, the cat took off around the side of the hedgerow. I followed him just in time to see Duncan, Hamish's pet red squirrel, throw his paws in the air and squeal in terror. Duncan leaped from Hamish's shoulder, bolted toward the willow tree, and ran up its trunk before Ivanhoe could reach him.

The gray cat sat at the base of the tree and waited for the squirrel to come back down.

"Miss Fiona!" Hamish said. "You have to do something about that cat!"

I sighed. "I know, Hamish."

Hamish muttered to himself as he got to work, and behind him I saw the fox with the blue eyes so much like my godfather's and my own watching me. Ever since Uncle Ian died, the fox had been a constant presence in the garden. Presha Kapoor, my friend from the village, had told me once that the fox was Uncle Ian come back in another form. I wanted to believe that, if only for the comfort it brought me to know Uncle Ian was looking out for the garden and for me. If anyone knew the secrets of the garden, it was him. I inched toward the fox. "Do you know if my dream means anything?" The fox bowed his head, and I felt my unease return.

I pushed back the anxiety rising within me. My nightmare hadn't been a vision of what was to come. It had just been a dream inspired by lack of sleep and worry over the busy days ahead. That's what I told myself as I walked back to the cottage. That's what I chose to believe.

Chapter Two

"The Merchant Society of Bellewick needs to stick together on this." Bernice Brennan's cheeks flushed pink as she spoke. She tapped her pencil eraser onto her clipboard in an erratic rhythm. She stood in front of a large stage that was in process of being built in the middle of the main road leading into the village of Bellewick, Scotland. I'd called Bellewick home for the last six months following a series of strange events, including a bad breakup, a sad passing, and the inheritance of my magical garden. Sounds like the beginning of a fairytale, doesn't it? If I was living in the fairy tale, I hadn't come to the happily-ever-after part yet. Also, I didn't remember any once-upon-a-time tales featuring committee meetings. Certainly they would ruin the story. Committee meetings ruined everything, in my opinion.

As Bernice went over the details of the concert for what felt like the hundred and fifteenth time, I found myself only half listening. I was still preoccupied with the terrible dream about my garden from the night before, or, more accurately, very early that morning. Even though I'd verified that the garden was fine, I couldn't shake an eerie feeling that seemed to hover just above my head.

Doing my best to look like I was paying the utmost attention, I watched the men and women working on the stage. It was like watching black ants build a fortress. All the members of the crew moved in sync. They knew what they were doing, how to do it, and the order it should all happen in, like they had done it thousands of times before. I suspected they had. In Scotland and much of the UK and Europe, Barley McFee was a household name, so of course he would have his own professional stage crew for all his concerts, even a concert held in the tiny village of Bellewick.

As much as I might dislike meetings and committees, when Bernice asked me to join the Merchant Society of Bellewick, I had jumped at the chance. It was the right business move. I had just opened my new flower shop, the Climbing Rose, in the village, and was hungry for an opportunity to become involved in the community. I wanted to be known for something other than being the "American woman living at Duncreigan." I knew I would never be able to drop the "American woman" moniker, especially with my Nashville drawl, not a common accent in these parts or on the entire island of Great Britain. At the very least, I would be known as the "American woman with the flower shop," and maybe, just maybe, that title would lead to a sale or two. I would take what I could get.

However, I'd agreed to join before I knew how much work the Merchant Society would be. It was also before Bernice had the idea to throw the biggest event the village had seen in its four- hundred-year history. It was Barley McFee's Coming Home Concert. Barley was a world-class fiddler who traveled all over the globe to play sold-out stadiums, and he was coming here to Bellewick, with its fewer than two thousand residents, to play a concert in his home village.

The Merchant Society had spent months preparing for the concert. Bernice, who was a jeweler and owned the local jewelry shop, looked at the concert in the same way she looked at the diamonds and gems in her store. She would accept nothing less than perfection, and if she drove everyone in the village mad trying to reach perfection, that was just the breaks.

I would have been more enthused to help if I'd had more time to devote to final preparations. The day of the concert was going to be incredibly busy for me, as I would be handling all the flowers and my parents would be arriving in Scotland from the States soon. Usually I would look forward to such a visit with excitement, but some facts about my birth had recently come to light. During the summer, I'd discovered a box in my godfather's wardrobe that held photographs and letters hinting that I was Uncle Ian's biological daughter. Right after the discovery, my mother had confirmed that he was my father in a brief phone call, but ever since she had been reluctant to speak of it. I still didn't know how Stephen Knox, the man I had known my entire life as my father, was listed on my birth certificate as my father and Uncle Ian was not. I needed answers, but I wasn't sure my taciturn parents would be willing to give them to me.

Also, if it had been a tad warmer, that would have been a help, too. I knew the concert had to be fit into the musician's schedule, but was it really a good idea to have a fiddle concert outside, in Scotland, in November? The threat of rain was always heavy in the air this time of year, and then there was even the chance of a late-autumn storm rolling over the little coastal village. No one wanted to be outside in a storm like that.

I shivered and burrowed down in my winter coat a little bit more. I was the only member of the Merchant Society wearing a heavy coat. The rest of them were perfectly comfortable in cardigans and light jackets.

Presha Kapoor, my closest friend in the village, a sixty-something Indian woman, was wrapped in a shawl. Being from India, she should have been as cold as I was, but after forty years in Bellewick, her body must have adjusted to the cold. As of yet, mine hadn't. My thin Tennessee blood wasn't up for the chill in the air. I wore jeans, calf-high boots, a flannel shirt, and a winter coat, and I was still cold. I wished I had thought to wear a winter hat, too. Early November in Scotland was like the middle of January in Nashville.

"Fiona! Fiona Knox, are you paying attention? What is happening with the flowers?" Bernice shoved her glasses onto the top of her head, and her short hair sprang up in all directions. I didn't know her well, but I would say the woman was close to the end of her rope. She might have thought hosting this concert was a grand idea four months ago when planning began, but with it less than twenty-four hours away, she was questioning that judgment.

Presha elbowed me in the ribs.

"Oh yes, the flowers," I said, and pulled my gaze away from the black-clad crew on the stage. "We're all set. The chrysanthemums are being delivered today, and we'll have them in place later this afternoon. They will be at their very best for the concert."

Bernice pressed her lips together, as if she wanted to catch me in some kind of mistake but couldn't think of what it might be. And then she sneezed. Bernice was horribly allergic to flowers, and mere talk of them could make her break out in hives. Which, I supposed, raised the question, why have flowers in the first place? I was very thankful her allergies didn't dictate her decisions where the village was concerned.

"If you ask me," Ferris Brown, a bait shop and fishing boat owner from the harbor, said, "I can't tell you why Barley McFee would want to come back to Bellewick for this concert." Ferris was in his seventies and had a long silver handlebar moustache, and his eyes were permanently in a squint from his time under the sun on the sea. "I do think it's smashing good luck that he's coming here, but I, for one, will be happy when this is over and I can work on the manor." His eyes lit up as he said this.

"Yes, yes," Bernice said, irritation in her voice. "We all know that you bought a manor house, but we must focus on the project at hand."

Ferris's face fell. Presha, ever compassionate, patted his arm.

Bernice tapped her pen on her clipboard. "It's Barley's homecoming concert. Where else would he have it other

than the village he grew up in? We must make a good showing of it. That means we can't let our minds wander to other
things."

Ferris smoothed his moustache; it was a practiced habit
and reminded me of someone lightly stroking a cat. "That
may be, but he would have found much more success if he
held the concert in the capital of County Aberdeen in Aberdeen City. He still could have called it a Coming Home
Concert, since he was returning to his own county."

Aberdeen was the county seat of Aberdeenshire on the
northeast coast of Scotland. A far more populated place than
my new home.

"It is no matter that Barley could have a bigger audience
in Aberdeen," Raj Kapoor, Presha's twin brother, said. The
pair of them had immigrated to Scotland together and created successful businesses in Bellewick. Presha owned the
local tea house, Presha's Teas, where she served the spiciest
chai I had ever tasted, and Raj had two businesses in the
village, the local laundromat and the pub, the Twisted Fox.
The pub was the most popular establishment in the village,
which was one reason I was grateful I'd been able to buy the
shop space right next to it for my flower shop. I knew my
close proximity to the Twisted Fox raised my profile in the
village. And it sure did guarantee plentiful foot traffic. Even
if the patrons of the Twisted Fox weren't buying while they
enjoyed their fish and chips and pints, they were seeing my
flowers artfully arranged. Many a resident had popped in
after or on their way to dinner to purchase flowers for special
occasions.

"The concert will be here," Raj went on. "And we will do our very best to accommodate it. I know it's a lot of work, but we must finish strong. We have come this far. In two days' time, the concert will be over, and we will return to our everyday lives. We should enjoy this brief moment of excitement in our sleepy little village." Raj always found the silver lining.

Bernice nodded. "Thank you, Raj. Now, the food trucks will be arriving this afternoon to set up."

Raj nodded. "Yes, everything will be ready. The food trucks will be here in a few hours, and the Twisted Fox will have a stand at the concert as well, selling ale and beer. Nothing too hard. If they want whiskey and the like, they can walk to the pub."

Bernice made a check mark on her clipboard. "Very good. Now . . ."

She was going to say more, but a black SUV limousine rolled up to the village's arched stone gate and stopped. It couldn't go any farther. Behind the SUV was a tour bus that said *Barley McFee* in bold letters on the side, next to an enlarged image of a redheaded, bearded man holding a fiddle under his chin and tapping his foot.

It was the kind of tour van I'd been accustomed to seeing in Nashville. A country-music star proved they'd hit the big time when they put their face on the side of a bus. Until then, no one in Nashville took them seriously.

Bernice looked at her watch and yelped, "He's early! He wasn't supposed to be here for another two hours. I'm not ready." She looked down at her plaid shirt and jeans. "I'm not dressed! I had another outfit picked out!"

"Bernice, calm yourself," Presha whispered. "The concert is not until tomorrow afternoon. Everything is ready for Barley at the guesthouse." She glanced at Eugenia Wilson, the owner of the village's only guesthouse, who nodded. Presha smiled. "See? He can go there and rest or practice. We can finish what we need to do. Now, pull yourself together if you would like to make a good impression."

Bernice looked as if she wanted to argue with Presha—which made me think that other outfit must have been something—but before she could, the driver climbed out of the SUV limo, walked to the back passenger side door, and opened it. A redheaded man got out, and judging from the larger-than-life wrap on the side of the tour bus, it was Barley McFee.

Two things I noticed about Barley right away. One, he was much older than the figure on the side of the bus. Like two decades older. Wrinkles fanned his eyes and mouth, and gray streaks threaded through his red hair. The photo made him appear to be in his forties, but I could see now that he was much closer to sixty, perhaps on the other side of it. Two, I knew we weren't in Ireland, but I swore the fiddler looked like a leprechaun. He had a full head of red-gray hair and a full beard, and he wasn't much over five feet tall. The picture on the side of the bus had given no indication of his small stature.

Bernice removed her glasses from the top of her head and patted at her hair. It wasn't much use. She had a curly bob cut, and it was sticking up every which way because she had been pulling on it for the better part of the morning. She shoved the glasses in the pocket of her coat and hurried over to Barley. "Mr. McFee, we are so happy you are here."

Barley smiled, and his straight white teeth glistened in the sun. He could have been a poster child for a toothpaste commercial. "I'm happy to be here. Can't say I have seen much of Bellewick yet because my stage is blocking the entrance into the village, but from where I stand here, very little has changed." He grinned from ear to ear. "It's surreal to be back, but I'm happy that I am." He held out his hand. "And you are?"

Bernice wiped her hand on her coat and shook his. "I'm so sorry, Mr. McFee. I'm Bernice Brennan. I'm the chairperson of the Merchant Society of Bellewick, and I have been working with your manager to put on this great event."

"Please call me Barley. I don't stand on pomp and circumstance. Is Owen Masters here?"

"Your manager?" Her brow went up. "No, I have only spoken to him on the phone. I believe he plans to be here this afternoon. That's when we had expected you as well . . ."

He grinned. "I like to keep the world guessing as to when I will show up. It makes everything much more exciting, doesn't it?"

Bernice didn't look the least bit excited about it.

"I would have thought he would make a point of arriving before me to make sure everything was ready." Barley's grin dimmed just a little, and then he shook his head. "I will catch up with him later, and I'm sure that everything will be positively lovely for the concert. I know how impressed Owen has been with your group of volunteers."

Bernice preened under his praise. I shared a smile with Presha, and Ferris cleared his throat loudly.

"Oh!" Bernice straightened quickly, as if the noise had brought her back to reality. "Barley, these are the other members of the Merchant Society. We have Ferris Brown, Presha Kapoor and her brother Raj Kapoor, Eugenia Wilson—you will be staying at her guesthouse—and Fiona Knox."

Barley shook all our hands in turn. When he shook my hand, he said, "Fiona, aye?" He still held on to my hand. "That's a very pretty name."

"Thank you. It's nice to meet you, Barley," I said.

He arched his brow. "You aren't from Bellewick. I can tell you that. Do I hear a Tennessee drawl in your voice?"

I raised my eyebrow, surprised. Because of television, most Scots could tell I was from the American South by my accent, but none of them had pinpointed it to my home state. "I'm from Nashville."

He nodded. "Thought so. Music City. I love that place and recorded my last two albums at RCA Studio A. If you want to make music, Nashville is the place to be. Are you musical, then?"

I shook my head. "Not at all. I run the flower shop here in the village."

"But I'm sure you know people in the music industry."

My wannabe-country-star ex-finance's face came unheeded to my mind. "I know a few," I said.

"Fiona lives at Duncreigan. You remember the MacCallister family, don't you?" Ferris asked.

"'Course I do." He studied me with interest. "Are you a MacCallister, then? None but MacCallisters have ever lived at Duncreigan."

"No," I said, thinking at least I wasn't in name. I wasn't going to explain my complicated family tree to a man I had just met when I had yet to tell my sister. "Ian MacCallister was my godfather."

He squeezed my hand hard and then let it go. "That makes more sense. I didn't think Ian had any children to claim."

To claim? His phrasing struck me as odd. "You knew my godfather?" I asked, looking at him with interest.

"Ian and I were old school chums. I was very sorry when I heard that he passed on. He was a good man and a damn good soldier in our Queen's army. It was a loss for Bellewick and for the entire United Kingdom." He studied me a little more closely. "The last name is Knox, is it? I remember Ian running around with a young man named Stephen Knox when we were in school."

"That's my father," I said. "Do you know him too?"

"I—" Barley started to speak, but then shook his head. "No," he said. "Only the name."

I wanted to ask him more, but Presha piped in, "Fiona's parents are on their way to Scotland right now." She glanced at the gold watch on her slender wrist. "They should be landing soon. Maybe you and Stephen can meet and swap stories about Ian."

Barley's eyes cut in her direction. "I don't think that's a good idea."

I opened my mouth and wanted to ask him what he meant by that, but the door to the van opened.

"My band is here," Barley said, and walked away. Bernice and the rest of the Merchant Society walked after him. All of them except Presha, that is, who stayed back with me.

"Did you find his reaction to my father's name odd?" I asked.

"So odd. There is something going on there, Fiona," Presha whispered back.

"That's what I thought too." I frowned.

Presha patted my arm. "Do not worry yourself over it. Whatever history he had with your father is long over." She went to catch up with the group, and I followed.

I wished the past had indeed been put to bed, but I was soon to learn it had not.

Chapter Three

Two men and one woman stepped out of the trailer. They all were dressed in jeans and graphic T-shirts under denim jackets. Both men were tall and dark-haired with matching dark beards. They looked if they could be brothers, and the woman had beautiful dark skin. Her hair was pulled back from her face in intricate braids that went from black at the roots to red to orange at the ends. It gave the effect that her hair was on fire. It must make quite an impression under the bright stage lights.

"Ah," Barley said. "My band has surfaced. I hope they got some sleep while on the road from London. That was our last concert stop. It's a long drive." He smiled at me. "But nothing like driving from tour spots in the U.S. Once I had a concert in Detroit and then one in Dallas two days later. I thought we would never get there. Since then, I fly whenever I'm in your country and let the band and crew deal with life on the road. I'm too old for road life now." He laughed at his own joke.

"You didn't ride with them?" Presha asked.

"Goodness, no." Barley laughed. "I have far too many other engagements that I must keep. I flew in this morning. Private. I only fly private anymore."

I supposed that explained why Barley had arrived by limo and the rest of the band was on the tour bus. It was interesting that they still seemed to have arrived in Bellewick at the exact same time. I wondered how the band felt about Barley flying private alone when they had to ride for hours in the giant bus.

"Let me confer with my band, and then we can chat more. I'm sure there are things you want to go over with me about the show tomorrow. I think this homecoming concert is going to be everything that the fans have been wanting."

Bernice nodded. "Take all the time you need."

Barley smoothed the sleeve of his jacket and flashed his winning smile before heading in the direction of the band.

"Do you have any idea what I had to put up with?" the woman with the braids yelled in a Scottish accent. "Ten hours in that bus with those two." She pointed at her band-mates. "I shouldn't be riding with them. I should have flown with you. You were making a point by having me ride in the bus. Point made. You'd better have a plane ticket for me on the way back."

Barley held up his hand. "Kenda, don't make a scene."

"I'll make all the scenes I want! You don't know what you have put me through by making me ride up with these two. The entire bus smelled like old gym socks and micro-wave meals. I almost threw up from the stench."

"But you didn't throw up," Barley said soothingly.

"I almost did. I can't believe you did this to me after everything I have done for you."

Barley tried to wrap his arm around Kenda's shoulder, but she shrugged him away before stomping back toward the bus. Barley followed her. "Kenda!"

She gave him a crude hand gesture in reply.

"She doesn't look happy," Presha said.

I shook my head. "No, she doesn't." I glanced at the others. "Does anyone know the band members' names?"

Bernice pressed her lips together. "The band has been together for close to ten years now. The two brothers are Jamie and Lester MacNish. They play guitar and bass, respectively. The woman is Kenda Bay. I have heard that she and Barley were an item for some time. Kenda plays backup fiddle."

"So she is his second fiddle?" Ferris asked, laughing at his own joke.

I raised my eyebrows. Barley had to be thirty years older than Kenda. Lots of older men dated younger woman, especially, it seemed, when it came to celebrities of Barley's level. "Are they still together?" I asked. I couldn't help it. My curiosity always got the better of me.

"Doesn't look like it," Raj said.

We looked on while Kenda waved her arms and shook her fists at Barley.

"He's got a fiery one on his hands," Ferris said.

Bernice, Presha, and I all gave him a look.

He grunted. "You womenfolk are too sensitive anymore."

"And you should know better and speak with more respect," Presha said.

Ferris dropped his eyes. Had anyone else said that to the old sailor, he might have said something rude in return, but Presha had the ability to speak with authority in a way that let others know they'd met their match. I wished I was more like her.

The MacNish brothers stood a little ways away with pained expressions on their faces. They didn't move a muscle. They appeared to be frozen in place by Barley and Kenda's very volatile argument.

We couldn't seem to look away from the dispute between Barley and Kenda as it unfolded in front of us. Barley tried to hug Kenda, but she pushed him away. He said something that we couldn't hear as Kenda slammed the bus door behind her. Shaking his head, Barley strolled back to us like he didn't have a care in the world. The five of us from the Merchant Society looked at the stage like we hadn't been openly gawking at the drama.

"It seems that we are having some issues with the music set," Barley said as he rejoined us. His face was still flushed from his argument with Kenda, which belied his calm. "Could you show us where we will be staying tonight? The band needs to meet and pick out music. Not everyone is happy with the choices. Could you show us the setup here later this evening?"

"Yes, of course," Bernice said. "Eugenia?" She smiled at the guesthouse owner, who smiled back with a nod.

"Eugenia will be able to host everyone from the band and your manager, Owen. You will find the guesthouse as nice as any place in Edinburgh," Presha said.

"The rooms are all ready for you," Eugenia said. "I am so honored that you will be staying in Thistle House the next two nights. It's quite an honor to have Barley McFee in my guesthouse. I told my family in Edinburgh, and they thought I was telling a tale."

Barley laughed. "Well, I am happy to help you impress your family. I'm always happy to help any way that I can."

"That young woman seemed to disagree," Ferris said.

Bernice looked like she wanted to wring Ferris's neck when he said that, but Barley simply laughed. "Kenda is one of those emotional young artists. Everything is the end of the world. Please don't worry about her. We are all professionals. Even though some of us can be more hot-headed than the rest, we will be on the stage on time and ready to play tomorrow. I never keep my audience waiting, and I don't plan to start now. It's rude, and the musicians who do that, in my opinion, are only trying to make a point that their time is more precious than the people in the audience. Nothing could be further from the truth. The musician is the least important person there because he would not exist if there weren't people in the audience to support him. It's what I want to teach all the young people in my band."

Ferris opened his mouth like he was going to make another comment on this. Bernice wasn't about to let that happen, and she jumped in. "I know you and the band need to practice and rest. I can also meet with your manager when he arrives to go over the stage setup, if that would be easier for you."

Barley looked over his shoulder. "That might be best, and if you could show the bus driver where to park within walking distance of the stage? I like to sit in the quiet of my trailer between sets."

"Not a problem," Bernice said quickly. She looked at the rest of us. "I think we all know what we should be doing. Let's get to work."

The group agreed with Bernice's plan, and it was clear that we were all more than a little relieved that we were being released early. I thought Barley arriving early and saving me from the rest of the meeting was just grand, as my Scottish friends would have said.

Bernice led Barley away in the direction of the village, and I watched them go. He looked over his shoulder back at the trailer with concern on his face. Perhaps he wasn't feeling as relaxed at Kenda's outburst as he would have us believe.

After the meeting broke up, I headed back into the village. As I walked, I passed the laundromat, the small Tesco, and a few other shops. Beyond those I could see the round sign with the fox face on it marking the location of the Twisted Fox, and beyond that was the cheerful yellow awning over the front windows of the Climbing Rose. Anytime I saw that awning, my spirits lifted. The awning had been an extra expense when I bought the building and renovated it to be my flower shop, but a much needed one. The shop faced south, and when the sun was bright, the entire shop filled with light. The awning broke up some of that light and saved the flowers in the front windows from being wilted in the sun's rays. Also, it was a beacon for my shop. There were no other bright-yellow awnings in the village, perhaps in all of Aberdeenshire.

I hadn't even opened the front door to the shop before my younger sister, Isla, popped out of it like a child at a birthday party yelling *Surprise!*

I jumped back. "Isla, you almost hit me with the door."

"Oh, I'm sorry. I wouldn't want to do that. I need your help," she shouted.

If calm Presha had looked so panicked in front of me, I would have had reason to worry. However, with Isla, it was different. Isla had the tendency to be dramatic, and she would play a part even if I was the only person in the audience.

"What's wrong?" I asked in my most measured voice.

"The mums are here! The mums are here!" She shouted with the same gusto Paul Revere had used to warn of the arrival of the Redcoats during the American Revolution.

"That's nothing to be panicked about," I said. "That's great news. We need to set them up. Did they deliver them to the store?" I thought maybe that was her reason for being so upset. It would upset me, too, because it would not be fun to haul sixty-some ten-inch pots of mums down the cobblestone streets of Bellewick.

She sighed. "No, they said they parked by the tour bus. I didn't have the foggiest idea what they were talking about. What tour bus?"

"It's Barley McFee's bus," I said.

"He's here?" she asked, and jumped up and down.

"What on earth has gotten into you?"

"I'm excited that Barley is here. I have been waiting forever for him to arrive." She stopped jumping.

"Isla, you grew up in Nashville. You saw famous people walking down the street all the time. You don't even listen to Scottish music."

"Shh!" she cried, and looked around. "Don't say that so loud."

I wrinkled my brow.

"Seth loves Barley McFee. Like he's a real superfan, and since Seth is my love, I must love Barley too. We love all the same things." She sighed happily.

"I know you two have a lot in common, but does it really count when you *make* yourself like something that he likes? You don't listen to Barley McFee."

"Shh! I do. Seth has played me some stuff, and I really got into it." She hugged herself.

"Okay," I said. "Name me one Barley McFee song."

"Do instrumental songs even have titles?" she asked dubiously.

"Yes," I said. "If you are going to be one of his number-one fans, you might want to know his songs."

She sniffed. "I don't see why. I absorb the music. I like what I like and I know what I like." She grinned. "Or in this case, I know what Seth likes. Same difference."

I sighed. "Let's just work on placing the mums, okay?"

Isla locked up the flower shop, and we walked back to where the stage was being set up at the end of the cobblestone road. There was a white delivery truck there from Aberdeen by the tour bus as promised. It must have arrived the moment I left the area. The driver unloaded the mums on the green space along the small creek that circled the edge of the village like a natural moat.

I thanked the driver, and Isla and I helped him unload the truck. As the last mums were removed, he closed the back of his truck with a clatter. "Wish I could come to the concert tomorrow. It's quite a thing to have Barley McFee back in Aberdeenshire to play a concert."

I raised my brow. "Why's that?"

He ran his hand under his bulbous nose. "You don't know the old tale? I thought everyone in the county knew, but then again, I can tell by your voice that you're a Yank. That explains why you wouldn't know."

I wrinkled my brow. "Wouldn't know what?"

"That Barley swore he would never return to County Aberdeen after he left some thirty year ago."

I blinked at him. "Really?"

"Oh yes, it was all over the county papers, and a lot of people said they wouldn't listen to his music because of what he said." He shrugged. "But a lot of time has passed. People forget the vows they make. Memories are short." He sighed as if this was a great failing of the world. He slapped the side of his truck. "Well, good luck to you. I think you are going to need it for this concert."

Chapter Four

Before I could ask him what he meant by that, Isla strolled over to me. "We have to place *all* these mums. There must be fifty."

"Actually, there should be sixty-four," I said.

The driver climbed into the cabin of his delivery truck, and I placed my hand on Isla's shoulder, pulling her away from the vehicle.

She shrugged off my hand. "I'm not a child, Fi. I can see the truck. I swear you still treat me like an eight-year-old at times."

I frowned. I supposed I did, and it was something I'd promised myself I would work on. Isla was eight years my junior, and I had spent most of my life watching over her. It was hard to change gears after twenty-some years of big-sister protectiveness.

"Let me grab the wheelbarrow. That will make this job faster," I said.

I had thought ahead and asked for the village ground-skeeper to lend the Merchant Society a wheelbarrow so we could move the mums easily around the concert area. I asked

Isla to count them to make sure they were all there and went in search of the wheelbarrow.

I found it right where I'd asked the groundskeeper to leave it behind the stage.

"You said we wouldn't have to deal with him anymore," a voice hissed on the stage. The voice was so hushed that I couldn't tell if it was male or female.

I looked around and didn't see anyone there.

"You're being ridiculous," a male voice returned. "I can't just walk away from Barley. He gave me my career."

I lifted the handles of the wheelbarrow and froze. I knew I shouldn't be listening to this conversation, but the nosy side of me, which was a very powerful side, could not be tamed. I listened harder.

"Barley, Barley, Barley. He's all I've heard about for the last ten years from everyone, including himself. When will it be my time? I've worked hard, and I play just as well as he does—if not better. He's trying to stifle me, and you are his accomplice in that." The voice went up an octave when it said that, making me believe the first speaker was a woman.

"Please. You need to think of what will become of you if you act too rashly. Barley has a lot of power in this industry. Look what he did—"

"I don't care what he did to someone else. I only care about me."

The male voice mumbled a response I couldn't quite make out.

"I deserve this, Owen," the woman said. "And I'm going to get it. Mark my words."

The voices faded away after that. Frowning, I rolled the wheelbarrow back to my sister.

"Sixty-four," Isla said. "It took me forever to count them. I hate math."

"Thank you," I said, still distracted by the conversation I had overheard behind the stage. "Just place the pots wherever you think they will be out of the way of foot traffic and most enjoyed."

"You're not going to tell me exactly where they should go? That's not normal Fi micromanaging."

"I'm turning over a new leaf." I smiled at her. "You're a college graduate now, right? You will know what to do."

She grinned and filled the wheelbarrow with plants. We both set to work.

A half hour later, Isla's lovely heart-shaped face was flushed from exertion as she pushed the wheelbarrow back toward me. "We had better make this quick. Mom and Dad are going to arrive at Duncreigan anytime now."

I groaned. "Don't remind me."

She grinned at me. "You aren't looking forward to their visit?"

"I want to see them. I miss them, but . . ." I didn't say anything more, because then I would have had to tell Isla the story of my birth. I wasn't ready to do that without talking to our parents first.

"I'm excited for them to meet Seth." She dropped the handlebars of the wheelbarrow, and it hit the ground with a thud. "I know they will love him!"

I wasn't so sure about that. Our mother was a hopeless romantic and did want both of her girls happily married—me especially, since I was over thirty—but I didn't think she'd be enthused about Isla's relationship with Seth because he was Scottish. Of course, our father was Scottish, but he had been willing to move to America and work on my mother's family farm for the rest of his life. I couldn't see Seth doing that or leaving Scotland. Having both of their daughters overseas would be tough for my parents. Our mother wanted one or both of us to take over the family farm. Unfortunately, neither of us wanted that life. I knew my mother would do her best while she was here to try to convince one or both of us to move back home.

I knew I wasn't going anywhere, not after I'd inherited Duncreigan from my godfather. Uncle Ian. My dad and Uncle Ian had been best friends at boarding school and then at university as well. What I hadn't known, until a few months back, was that the old friends had been in love with the same woman, my mother. Nor had I known Uncle Ian was my biological father until I found evidence in the cottage in my godfather's wardrobe. My mother later confirmed my suspicions over the phone. That call, which had taken place months ago, was the last time we'd spoken of my birth. It was a conversation Mom deftly avoided anytime I tried to bring it up. I knew my parents were busy, and my mother didn't have much time for chitchat while running the farm, but it still hurt that she didn't want to talk about what had happened when I was born or tell me why she'd left for the

United States with my father instead of staying with my godfather/biological father in Scotland.

What made it even odder was that two weeks ago, Mom and Dad had called Isla and me and said they were coming to Scotland for a short visit, which was out of character for them. It was autumn and the height of harvest season. It wasn't the usual time my parents would be willing to leave home. I hoped that during this visit I would get some answers. In fact, I didn't plan to let them leave until they answered some of my questions.

I set the mum I was holding on a wooden plant stand by the stage. I filled the stand to the brim and stepped back, admiring my work. The mums were the easiest way to decorate for the concert. They would be vibrant throughout the event, and then the village could split them up afterward to plant in their front gardens. Hearty plants, with a good tolerance for colder weather, they would come back year after year. I planned to plant a few at Duncreigan as well.

Isla pointed at the last few mums at our feet. "Where else would you like these?"

Before I could answer her, Kenda Bay stomped out onto the stage. "I won't stand for this. I have put up with too much! Gave up too many opportunities for Barley and for his tours. I deserve my shot."

A tall man in a button-down shirt and dress pants followed her onto the stage. "Kenda, I wish you would listen to reason. It's just a few more weeks. I'm begging you to be patient for a little while longer, please."

"Patient? You want me to be patient? Haven't I proved that over the last decade? I've given up my dreams for him!"

"I don't think you should look at it that way," the man said with a slight whine in his voice. "You have traveled the world and played in grand concerts as part of the band."

She spun around and marched toward him. Then she jabbed her long red nail into his chest. The man winced.

"You promised me, Owen," she said. "You said Barley was going to give me a shot. You said *and* he said that I would co-headline at this homecoming concert, and everything just has his name on it! He lied to me. *You* lied to me."

Owen? This must be Barley's manager, and Kenda and Owen must also be the two people I'd heard fighting behind the stage earlier. The woman in that conversation had called the man Owen.

"Barley wants to give you that chance, but he believes this Coming Home Concert isn't the right place. I think he's right. You aren't from this village. You aren't even from Aberdeenshire. It would not make sense for you to co-headline here. We'll find another concert, something bigger where you can have even more exposure."

"So it was his decision to cut me out of it. I knew it! That snake. He's so selfish. I could just kill him!"

Isla and I stood there, dumbly holding potted mums in our hands.

"What are you looking at?" Kenda shouted at us.

I jumped. "We're just putting flowers out for the concert."

Kenda glared at each of us in turn. "This place is so *provincial*." She ran off the stage.

"You would think *provincial* was a swear word by the way she said it," Isla whispered out the side of her mouth.

"Maybe it is to her," I whispered back.

Owen removed a white handkerchief from the pocket of his charcoal trousers.

"I should apologize for that," Owen said. "The flowers look lovely." He then ran after Kenda.

Isla and I shared a look.

"Who even carries handkerchiefs anymore? Is it 1930?" Isla asked.

It was a fair question.

"What was that about?" my sister whispered.

I shook my head. "None of our business."

"Since when are other people's problems none of your business, big sis? You make a point of poking your nose in everything."

"Consider my nose unpoked. I can't take on any more stress, with our parents coming to town and with this concert. I can't wait for it to be over. I think Bernice is at a real risk of collapsing from the stress."

"I wouldn't tell her about what we just witnessed, then." She set her pot on the corner of the stage.

"I don't plan to. Now, let's finish up here, so we can beat Mom and Dad to Duncreigan."

She nodded, picked up the handles of the wheelbarrow, and walked it to the other end of the stage. I put the argument we'd witnessed out of my mind. Little did I know it would come back to me sooner than I would have liked.

Chapter Five

"My land! Duncreigan hasn't changed one bit," my mother declared as she opened the door to her and my dad's rental car in front of my little cottage.

Isla gripped my hand tightly as our parents climbed out of the rental SUV they had picked up at the Edinburgh airport. It was the biggest SUV I'd ever seen. I guessed that was my father's doing. He was Scottish by birth, but when he moved to Nashville to marry my mother over thirty years ago, he'd immediately adopted the American habit of giant cars. He said it was something he needed as a farmer. I didn't know why he would need it for his two weeks in Scotland, but that was the least of my worries upon their arrival.

Educated in British prep schools and then at St. Andrews for university, I wondered if my father ever thought that one day all that fancy education would lend itself to being a farmer. He was a good farmer. Since my father had taken the helm of my mother's family farm, it had grown by leaps and bounds, and it pained my dad to leave it. When it was planting or harvest time, Isla and I knew to leave our father alone, as he stressed over getting the seeds in during the spring and getting the crops out during the fall, which again made me wonder why they were here and why now.

I'd moved to Scotland to accept my inheritance of a cottage and garden in Aberdeenshire. I hoped that during their visit we would have a chance to sit down and talk about what had happened with Uncle Ian before I was born. But how could I ask my parents, "Why did you lie to me for the last thirty-some years, and why did Uncle Ian go along with it?"

In general, my family wasn't open with their emotions. Except for Isla, of course; she felt everything and said everything she felt. Everything was the best day ever or the pit of despair. There was no middle ground with her. Sometimes I wished I was more like her. However, I was more measured in my emotions, much like our mother.

Isla rushed forward. "Mama, Daddy! I'm so glad you're here. Fi and I have been looking forward to your visit so much!"

I was glad my parents were distracted by my sister, so they couldn't see my face when she said that. Not that I didn't want to see my parents; I did, very much. Seeing them stand there made me realize how much I'd missed them. Before I moved to Scotland, I had seen my parents once a week, even though I lived in downtown Nashville and they lived an hour outside the city on the farm. Every Sunday, I would go back to the farm for Sunday dinner. The four of us and sometimes my good-for-nothing fiancé would sit down for a home-cooked meal made by my mother's hand, which meant everything was dripping in butter and half of it was deep-fried. It was delicious.

But now that Isla and I were in Scotland, I wondered what my parents' Sunday dinners were like. Did they sit down at all? The idea of that tradition dying away made me sad.

Isla squeezed our father tight and then let go. "I can't wait to show you Fi's flower shop. It's so pretty, and I want you to meet my—"

I stepped forward and hugged them too. I made it just in time to stop Isla from telling our parents about her boyfriend Seth, a medical school dropout with a gambling problem. Seth MacGregor was working on the gambling problem; going back to school . . . not so much. He'd gotten a job as a janitor at the school in the village. It was a good job with reliable hours, but I knew it wouldn't be the kind of career my parents would want their youngest daughter's significant other to have.

My mother hugged me, and she smelled just like the farm, even after traveling across the ocean. I thought the smell of the open field, fresh-baked bread, and drying hay must have been infused into her very pores. There was no other explanation for why the smell would still be on her.

"It's good to see you," I said, and was surprised when tears pricked the back of my eyes. Anytime I spoke to my mother on phone and brought up Uncle Ian, she deftly changed the subject. It was to the point I had stopped calling and answering calls because I was so hurt that she wouldn't talk to me about him. Now they were here. I wished I knew why.

"Let's go in the cottage," I said. "I made some tea, and my friend Presha sent over some of her world-famous scones."

"Oh my, yes," my father said. "As desperately as the Americans try, you cannot find a well-made scone back in the States. There must be something in the British air to make them just right."

"These will knock your socks off, then," I said.

My parents stepped into the cottage, and I bit my lip as they looked around. In the months I had lived there, I had made some changes. I'd given away some of Uncle Ian's things I didn't need, filled the room with flowers, and bought my own living room furniture in Aberdeen that was more my style. It was less bulky than the large leather pieces he'd had. My selections made the tiny space feel twice as big. However, some things were still the same. Baird MacCallister's painting still hung over the mantel, and my godfather's medals remained on display.

"The cottage is as charming as ever," my mother said. "I can't remember the last time we were here. Can you, Stephen?"

My father walked over to the mantel and picked up one of Uncle Ian's medals. "It must be five years, at least. It's a damn shame we didn't make the time to visit Ian more often." He pressed his mouth closed in a tight line.

There was an awkward moment while we all waited to see if my father was going to cry. Dad never cried. Even when a tractor ran over his foot and broke it, he didn't cry.

"Meow!" Ivanhoe saved the day as he sauntered in from the one bedroom in the back of the cottage.

"Who is this?" my mother asked, and bent down to pet the cat's head. We gave a collective sigh of relief that the cat had interrupted the emotion heavy in the air.

The Scottish Fold leaned into the caress.

"Ivanhoe," I said. "I thought I told you I got a cat. I adopted him not long after I moved here."

She frowned and straightened up. "I suppose you did. The farm has been so busy that it's hard to remember everything. Your father is making a name for himself in the farmers' markets back home." She paused and looked at both Isla and me in turn. "He could use help."

I shifted my feet, and Isla looked at the floor. Although neither of us had come right out and said we didn't want to run the farm, we had given every indication with our life choices. It appeared our mother was stilling holding on to the hope that we would come around.

"You know that we aren't getting any younger," Mom added in an effort to hit her point home. We all knew what she was getting at. My mother was a pro at laying guilt on thick.

"Then hire some help," Isla said. "I mean, if the farm is doing well, you can afford it, right? I bet there are a couple high school kids who could use the part-time work."

Mom patted her hair and frowned.

My little sister had always been immune to our mother's guilt while I suffered from it. I thought it was the luxury of being the youngest. There were many times growing up that I'd envied her ability to ignore Mom's thinly veiled hints.

Mom wasn't done with trying to convince us to move back home. I knew that.

She pointed at the bedroom. "You sleep in there, Fiona?"

I wrinkled my brow. "Yes, it's my bedroom."

"Where is it that you sleep, Isla? The couch?"

"I don't live here. I have a little apartment over the laundromat in the village with my—"

"Isla is renting from Raj Kapoor. You might remember him when you visited Uncle Ian in the past," I said. I stopped her from telling them she lived with her boyfriend. My mother was a southern woman and very traditional when it came to that sort of thing. It would not go over well. However, I didn't think she could get on Isla's case about it too much, considering her own romantic history. Even so, I would much rather save that awkward conversation for another time, preferably just between the two of them when I wasn't around.

"I don't know anyone by the name of Raj," my father mused.

"He also owns the Twisted Fox pub. It's right next door to my flower shop. I'm sure we will go there quite a few times while you visit. Other than Presha's Teas and the fish-and-chips stand at the docks, those are the only places to eat in the village."

Dad nodded. "I remember that. I'm surprised that after all this time, Bellewick has been able to stay as small and quaint as ever. I think Ian would have liked that. He liked the smallness of the place."

"My, Isla," said my mother, who was not finished grilling my sister. "I do like your initiative to find work in Bellewick.

There must not be many options, but do you think it's wise to sign a lease when you don't plan to be here very long?"

"Oh," Isla said. "I don't plan to—"

"Oh!" I cried. "The tea! Have a seat, and I'll grab you those scones too."

"I can't wait for the scones." Dad rubbed his hands together. "I have been craving a proper Scottish scone since we purchased our plane tickets."

Isla shot me a look. I gave a subtle shake of my head and mouthed *not now*. I knew she needed to tell our parents her plans about staying in the village and eventually marrying Seth, whom she was preengaged to. Preengagement was a concept I found absolutely ridiculous, but I supposed, after what I'd gone through with my ex-finance, I was a little down on engagement as a rule.

"You arrived at a good time," I said as I set the tea and scones in front of them at my small table. "Bellewick is having a giant concert tomorrow afternoon, and the village expects over three thousand people to attend."

"Three thousand?" my father asked. "That's bigger than the population of the village."

I nodded. "They are expecting a crowd from the city of Aberdeen and the surrounding villages too."

"What's the concert for?" Mom asked.

"A local celebrity," I said. "Barley McFee. He's a famous fiddle player who is coming to the village to play a Coming Home Concert." I glanced at my dad. "He said he went to school with Uncle Ian and the two of them where friends, but when I asked him if he knew you, he said he didn't know you."

"No," Dad said. "I don't know him. The name is vaguely familiar, but that could be from his music." He took a huge bite out of his scone.

"The concert is going to be amazing," Isla gushed. "You'll even be staying at the same guesthouse with Barley and the band. Maybe you will get to chat them up at breakfast. I always wanted to be in a traveling band. I think I'd look good onstage."

Isla would look good onstage and just about anywhere else. She was beautiful. However, just like all the Knox relatives we knew, she had no musical talent.

Dad gulped from his teacup. "Why are we staying at the same guesthouse?"

"It's the only one in the village," Isla said.

"Won't that be fun?" Mom asked. "We do love music."

My father, who wasn't the most talkative of men to start, seemed to be extra quiet.

I sipped my tea. "Dad, is everything all right?"

He held out his teacup for a refill. "Everything is fine, Fiona. Completely fine."

That's when I knew he was lying.

Chapter Six

The next morning, I arrived in the village early. I knew Bernice expected every member of the Merchant Society to pull their weight during the concert. I made a quick stop at my flower shop before I joined the rest of the society members in the concert area.

As I unlocked the door, I was hit with the lovely scent of flowers. I inhaled deeply. I was most at ease when I was around flowers. It had always been that way for me. When I was as young as four, I'd asked my parents if I could have a bit of earth on the farm to grow my own garden, just like Mary in *The Secret Garden*. They turned an old sandbox into a garden for me, and I planted daisies, dahlias, and lilies in that little garden. I sat for hours by the garden, nurturing it and pulling weeds. I was obsessed with making sure my beauties had enough soil, sunlight, and water. I checked on them every day before and after preschool.

As I grew older, my parents gave me more and more area to grow flowers until caring for the flower gardens was my main job on the farm when I was a teenager. Most of what

I learned about gardening had come from Uncle Ian. Every time I visited him in Scotland, we spent hours in the walled garden at Duncreigan. I didn't know then that he was preparing me for my job as Keeper of the garden. I didn't know I was the one who spent time with Uncle Ian in Scotland instead of Isla because I was his daughter. I wished I had known. For myself and for my godfather, but there was no hope for that now, at least in the way I would have wanted.

Even earlier that morning before I came to the village, I had stopped by the garden like I always did to make sure everything was all right. I'd checked on the flowers, the menhir with the yellow climbing rose wrapped tightly around it. The fox was there with his blue eyes that reminded me so much of Uncle Ian's and of my own. At times I believed they were the eyes of my uncle like Presha did. That it wasn't just a wild animal that liked to hang around Duncreigan but my uncle who had come back in another form. Presha had told me the fox would stay with me in the garden until Uncle Ian felt I didn't need to be watched over any longer.

If that was true, I wondered if the fox would leave the garden soon. Over the last few months, I'd fallen into a comfortable life in Duncreigan and in Bellewick. I didn't think I needed much watching over anymore. My sister Isla, on the other hand, could always use a little bit more supervision.

It wasn't yet eight in the morning when I left my shop. I would be back at ten to open up, and then Isla would watch the shop for most of the day while I helped out at the concert. At some point I planned to give her a break so she could enjoy a portion of the concert, but I did hope some visitors in the village here to see Barley McFee would wander down the street and buy a flower or two.

I locked up the flower shop and walked down the street toward the village's main entrance.

I heard the commotion long before I saw it. There was a soft roar in the air from all the people, and some of the food trucks played Celtic music from their stereos as they waited for the concert to begin.

People by the dozens were already arriving, and it was only eight in the morning and the concert was at two in the afternoon. They walked over the troll bridge carrying lawn chairs, coolers, and blankets. It was clear they were in this for the long haul. The food trucks were already up and running, and I saw Raj setting up his beverage stand for the day. At the moment, he was serving coffee, but in the afternoon it would turn to ale and beer.

It was a very good thing Bernice had gotten permission from the village to close the main entrance into the village the night before. There was no way a car could have gotten through this crowd.

Even though there was a lot of activity on the street, the stage was quiet. There was no sign of Barley, his manager, or the band. Looking at the stage, I thought about the argument Isla and I had witnessed yesterday between Owen the manager and Kenda the second fiddle. I hoped Barley and Kenda had been able to settle their differences so the concert could go off without a hitch. I knew that if anything went wrong, Bernice wouldn't recover from it. She had so much riding on this concert's success. When she started the

Merchant Society of Bellewick, there had been many naysayers in the village. By tradition, Scots were individualistic people who didn't hold much value in organizing. If the concert failed, it would be proof to those naysayers that the Merchant Society was a waste of time.

I assumed Barley McFee was at the guesthouse, waiting to make his big return to Bellewick.

"Now I feel a lot better about this day," a deep male voice said behind me. "If I have to spend the next twelve hours here, at least it's with you."

I smiled as I turned around and looked into Chief Inspector Neil Craig's dark-blue eyes. "I didn't expect to see you here this early."

Craig was a broad-shouldered, six-feet-five-inch-tall man with a full dark-auburn beard. On this occasion he wore jeans, a button-down shirt, and a sport jacket. I knew under that jacket he had his badge and gun. It took all my strength not to wrap my arms around him and give him a giant hug. Craig gave the very best hugs.

He smiled down at me. "You can trust that Bernice Brennan has been texting me nonstop these last few days and told me where to be and how many constables to bring with me. If this concert doesn't go well, the woman is going to snap."

I chuckled. "I was just thinking the same thing. And I don't know why she would ask you to be here. There's always Kipling."

Kipling stood a few yards away from us next to the larger-than-life unicorn statue near the village arch. The unicorn stood on its hind legs, and his front hooves were in the air as if ready to strike. Kipling looked far less fearsome as he stood next to the statue in his navy-blue volunteer-police-chief uniform that was covered with brass buttons and gold medals, all of which meant nothing at all.

"Kipling is not adequate security for an event this size. Not when a big star is coming to Bellewick, and I'm looking forward to the concert myself. It was a nice excuse to spend some time with my favorite florist, too."

I blushed. "You like fiddle music?" I asked, surprised. This was the first I had heard of it.

"I'm Scottish, aren't I?" He feigned offense.

I laughed. "You very much are. You might be the most Scottish Scot I have ever met."

He wrinkled his brow. "I'm choosing to take that as a compliment."

"You should, because that's how it was meant." I smiled up at him. "I'll be here for the concert, of course. Bernice is not going to let me escape that. 'Every member of the Merchant Society has to pull his or her own weight,'" I said, quoting Bernice. She had said that more than once over the last several weeks. "The whole village is coming, and I think that's more because everyone wants to see what it's like to have three thousand people in one place. And my parents . . ."

"They arrived safely, then?" Craig asked, studying me.

I nodded. "Last evening. I haven't seen them this morning. They are staying at Thistle House."

"Will I get to meet them?" He searched my face.

"Umm . . ."

He arched his brow. "You don't want me to meet them?"

"It's not that. I do want you to meet, but I think it would be better for me to get some answers from them before I introduce them to my new boyfriend. Mom and Dad are going to be suspicious of you." I swallowed. "I was with my ex-fiancé for a very long time. They'll be surprised I'm dating again. I'm surprised, actually."

He smiled. "You couldn't resist me."

"That's part of it." I winked.

He laughed at my honest answer, and I reveled in the sound of his deep-throated chuckle as the unease I had felt the day before dissipated just a little.

"When you say you want to get answers before you introduce me to your parents, you mean about Ian," he said. Craig was the only person I'd told about my birth. I had told him months ago, right after I found out. I'd had to tell someone, and he was the person I trusted most to keep this secret for me. Isla would be crushed if she ever learned I'd told him before her, but I trusted him, and he was objective about it. Isla would not be objective about us being half sisters since she wasn't objective about most things.

"Right, and I think telling them, especially my mom, that I have a new boyfriend will just distract her. She very much wants Isla and me to move back to the States and take over the family farm."

"Are you considering that?" he asked in a careful voice.

"No, of course not. The garden would die if I went away for that long." I lowered my voice. "You know that as the Keeper of the garden I have to be the one to tend it. I can't abandon it."

Craig knew all about my garden and the role I had with it as well. Early on, when I first moved to Scotland, he had been there when the garden helped me solve a murder. I had found a dead man in the garden on the very day I arrived in Scotland. Through the visions it gave me, the garden helped Craig and me solve the murder. Craig had even been present when I got the vision.

He cocked his head. "Is that the only reason you wish to stay? Out of duty to the garden?"

"Well, there's my flower shop too," I teased.

Craig made a face.

"And I have grown very partial to the scones."

Craig scoffed.

"And you," I finally said. "You know I don't want to leave you."

"I'm glad that I play second fiddle to the garden and the flower shop."

I grabbed his hand and squeezed it. "You aren't second fiddle to anything or anyone, Chief Inspector Craig. I would think you knew that by now."

He squeezed my hand in return before releasing it. "It is still good to hear."

"Your point about second fiddle reminds me of something," I began, then went on to tell him about the argument Isla and I had seen between Owen and Kenda.

"So you were being nosy," he said with a smile.

"I wasn't," I said defensively. "They were having a terrible fight right in front of us. What could we do?"

"Move away and give them privacy."

I made a face. If Craig knew anything about me, he would know moving away was something I wasn't prepared to do in that sort of situation.

He laughed. "Fight or no fight, the concert will go off swimmingly. They are professionals."

"I hope so. This concert could be just the beginning of great things for the village," I said.

The corner of his mouth turned up. "That's where your Americanness is showing."

"Americanness? Did you just make up a word?"

"Maybe, but it's true. The American tendency is more and bigger and better and new. We don't always buy into that in Scotland. We appreciate old and tradition. Why change something that has worked for hundreds of years?"

"Can't you have both?" I asked. "Wouldn't it be better for everyone with both?"

He nodded. "And that's why I have you. You're my opposite, my balance."

I felt my cheeks grow hot, and a warm feeling grew in my chest. When my ex-fiancé left me for our cake decorator, I'd never thought I would find someone who cared about me so much again. I certainly hadn't thought it would happen so soon, not even a year after my broken engagement. I wasn't ready to use the *love* word just yet, but I felt like we could get there. At the moment, my heart was still too bruised from my last relationship to say those three precious words out loud. Craig was bruised and battered too when it came to relationships. His ex-wife, whom I'd had the misfortune of meeting once, was a piece of work, to be sure. We both were treading lightly.

He kissed me on the cheek, which was a rare display of affection when we were out in the open, especially around so many people. I felt myself blush with pleasure. I was happy Craig wasn't afraid to show he cared for me.

"I should do a loop before Bernice gets on my case. I want to make sure all my constables are in place," he said.

I nodded. "I should see what help she needs, too. I just want this to go as smoothly as possible, as much for the village as for Bernice's blood pressure."

"You and me both," Craig said, and walked away. He paused. "The mums look beautiful, by the way. Almost as beautiful as you on this lovely morn."

I beamed back at him.

I watched him go. Beyond him and the stone arch was a field, which was being used for a car park. Teenage volunteers directed the long line of cars, and it was still hours before the concert. The stage was set up at the end of the street, and as I walked to it, I could see men and women in black jeans and T-shirts making the finishing touches. From the back, the stage just looked like a giant black rectangle in the middle of the cobblestone road, but when I came around the side of it, I saw the hard wood stage. Amps, guitar pedals that could change the tone of the guitar's sound with just one press, and drums waited under a white stage awning. I hoped that the awning wouldn't be needed, given the unpredictable November weather.

I looked up at the sky. It was blue and clear. I felt suspicious. The weather in Scotland could turn from beautiful to terrible in a blink.

The stage took up the entire width of the street, which was about two compact cars across. Roads in Scotland were much narrower than in the States.

Even though things were still being set up as the crew moved around the stage, running wires and plugging in instruments, concertgoers were finding their spots. Bernice had been right. This was the biggest event Bellewick had ever seen.

People poured into the village, walking past the seven-foot-tall unicorn sculpture that met them at the village gate and over the old stone bridge. I was convinced that a troll lived under that bridge, not that I had ever seen one. My ability to believe the impossible had grown by leaps and bounds when I moved to Scotland and learned I had inherited a magical garden. I didn't think trolls were real, but if you had asked me a year ago if there was real magic in the world, I would have said no to that too.

Chapter Seven

Barley waved to the crowd from the stage. "Thank you all! The band is going to take a fifteen-minute break before our next set. Take a load off and grab some food. You have been a fabulous audience!" He and the band marched off the stage. All appeared to be in high spirits. No one watching the performance would know there was any kind of rift between Barley and Kenda.

A cheer rose up from the audience, and the general mood in the village was jovial. I couldn't believe how well everything had come off. Barley and his band had arrived on time to the stage for their sound check and promptly started the concert at two. The crowd was large but civil, and everyone seemed to be having a fabulous time.

Bernice beamed at me. "One more set and this is over. It is like some kind of Scottish miracle," she said. "Did you and your garden have anything to do with the good weather?"

I wasn't surprised she asked that. All the villagers knew the tales of the garden and its magic. However, they believed it to varying degrees. I didn't think Bernice was one of the people who really thought the garden was magical. She was just trying, in her way, to make a joke. It didn't bother me in the least.

"I had nothing to do with the weather. You should be very proud of the event. You did a fantastic job steering our ship. To be honest, a week or two ago, I thought we were going to sink."

"Between you and me," she whispered. "I did too. I'll be happy when it's over, and when I have recovered, I would like the Merchant Society to meet again and talk about how we can do more events like this in the village." She paused. "Just not at this scale."

I was happy she said that. I wanted it to be a very long time before I was involved in planning such a giant event. Like forever long.

I answered tourists' questions about the village as I waited for the band to return to the stage. Just like Bernice, I was looking forward to when they finished the concert so everyone would pack up and leave. I hadn't realized how much I loved my sleepy little town until it was overrun with outsiders.

I saw my parents chatting with some of the villagers while standing in line for one of the food trucks. They too seemed to be calm and having a good time.

My stomach growled. The wraps the food truck was selling looked delicious. I was overdue for lunch, but I told myself to wait until after the concert, when I could grab a proper meal at the pub. Raj's tikka masala would be the perfect end to a long day.

When the fifteen minutes were up, the band was back onstage, and Owen, the manager, waited in the wings. There was no sign of Barley. Ten more minutes ticked by. The crowd was starting to talk among themselves. I spotted Bernice across the audience, and she gnawed on her thumbnail.

Owen waved me over. Maybe because I was wearing a Merchant Society sweat shirt, he pinned me as someone who could help.

"Can I help you?" I asked.

He licked his lips. "You were the girl setting out flowers when we arrived."

I nodded.

He flushed red. "Yes, well, I think you might be able to assist me. We need Barley to return to the stage. We can't keep the audience waiting for this long. You can go look in the tour bus for him. I think that's where he went for intermission."

He glanced over his shoulder at Kenda, who was glaring at him.

She waved her bow. "We have to start whether or not Barley is back. I can lead the next set."

He waved his hands like he was directing a plane in for a landing. "No, no, Kenda, that wouldn't do. It would insult Barley if we began the set without him. He has a very clear vision for each and every one of his concerts."

"I would hate to insult Barley," she said sarcastically.

The manager turned back to me. "As you can see, I can't leave my spot. I need to, well, keep an eye on things here."

"I can go look for him for you," I offered.

His face brightened. "Would you?"

"Or I can stay here and make sure everyone stays in line while you check," I said.

"No!" he said, a little too forcefully. "I know better than to disturb Barley on a break. Maybe if the time reminder came from you, he would be less upset."

I frowned and pulled my cell phone out of my pocket. The fifteen-minute break had already run twelve minutes longer than promised. I wanted this concert over as much as Owen and the band did. "I'll go look for him."

He smiled. "Thank you. This village has been nothing but hospitable to us. We're so grateful to you for hosting this concert for Barley. Coming home has meant a great deal to him, and everyone has been wonderful."

I nodded and was happy to hear it.

"I would give him some space, though. He can be a real bear when he's in the performance zone," Owen warned.

I frowned. Great. Sounded like it would be great fun to find him.

"I'll go now." I turned and headed around the stage in the direction of the tour bus parked in the corner of the field just on the other side of the village gate.

As I reached the field, I started when I saw the man across from me was Carver Finley. He was a handsome man in a polished way. He had a mane of golden hair brushed back from his face, even features, and just enough stubble to give his otherwise perfect appearance interest. I hadn't seen him since the summer when he was in the village to work the restoration of the village's original chapel, which had been built in the fourteenth century. By the time Carver got to the chapel, it had been little more than one standing wall, a wall that sadly fell down during restoration. It would take a lot more work and funds to get the chapel pieced together again.

He smiled at me. I debated walking over to him and asking him what he was doing back in the village, but I thought better of it. Carver and I had not gotten off on the right foot. He was a historian who was determined to study the menhir in my garden, to the point that he'd tried to force the issue last summer. At the time, I was still learning my role as the garden's Keeper and was afraid Carver would use the garden for his own purposes—to further his career.

The less contact I had with him, the better. Besides, there was no rule that said he couldn't come to the concert, and he might just be a fan of Barley's music. Even still, seeing him back in the village put me on edge.

Isla pulled on my sleeve. I had been so caught up in seeing Carver that I hadn't even known she was there. "Fiona, you were supposed to come back to the shop and give me a turn watching the concert. I have been stuck in the shop *all* day, and Mom has been in and out of it like fifty times. If she tries one more time to talk me into moving back to the farm, I will scream. I really need to tell her about Seth and me getting married. I think then she will finally back off."

I shook my head. "No, Isla, Mom will double her efforts, and then she will torment Seth as well."

"Gah! Now, I wish they never came," she whined.

I didn't even touch that bratty comment. Instead I homed in on her standing here and what that meant. "You left the shop in the middle of the day with no one there?" I asked, concerned. I needed to find Barley to get this concert over with, but I didn't want to leave my shop unattended, especially with so many potential customers in the village.

"I locked it up. We didn't have any customers anyway. I mean, except for Mom, and she didn't buy anything," she groused.

"There might be some customers when the concert is over. I'll take it from here just as soon as I find Barley. Have you seen him?" I asked. "The next set should have started twenty minutes ago. It's growing colder by the second, and we need to keep the concert on schedule."

"Maybe he's just hanging out at the end of the rainbow."

"Isla!" I hissed. "Don't say that. It's not nice."

"Oh come on, Fi. He does kind of resemble a leprechaun, doesn't he? I mean that as a compliment. Leprechauns are lucky."

"I'm not sure he or anyone else would take it that way," I said.

She rolled her eyes. "He's probably just chilling in his tour bus. Let me tell you, from working concerts in Nashville, some performers can be real divas. It's when they are nice and on time that's more notable."

"I'll go see what's taking so long, and then I'll head over to the shop. You can hang out at the rest of the concert. I know you're a big fan of Barley's music."

She made a face. "Just like Seth."

It was my turn to roll my eyes, but since I was an adult, I refrained. At least outwardly.

She hopped in place. "Awesome. I need to find Seth. He said he would he helping out at Raj's booth. He's so thoughtful like that."

I knew Raj paid Seth to work at the booth. I wasn't sure thoughtfulness had much to do with it at all. I felt pretty proud of myself that I refrained from commenting about that as well.

I walked up to the tour bus and marveled yet again at the huge likeness of Barley plastered on the side of it. He smiled down at me from the bus with bright white teeth. I shuffled away from that image. Something about it made me edgy.

I knocked on the small trailer door, but there was no answer. "Mr. McFee!" I knocked harder. "Mr. McFee, the band is ready for you to join them on the stage," I called through the door. "Everyone is waiting for you, sir. The audience loved the performance."

I opened the screen door and knocked on the second aluminum door. When I did, the door opened and banged against the wall on the inside of the bus. The most disconcerting thing about the noise was that nothing happened. No one yelled at me and demanded to know what I was doing there. No one yelped or screamed or made a single peep.

Against my better judgment, I stepped into the trailer, telling myself everything was fine. I was just being a scaredy-cat, worried about going inside. Maybe I was a little nervous. I didn't want to walk in on Barley McFee in some kind of compromising position.

"Mr. McFee?" I asked in a quieter voice, like one I would use in a church.

Then I saw why he didn't respond. All was not fine. Barley McFee was dead on his trailer floor with a fiddle cord around his neck. His luck had finally run out.

Chapter Eight

I gasped, and my stomach dropped into my boots. It was a violent scene. Papers, dishes, and musical gear like pedals and microphones were strewn all over the floor. Barley's hands were bloody, as if he'd tried to pull the cord away from his throat and ultimately failed. He'd put up a fight, which made it somehow worse. He'd known what was happening at the end. How terrifying that must have been.

I closed my eyes and willed the image away from my mind. When I opened my eyes again, it was still there. This was not a dream, vision, or hallucination. This was real. I had found another dead body, another person killed at the hands of violence. This wasn't the first time this had happened since I'd come to live at Duncreigan, but it wasn't a claim to fame that I wanted or needed.

I backed out of the tour bus, trying to remember everything I touched so I could tell Chief Inspector Craig. I knew he would want to know when the crime scene was processed. I had been a murder suspect in the past, so my prints were on file. Sadly.

Outside the trailer, I doubled over and gulped air. Of the dead bodies I had seen, this was the worst. Really, how horrible was that—dead *bodies*, as in plural? But I wouldn't dwell on previous tragedies. My mind was firmly locked on today's events.

I couldn't block the look of horror on Barley's face out of my head. As I was gasping and bent at the waist, Bernice Brennan marched toward me. I noted that Bernice never walked anywhere; she always marched like she was a soldier about to lead a siege on a castle. She would have done well as a medieval knight. There was a righteous Joan of Arc quality about her, but instead of a sword she wielded a clipboard.

"Where's Barley?" She wanted to know. "The set was supposed to start almost half an hour ago. The audience is restless, and Owen Masters refuses to let the other band members play to pass the time. It's utterly ridiculous. I have tried to call Barley's cell four times, and it always goes to voicemail. Owen said he sent you to go look for Barley. Did you find him?"

"I did," I said.

"He's in the tour bus, then. He needs to come out. The show must go on. He should know that. He's been in this business long enough to know that!" She walked up the steps into the trailer.

"No!" I cried. "Bernice, don't go in there!"

She sniffed at me. "I will go wherever I please. It's up to me to make this concert a success, and I'm going to make sure it's just that."

She pushed her way into the tour bus. A moment later, she came out of the bus, her face pale, and threw up.

I had to look away, because I was at real risk of getting sick to my stomach as well. I knew I would have already if I hadn't taken the time to gulp that beautiful fresh air. However, now I realized my error. My delay had given Bernice enough time to see the inside of the bus. I didn't wish her to have that image in her head. I didn't want it in *my* head, that was for sure.

I hadn't noticed that a small crowd was gathering around the trailer. I was sure they were attracted by the commotion Bernice and I had made.

"What is going on over here?" The question came from Chief Inspector Craig.

I was so relieved to hear his voice. "Craig!" I called, and waved over the crowd.

He pushed his way through the cluster of curious concertgoers. Then he looked back at the encroaching audience. He removed his badge from the inside of his coat and displayed it as he encouraged people to "make way." Wondrous what that medal could do. I wished I had that kind of authority. Then again, maybe not. I was fine not walking in Craig's proverbial shoes, because crime was something Craig had to deal with on a daily basis and I'd much rather live in my world of flowers.

He glanced at Bernice, who was sitting on the ground with her head between her knees. I didn't blame her. I wanted to do the same, but one of us had to keep it together.

"Fiona, what's going on?" Craig asked.

"Barley McFee was late from getting back to the stage after the break, so Owen, his manager, asked me to go see if he was in the tour bus."

He nodded. It was clear that he wanted me to continue with my story.

I took a breath. "I found him." I pointed. "He's in there."

"And . . ." Craig said.

"And he's dead," I whispered.

Craig jerked back. "Dead. Did he have a heart attack? I mean, I saw him onstage and his face was getting dangerously red from the exertion of the performance."

"No," I whispered. "He was murdered."

He closed his eyes for the briefest moment. I wondered if he was wishing he was on a desert island, free of the murder and mayhem that seemed to follow me wherever I went.

"You're sure?" he asked.

"Very. Go see for yourself. There is no doubt. A fiddle cord is wrapped around his throat." I placed my hand to my own throat and rubbed it as if I could feel the metal cord biting into my flesh as well.

He jerked back and looked at the trailer. "In there?"

I nodded. "Neil, it's bad. One of the worst things I've ever seen."

He raised his brow. Craig knew this wasn't my first time finding a dead body. I dared to hope it would be my last.

"Bernice saw it?" he asked.

I nodded. "After I did. I tried to stop her from going in there, but I was too late."

He nodded and removed his phone from the pocket of his sport jacket. He made a quick call, and two of his constables were almost immediately on the scene.

Craig looked at them both in turn. "Clear the area, and tell the crowd to go back to their seats so the concert can continue. I don't want them leaving the village just yet. We might have witnesses among them. Call in another squad of constables and crime scene techs from Aberdeen. And we're going to need the coroner's services again."

"It's hard to believe there's been another killing in Bellewick," one of the constables said. "It's almost like this place is cursed."

I shivered. Could he be right? Curses were another thing I would have categorically said didn't exist if you'd asked before I moved to Scotland, but now . . . It did seem odd that there was so much violent death in such a small and remote fishing village.

"Go," Craig said, and his voice left no room for speculation. He wanted the scene secured and now. The constables went off to do what he asked.

He glanced at me. "I'm going to go in the bus. Are you all right to wait here?" He studied my face as if he was searching for even the slightest hint of a breakdown.

I straightened my shoulders. "I'll be fine. Do what you have to do."

He nodded and entered the tour bus. While he was thus occupied, Bernice came out of her stupor. I went to sit next to her in the grass.

"This is awful," she said, in a voice halfway between a wail and a whimper. "More awful than I could have ever imaged. I would have thought something would go wrong with the food truck or the sound system would fail. I never thought the main act would be killed. Who would ever think something like that was going to happen?"

"No one would," I reassured her. "How could we?"

"Someone did," she said, looking me in the eye for the first time since she'd come out of the bus. "The person who killed him did it, and he did it in my village!" She jumped to her feet and stomped her foot. "I take it as a personal insult. Barley travels all over the world. Why here? And why now? The concert was going so well. I did a good job!"

I stood up too. "You did an excellent job, Bernice," I consoled her. "You should be very proud of yourself."

She looked like she might cry. "And now it's ruined."

I patted her arm in the hope that I was being encouraging. "Bernice, I know this is very upsetting. I'm upset too." I shivered as the image of Barley's body came back to me. "But this is no time to overreact. We need to help Craig and the rest of the police as much as possible. We need to stall so that the crowd doesn't leave. Ask the band to play something."

She nodded. "Owen already told me no."

"That's just too bad."

She nodded. "You're right. I will tell Owen what has happened, and then they will play."

"No," I said, a little too quickly. I cleared my throat. "I mean, no, on second thought, why don't I go talk to the band, and you have a seat on the grass right there." I pointed at the ground.

"Right there?" she asked, looking at the spot like she'd never seen anything like it before.

"Yep," I said. "Since you are in charge of the concert, the police might want to talk to you again. It's a better idea if I talk to the band."

She sat back down on the grass. "I suppose you're right. I'm far too upset to make much sense."

"I'll be right back." I hurried to the stage, taking one last look over my shoulder. Bernice was sitting on the spot on the grass I had suggested, just like a docile child. I hated to leave her there like that, but someone had to reach the band before the concert broke up too early.

I pushed my way through the crowd and was almost to the stage when a man grabbed me by the shoulder. "Tell me what's going on over there at the tour bus!"

I stared into the man's piercing green eyes, as he still had a grip on my arm. He had bright-red hair and was clean-shaven with a pale complexion. "Let go of my arm."

He held me a little more tightly. "I need to know what's going on over there."

"Let me go," I snapped.

"Not until you answer me. It's important." He shook me.

"It's important that you let go of my sister's arm before I use the self-defense-class skills my boyfriend taught me," Isla said as she popped up at my side. "Any guesses where I was instructed to hit first?"

The man dropped my arm and glared at us. "You don't have a right to keep this from me. I'm his family."

"Who's family?" I asked.

"Barley's," he spat. "That ungrateful miser. I wish I could disown him just like he did the rest of us."

I tried to keep my face neutral. If Barley was in some kind of dispute with his family and now he was dead, there was a murder suspect standing right in front of me. "How are you related to Barley?" I asked.

"It's none of your business." He leaned in, and I could smell the pipe tobacco on his breath. "You tell the good-for-nothing Barley that I'm not going to make it easy for him to come back here. He should have stayed away forever, just like he said he would. Now that he's returned, I'm not holding anything back."

"What are you talking about?" I asked. The crowd attending the concert seemed to be closing in around us, forcing me an inch closer to the man.

"Just give him my message. He will know what I mean." The man let go of my arm. "Do as I ask, or you will be as sorry as Barley is."

Was that a threat? It sure sounded like one. I didn't tell him I couldn't deliver the message because Barley was dead.

He stalked away, disappearing into the crowd.

"Wait!" I called after him. I still didn't know his name.

Isla turned to me. "Did you see how I protected you like that?" She bent her arms as if to show off her biceps, which were impossible to see under her winter coat. It might be autumn in Scotland, but according to our thin Tennessee blood, it might as well have been the middle of winter. "Those classes were a great idea."

"I think a self-defense class is a good idea for any woman. I'm not sure Seth is the best teacher," I said, thinking of how tall and thin her boyfriend was. He looked as if a stiff wind from off the North Sea could break him in half.

The man who'd grabbed my arm was long gone. I tried to commit what he looked like to memory because I knew Craig would want to talk to him. Was it true he was Barley's relative? When the Merchant Society started to plan the concert, I had asked Bernice if there were any members of Barley's family still living in the area, and she had said no. Who was this man, then? And how far had he traveled to deliver his message to Barley—a message that would never be received?

"Did you find Barley?" Isla asked.

I pressed my lips together. I didn't think Craig wanted me to tell others yet what had happened.

"Oh no! Don't tell me he's dead." She threw up her arms.

"Shh!" I hissed, looking around. "Dead? Why would you think he was dead?"

She held up her hand. "One, you're not answering my question. Two, I saw the police officers walk over to the trailer. Three, it's not like this will be the first time. You find dead people a lot."

"That's not true." I frowned, wondering if she might be right. It was a terrifying thought.

"Has it happened more than once?" She cocked her head.

I didn't answer.

"I'll take that as a yes, which means you have found them a lot more times than anyone else living in Bellewick, more than anyone else living in Scotland, if not the world."

"Please don't remind me."

"Omigosh, he is dead. I was saying it as a joke." Isla paled. "What happened? Did someone kill him?"

"What's this about killing?" Owen Masters, Barley's manager, walked up to Isla and me.

I closed my eyes for a moment and willed my sister to just be quiet for once in her life.

Chapter Nine

I needed to distract Isla before she said too much to Owen. "Isla, is that Seth over there by the Greek food truck?"

"Where?" My sister perked up, and her long blonde hair hit me in the face when she turned to see where Seth was. "He said he wasn't able to leave the pub's beverage booth until after the concert. As you can imagine, it breaks his heart, since he's such a huge fan of Barley. Oh no! Now that Barley's—"

"You really should go see if it's him." I interrupted her just before she could announce Barley's death in front of his manager. I knew Owen deserved to know what had happened to his client, but this wasn't my first rodeo when it came to murder. I knew Craig would want to tell him himself. He was very careful with the information he shared with suspects, and just by his close relationship with Barley, Owen was undoubtedly a suspect.

He wasn't the best one I could think of, though, I noted as Kenda walked across the stage. She was clearly annoyed that the concert was delayed.

"You're right. I need to comfort my love in his time of need," Isla said. "He will be brokenhearted. I think the only saving grace is that I will be there with him. He won't have to walk this road of grief alone."

Owen frowned at her as if he was contemplating asking her what she was talking about, but then thought better of it.

"I'll go now," Isla said dramatically. "I know they were swamped at the Twisted Fox cart." She pressed her hand to her chest. "He works like a dog. My poor love."

I tried not to gag. Of all the people I knew who might be considered hard workers, Seth MacGregor wasn't even in the top thousand.

I cleared my throat. "Well, I thought I saw him over there by one of the food trucks." I shrugged as if it didn't matter. "Maybe he's on break."

She pouted. "How could he be on a break without telling me? We're a couple. He is supposed to tell me where he is at all times. That's how it works!"

I made a face. I wondered how long it would be before that requirement of my little sister's grew old on Seth. I couldn't imagine asking Craig where he was at all times. In fact, I didn't want to know. He had a dangerous job as chief inspector of the county, and I was certain if I knew where he was, sometimes it would only cause me more worry. Honestly, I didn't want him to keep such close tabs on me either.

"I'll go find him," she said. "And remind him what his duties are as my almost-fiancé." She flounced away. My little sister was one of the few people in the world who could flounce and look good doing it.

"What's going on?" Owen asked. "I sent you over there to retrieve Barley, and now people are complaining because the next set hasn't started. We need him onstage. If this goes on much longer, he could hurt his reputation."

Barley's reputation was the least of his concerns.

"Can the band start playing?" I asked. "I'm sure they can do some pieces without Barley. They all seem to be very talented."

Owen shook his head. "No way. Barley never wants his band to play without him. He says everyone comes to his concerts to hear him play and we shouldn't pad the time with some other act."

"Well, you're going to have to do it this one time." I shifted my feet.

"Why?" He glared at me. "Do you know where Barley is and you're not telling me? Because if I find out you're keeping information from me, I'll have your job."

I frowned back at him, not knowing what a music manager could do to ruin my job as a florist. It wasn't like the careers overlapped each other in any way. "Barley's not available," I said, a little more bluntly than I would have two minutes before. "You will have to go on without him."

"Where is he? Tell me now!"

I suppressed a wince. "He's in the tour bus." It was technically true, unless the body had been removed by now. I closed my eyes for a moment. Any mention of the tour bus made me remember the scene when I'd found Barley's body, and I got a bit queasy. I took a breath. I refused to get sick to my stomach as Bernice had.

"Then we can wait. If he's sick, we can tell the audience the concert had to end early, but it would be best for him to do it himself."

"I don't think you should. Barley is under the weather." That was one way to put it.

He folded his arms. "I don't believe Barley is too ill to play. I've seen him go onstage with the stomach flu. He's a professional, and he knows what the fans want. He would never let them down like this. There's something more going on here."

He was right. There was definitely something more going on, but that didn't mean I could tell him what it was.

He pointed at me. "And you are going to tell me what it is right now!"

"Sir," I began.

He leaned forward. "Do you even know who I am? I'm one of the most sought after music managers in the UK. I can put your village on blast, so much that no one will ever dare to come back. I have over a million followers on Instagram."

I tried very hard not to roll my eyes. I doubted his social media following was going to have any impact on the village of Bellewick.

"I'm sorry, Mr. Masters, but I can't tell you any more than what I have said. You should have the concert begin again without Barley. That's my best advice, and trust me, it's sound advice too."

"You can and you will." A bead of sweat appeared on his temple. "It's my job to keep Barley on schedule and make sure he's everywhere that he promises to be. We can't have him leaving. It's unacceptable."

I shook my head. "No, we can't wait. You said yourself that the audience is restless, and Barley isn't coming back to the stage. Play the last set and wrap everything up without him."

One of the MacNish brothers stomped to the end of the stage, carrying a guitar. "What the hell is going on? Where's Barley? People are starting to leave. If this keeps up, we're going to get roasted on the Internet."

Kenda came up behind him. "We can't wait for Barley any longer. I'm taking over the stage." She nodded to the two MacNish brothers. "Boys, let's play." She didn't wait for an answer and walked up to the mic. "Hello, everyone, we would like to do something a little special tonight. Barley had asked me to come onstage and share with you one of my original pieces. It's called 'Purple Thistle.' I hope you enjoy it." She lifted her fiddle to her chin and began to play. After a beat, the MacNish brothers joined in.

"Kenda!" Owen hissed, even though it would have been impossible for her to hear him from where she played on the stage. "You can't do this. Barley will kick you of the band. He will kill you."

The *kill you* comment stuck out at me. Barley wasn't going to be killing anyone now because he had been killed. But had someone killed him first because he was a threat to him or her?

I frowned. Barley would have kicked her out of the band if she played without him onstage? Kenda had fought with

Barley the day before, and she and Barley were a former couple. She had the very best motive, or, I should say, *motives* for murder. As I thought of this, I remembered Barley's relative who had accosted me just a little while ago. Barley hadn't even been dead an hour, and there were already several strong suspects. It made me wonder who else had wanted to kill him, because I had a sneaking suspicion these folks were just the tip of the iceberg when it came to people who wanted Barley McFee to take a final bow.

The hardest part of this investigation for Craig would be the sheer number of suspects. I glanced out at all the concertgoers and cringed.

Kenda tucked her fiddle under her chin and continued to play. The MacNish brothers jumped in with their own instruments, and soon a jaunty tune filled the village of Bellewick.

The audience loved it, and even though I wasn't well versed in the world of fiddle music, I could tell she was good. She played with a new energy she had been lacking in Barley's shadow.

The audience murmured about her performance, and I caught some of what they were saying.

"She's better than Barley himself," a voice in the audience said.

"She's gifted. I have never heard the fiddle played so well," someone else commented.

"It makes me want to dance. I think I like her better than McFee."

"Aye, I do as well. She brings a new take to the instrument. It is always good to hear a different style."

"Does the girl have an album? Because I would buy it if she does. It's the perfect music to listen to when you need a little extra pep."

"Aye," another agreed.

Owen ran his hands through his hair. "This is an utter disaster. She has gone mad. She doesn't know what she's doing. Barley can ruin her career if she doesn't stop. It might already be too late, and he will ruin her now. She's playing a very dangerous game." He lowered his voice. "She doesn't know what he is capable of, the power he has. She just doesn't."

"How could Barley ruin her career?" I asked.

He looked at me as if I had pulled him out of some type of nightmarish vision. Having had a few of those in my life, I knew the expression well. "You've been no help," he said, and stomped away.

I watched him go. Kenda and the MacNish brothers played a full set. The sky grew dark as evening came on, and the concert would be over soon.

"Thank you all for your love and support," Kenda said into the mic as the concert came to a close. "If Barley were here, I know he would say the same thing. I do thank you for this chance to share my music with you. My name is Kenda Bay, and it won't be a name you will soon forget. You will see it in lights!" She threw up her arms, her bow in one hand and her fiddle in the other.

Another man walked on the stage, and I was surprised to see Chief Inspector Craig take the microphone from Kenda.

She stepped back from the mic, and the two whispered back and forth. Then she covered her mouth and ran off the stage. The MacNish brothers stared at Craig as if they were frozen in place.

"Thank you all for your patience," Craig said into the microphone. "I'm Chief Inspector Neil Craig of the County Aberdeen police. I know you are eager to leave now that the concert has ended, but there has been an incident at the concert this afternoon, and I'm very sorry to report, Mr. McFee has passed away. If anyone could provide me or one of the constables information as to what might have happened that led to Mr. McFee's death, we would be most grateful."

A murmur rushed through the concert. Some people were crying. Others shouted out their disbelief. "It's just not possible. We just saw him."

"How can he be dead?" another bystander asked.

"When he said his 'Coming Home Concert,' I didn't know it would be his last concert," another replied.

"I don't think he did either."

I knew he didn't.

Chapter Ten

The concert started to break up. As people crossed the troll bridge to walk back to their cars, Craig's constables asked them questions about what they might have seen or heard around the tour bus and in relation to Barley's sudden death. Some of the concertgoers were happy to chat with the police, while it was clear that most just wanted to leave and not get involved in a murder investigation. I couldn't say I blamed them.

"Fiona, what on earth is going on?" my father asked as he and my mother walked up to me. It was the first I had seen either of them all day.

"Did we hear right that Barley McFee is dead? That's what Isla said as she walked by us." My father removed his glasses and polished the lenses on the bottom of his shirt before replacing them on his thin nose.

"Yes," my mother said. "Isla was with a tall young man when she walked by, and she seemed to know him well. Who is he? I would have expected you to tell me if anything was going on with her. We all know what a flirt Isla can be.

She shouldn't be wasting her time with a flighty Scottish boy when she will be moving back home at the end of the year."

It didn't surprise me in the least that my mother was more concerned about the guy my sister was walking around with than the fact that a man had been murdered just a few hundred yards away.

I didn't think it was because my mother lacked compassion. It was just that she couldn't process what was happening. Murder wasn't something my parents had had to deal with before. Isla and her long string of boyfriends was something much more familiar, and so my mother latched on to that.

"Isla is moving back home?" I knew this wasn't true, and I hoped Isla wasn't stringing our parents along into believing that. That was the worst thing she could do. It would come back to haunt her and me.

Mom sniffed. "She didn't say that in so many words, but of course she's coming home. She told us when she decided to stay beyond just the summer that she would be home at the end of the year. I know you have Duncreigan and the flower shop, but what could Isla possibly have in Scotland? There is nothing for her here. Nothing at all."

Ah, that made more sense. My sister was just putting our parents off for a little while. I didn't blame her. When Isla told them she wanted to stay in Scotland, that would be a hard pill to swallow for both our parents but especially our mother.

"You would tell me if something was going on with your sister, Fiona, wouldn't you? I would expect you to." My mother examined my face as if she were trying to peer into my very mind.

I turned away. I wasn't going to be pulled into this conversation right now.

To my father, I said, "Yes, Barley McFee is dead. It was terrible." I shook the image from my head yet again. I supposed it was futile. I expected the scene inside the trailer to be in my mind for a very long time.

"Wait!" Mom said. "How do you know? Did you see him?"

I pressed my lips together. This wasn't something I wanted to talk to my parents about.

Dad shook his head. "I'm glad I was able to talk to him. It was my only chance."

"You spoke to Barley? Why?" I asked.

"Fiona," Mom said. "I don't like the tone you are taking. There is nothing wrong with your father being nice to a stranger, even if he is a celebrity. He's still a person."

I knew that, but I also knew my father wasn't the type to go out of his way to speak to people he didn't know. If it had been my mother, I would have believed it, but Dad was the one who'd said he was glad he had spoken to Barley. Also, he'd said it was his only chance, implying he had wanted to talk to Barley all along. Why? Both men had told me they didn't know each other. Both had seemed to be upset when I spoke about the other to them as well.

"Dad, did you know Barley McFee before yesterday?"

"Fiona, you should not question your father like that," my mother said. "Show some respect. You should take the things your father tells you as facts. He told you he didn't know Barley. His word should be enough for you."

"Just like everything you tell me is true?" The words were out of my mouth before I could stop them. I wanted to talk to my parents about my birth and why my dad's name was on my birth certificate and not Uncle Ian's, but not this way.

All the color drained from my father's face. Both he and my mother knew what I was talking about even though I hadn't come right out and said it. My heart sank. I wanted to grab the words out of the air and shove them back into my mouth. But it was too late for that.

An apology was on my lips, although I didn't want to apologize. I didn't want to let my parents off the hook this time. Perhaps my timing was awful. I *knew* it was awful, but that didn't mean I didn't have a right to know the truth.

"Fiona, how could you speak to your father in such a way?" Mom asked. "That's the man who raised you. He was there the day you were born. Was Ian? You should never speak to your father like that."

"It doesn't change the fact that you two lied to me my entire life. What am I supposed to do with that? Don't I deserve to know my real history?"

My father cleared his throat. "Excuse me." He melted into the crowd.

I wanted to run after him and I didn't, all at the same time. I supposed it didn't matter because I couldn't follow him, as my mother stepped into my path.

She glared at me. "Your real history is that you grew up on a farm outside Nashville, Tennessee, and Stephen Knox is your father. That's all you need to know."

"Mom, I'm an adult. I have a right to know the truth about how I came to be." I took a breath. "I'm sorry that Dad is upset. I'm sorry how I brought it up. It's not the way I wanted to do it, but I still have a right to know."

She shook her head. "I think you lost that right the moment you spoke to your father in that way. You broke his heart. You might as well have wrung his neck."

I swallowed. Did my mother know that's how Barley had been killed? By being strangled? How would she know unless . . . No, I was being ridiculous. My parents had had no idea Barley McFee was dead until my sister told them.

"Did you hear Craig's announcement about Barley?" I asked.

My mother shook her head. "The concert was becoming too crowded, and we went back to Thistle House to rest a bit. We were just coming out again in search of dinner when we ran into Isla and the tall young man. She told us." She narrowed her eyes at me as if to see if I would crack and tell her who the guy Isla was with was.

That wasn't going to happen. Isla's relationship was hers to tell our parents about. I still hadn't mentioned Craig to them. I wasn't one to talk.

When I didn't say anything, she scowled. "Now I'm going to go find your father and make sure he's all right. If you need us, we will be at the guesthouse." She spun on her heel and walked away.

I stood in the middle of the crowd of concertgoers and watched her walk away. I bit my lip. I should have done a better job of bringing up my birth with my parents. I felt bad about the way I'd handled it. Really bad.

I moved through the crowd and walked to the steps beside the stage. From there I could get a good view of what was happening as the concertgoers left the village. Many of them were bottlenecked by the constable on the other side of the troll bridge, who was gathering any information they might have about Barley's death.

Some people who were tired of the line not moving were jumping over the creek and avoiding the bridge completely. I scanned the faces in the fading light for Bernice but didn't see her. I hoped she was okay. She hadn't taken Barley's untimely demise well.

I promised myself I would find Bernice and then go look for my parents and try to smooth things over. No matter what decisions they'd made before I was born, they were still my parents, and I loved them. I knew they loved me too. I supposed I just wanted to know the choices they'd made. I wasn't so much upset that they'd taken me to the United States. I more wanted to know why Uncle Ian had let me go.

I hopped off the stairs and headed back to the tour bus. I had a hunch that's where I would find Bernice. I was still a few feet away when I heard Bernice before I saw her. "The village's reputation is in shambles."

I stepped around a cluster of visitors and finally spotted Bernice standing with Presha.

Presha had her arm around Bernice. "No, Bellewick's reputation is not ruined," Presha soothed. "There were many people here today for the concert. Most of them are not from the village. Any one of them could have killed Barley."

"But why did it have to be in our village?" Bernice whined. "He plays in a new place every week. Why couldn't it have happened in one of those other places?"

"And you would wish this difficulty on someone else?" Presha's black eyebrows pointed up.

"Yes, I would," Bernice said, missing the irony in Presha's question. "I would give this problem to someone else in two seconds flat."

Presha shook her head. "Ah, Fiona is here. What is it?"

"I just wanted to see if Bernice needs any help." I pressed my lips together and widened my eyes at Presha.

She smiled. "She will be fine. She's coming to terms with what happened, right, Bernice?"

Bernice shook her head. "Why did it have to be in our village?"

Presha shook her head. "You're going to have to break that script, Bernice, because it's not helpful. This village has been here for over four hundred years. Many have lived and died in this place. One event will not destroy it. We have much to do to clean up after the concert and make sure everyone leaves safely. I think it would be more productive if you concentrated on that instead of what-ifs."

Bernice blinked at her. "Yes, of course, you're right. I'll start making a list of what all needs to be done, and I have to talk to Barley's manager as well."

"That's a good idea," I said. "This will blow over for the village. It won't blow over quite as well for Barley's band and the others who might have known him."

"This is true," Presha said. "I will say a prayer for him when I return to my altar at the tea shop."

"His family would also be affected," I said. "There was a man I met a little while ago who claimed he was Barley's relative. When I asked at one of the society meetings if any of Barley's relatives still lived in the village, everyone said no."

"There are certainly none in the village," Presha said. "However, this concert has been widely advertised, so I guess any relative of his could have heard about it and come to the concert to reconnect. Did he say who he was?"

"Only that he was Barley's relative. He didn't give me a name, and this was right after I found Barley . . ." I trailed off.

"Barley is a bit older than me," Presha said. "His parents are long dead, and I don't know of any siblings. Perhaps it was a more distant relative? Can you think of any, Bernice?"

The other woman blinked at her. "No." Her answer was clipped.

"Maybe Raj would know," Presha said. "My brother talks to everyone, and if someone is staying in the village, he will have to have eaten at the pub at some point. Raj has a way of getting everyone to tell him his or her life story."

I nodded. "I'll ask him about it. I need to tell Craig too."

"Tell me what?" a deep voice asked behind me.

I turned and found Chief Inspector Neil Craig looking down at me. He stood straight and kept an eye on the people leaving the concert as if he were documenting their every feature in his mind. However, on closer inspection, I noticed bags under his dark-blue eyes.

The violence that seemed to hang over the village was starting to take a toll on the chief inspector, and it broke my heart to see it. I wanted to reach up and touch his tired face. I stopped myself from doing it. There were too many witnesses.

Chapter Eleven

The members of the Merchant Society were the very last ones to leave the concert, and it was well after dark when I shuffled down the cobblestone street toward the flower shop. I could have lost out on some business today because the shop had been closed since before Barley's body was discovered. But honestly, after hearing about Barley's death, no one was probably thinking about buying flowers.

I had parked my little compact car in the small community lot just outside the city gates, and I could have gone straight home after the Merchant Society broke up for the night. Habits were hard to break, though, and I always stopped to check on my shop before I left the village at night, no matter where I was or what I had been doing.

My pace was slow as I walked toward the shop. I just wanted to return home to Duncreigan. The day had not gone as planned.

As I drew closer to the Climbing Rose's yellow awning, I saw that people were standing idle in the middle of the street near the shop. They were clustered around the lone lamppost between the Twisted Fox and the flower shop. It wasn't unusual to see people standing outside Raj's pub in the evening; the pub didn't have as much seating as the number of villagers who ate there every night, so waiting for a table was a common problem. There would have been more tables if Raj had been willing to kick out some of the old fishermen who hung around the pub day and night, but he was too much of a softie to try. The ringleader of the group was a man I called Popeye because he looked just like the cartoon sailor, all the way down to the tattoo and pipe. For the record, I had never seen the village's Popeye eat canned spinach, but I wouldn't put it past him.

"There she is!" a woman's voice rang out.

All twenty people moved toward me in a wave. For a moment, I was transported back to the zombie movies I'd sneaked in and watched with my friends back in middle school, where mindless zombies walked through a town eating everyone's brains. No one was taking my brain.

I held my hands up in the universal sign for *stop* and shouted, "Stop!" just to put a fine point on it.

The group froze. Most of them were women in late middle age, although three men were intermingled with the group. I didn't know if the men were there of their own accord or if their wives had dragged them along. By the irritable and tired looks on their faces, I guessed the latter.

"We need to buy flowers!" a crying woman said. Tears ran down her face in rivulets.

"Yes," another agreed. "We need to put them out in front of the tour bus where Barley died." She choked on a sob. "I can't believe he's gone. He was so incredibly talented. The world has lost a bright and shining star."

"The world didn't just lose a star. Someone snuffed it out," a taller woman about the same age said.

"It was the young woman who did it. Mark my words, it was her," the crying woman said.

"Kenda?" the first woman asked. "Why would she? She and Barley were an item, and he certainly gave her the life the rest of us could only dream about."

"They *were* an item. They aren't anymore. I read online that they broke up a month ago."

The first woman gasped. "You read that and didn't tell me? I should be the first to know, as the president of the Barley McFee Grannies."

I blinked. "Barley McFee Grannies?" The question popped out of my mouth before I could stop it.

The first woman turned back to me. "Yes, we are Barley's longest-running fan club. You can call us the BMGs for short. We have loved him so much. We've gone to all his concerts for the last thirty years. I'm Gemma Gemel, club president."

"I've been to one of his concerts in Norway," one of the women spoke up.

Gemma scowled at her. "Yes, yes, please stop rubbing it in. It's unattractive."

"You're like fiddle groupies?" I asked.

Gemma frowned. "I wouldn't say that. No one is throwing her bra on the stage. We are all grandmothers and have more self-respect than that."

"Gemma," said the woman who'd seen Barley in Norway. "I think you threw your cardigan on the stage at Barley the last time he played in Brighton."

Gemma pressed her lips together. "That was a very different scenario."

I wasn't sure I wanted to hear what scenario would make a grandmother throw her sweater on stage.

Gemma put her hands on her hips. "If Barley and Kenda are no longer together, why is she still on his tour? He should have broken up with her and kicked her out of the band. Barley was so gifted with the instrument that he doesn't need a second fiddle to back him up. Honestly, he doesn't need the band at all. I could listen to him play all day long." She sniffled. "And now we will never hear him play again."

"There are always CDs," another woman suggested.

"I can't believe you still listen to CDs," another woman said. "It's the twenty-first century. Learn to stream music already."

"Any way we listen to Barley's music," Gemma said, "it won't be the same. I have traveled all over the country for Barley's concerts. He expected me to be there. I was his number-one fan. I know he cared about me. He might even have loved me if that floozy Kenda wasn't in the picture."

I did my best to control my expression, but this was getting into stalker-level adoration of Barley. In the back of my mind, I thought, *Some stalkers even kill.*

"She wasn't in the picture before he died. Had you known that, you could have made your move on him."

"Excuse me?" Gemma asked. "I am a proper lady, and a proper lady doesn't make a move on a man. It is not the way things are done."

"That's antiquated thinking," the pro-streaming groupie said. "I asked my third husband on a date, and now we are happily married."

"If you weren't so forward, you might not be on your third husband." Gemma sniffed.

"Ladies, what are you doing in front of my shop?" I shouted over their bickering.

"Finally, yes, get to the point," one of the men muttered. "I don't want to stand out in the cold all night long while they fight over who loved Barley McFee the most. I know you are just all a bunch of crazy old hens."

"What?" Gemma cried.

"Barley wasn't going to pay you no mind, and he wouldn't have given you the time of day either. You can mark my words on that, just to be sure and certain. You're all too old," he replied.

There was a collective roar from the women as they turned on him. One of the ladies stepped in front of the man spouting off his very unpopular opinions. "Ladies, please. Give Guthrie a chance. He's had a ministroke and he doesn't know what he's saying. He's not been the same since the stroke. It messes with your mind, you see."

"I never had a ministroke," Guthrie complained. "My brain is more fit than yours, you crazy old bat. How do you go saying to this batch of crazy hens that I had a ministroke? It's not right, if you ask me."

"See, he doesn't even remember when he had his stroke. That's how bad it is. Trust me, ladies," Guthrie's wife said. "He doesn't know what he's saying."

"I know exactly—"

"Please!" I interrupted. "Would someone please tell me what's going on? And why you are all standing outside my flower shop on this cold night?"

The woman who had been sobbing over the untimely demise of Barley wiped her eyes. "We need to buy flowers to put in front of his tour bus right now. We have to pay our respects to this great talent."

I looked at them. "All right." I wasn't sure it was a good idea to let Barley's superfans into the flower shop after closing. I edged around them. "Will you just let me have a second to unlock the shop?"

They crowded around me under the yellow awning while I unlocked the door. So much for giving me some space. I guessed the Barley McFee Grannies didn't know what that meant.

I unlocked the door, and the group of twenty-some concertgoers poured inside. I hadn't had this many people in my shop since the grand opening months ago.

"Oh! She has roses. We must have roses. Red for love and white for purity. Barley was beloved and pure of heart," a white-haired woman exclaimed.

"And purple thistle too," her companion agreed. "It's the symbol of Scotland. He was a Scotsman through and through."

"Aye, that he was."

The three men stood in front of one of the two large display windows in the front of the store, the scowls on their faces so fierce that I gave them a wide berth. I couldn't figure out why they were even there if they were so miserable. Couldn't they have waited outside for the women?

Maybe these three guys had come a long way to make their wives happy by going to a Barley McFee concert. Maybe they'd thought they were just on the brink of leaving Bellewick forever and going home when the women learned Barley had died. There was no leaving now until the women had paid Barley all the respect they believed he deserved. I guessed that if I'd been one of those men, I'd be a little bit frustrated too.

I watched in awe as the women flew about the shop, picking up every bouquet, touching the flower petals and buds, smelling them and holding them a little too tightly. "I can show you flowers you can have for free," I yelled over the din. I had to do something before they mangled every single blossom in the shop.

"No, dear, you're a businesswoman, and we support women entrepreneurs," the ringleader said. "We would never take money out of another woman's pocket. We will pay for all of these."

The women rushed the counter. All were holding bouquets they had stripped from other arrangements. Behind them my shop looked like it had been hit by a cloud of grasshoppers. There were just a few leaves and stems left in the women's wake.

Considering the mess they had made of the shop, I was inclined to let them pay for the flowers.

Forty-five minutes later, I'd rung up the last woman. She held her bouquet of thistle, roses, and dahlias close to her chest. I handed her credit card back to her. "Thank you for your business."

Tears shone in her eyes. "No, thank you. If your store hadn't been here, I don't know what we would do. Barley deserves our respect."

I studied her. "He seems to have been quite a guy."

"He was." She nodded solemnly. "He didn't have an easy life and made a name for himself just by his incredible talent. He's a real rags-to-riches story. It's inspirational." She gathered up her makeshift bouquet and toddled out the door in the direction the other women had gone.

After she left, one of the three men remained in the store. Before he went out the door, he angrily grabbed a final rose from the vase in the front of the shop and marched out without paying.

After they had gone, I stared at the mess that was the Climbing Rose. I'd made a good deal of money from the women, more than the shop typically made in a month, so I tried not to be too upset at the disaster they had left behind.

I yawned. What I should have done was lock up the shop and go home, but it wasn't something I was capable of. I knew I wouldn't be able to sleep if I knew the mess and overturned vases were waiting for me in the morning. As I worked, I thought about how little I knew about Barley McFee. The last woman in the shop had said he was self-made. That made me wonder what his life as a child had been like, and about his mysterious relative who'd gruffly stopped me at the concert.

I yawned and was half tempted to leave the rest of the cleanup for the morning, but I couldn't do that. "Be kind to future Fiona," I whispered to myself. Today's Fiona was tired, but there was no guarantee tomorrow's Fiona wouldn't be tired too.

I rolled up my sleeves and got to work, having no idea what was in store for poor future Fiona. Had I known, I would have left the shop just as it was.

Chapter Twelve

I rolled over in my bed and groaned. It was still dark outside. I reached for my phone. Even though it was dark, it was time to start the day. I was expecting a flower delivery that morning, and the van usually came in early. I flipped onto my belly and put my pillow over the back of my head. Everything was sore. I hadn't arrived home from the flower shop until well after midnight. After I had cleaned the place up, I'd seen how low I was on flowers, put in an emergency online order with my supplier in Aberdeen, and prayed that they would be delivered this morning with my usual order. I'd paid extra for the quick turnaround.

There was a meow, and then I let out a grunt as Ivanhoe jumped from the floor to the middle of my back. He wasn't a dainty cat. Scottish Folds were known for their sturdy and stocky build, which served them well in Scotland's rugged terrain. Not that Ivanhoe had to experience any of the steep Scottish mountains. He spent his days strolling around the cottage, lounging around the garden, and occasionally accompanying me to the Climbing Rose to have an audience with his admiring public.

"Ivanhoe, you are getting heavier. How many mice are you eating around Duncreigan?" I said into my pillow.

He mewed his sweet meow that belied his size and stature. I found this the funniest part of the cat. He was a hardy boy with the sweetest kitten meow you had ever heard.

Ivanhoe bonked me on the back of the head with his paw. I was glad his claws were sheathed, but he was still a powerful cat. I felt the impact all the way to my forehead.

"Leave me alone," I said into the pillow. "Don't you know I have another dead body on my hands, and my parents are in Scotland? A girl can only take so much."

Bonk. He hit me again. He didn't care I was in a bind. He wouldn't have cared if I was the prime minister making wartime decisions. He would still bonk me on the back of the head to remind me when it was time for breakfast.

"We both know you can catch your own meal outside, but . . ." I started to move, and he jumped off my back, literally.

My feet hit the floor. "I'm up," I grumbled, and padded out of the bedroom.

After I fed Ivanhoe and was dressed for the day, I left the cottage, locking the door with the old-fashioned skeleton key Hamish had given me on my first day in Scotland. That was the day I'd learned about the magic in the garden.

Ivanhoe had followed me outside. Usually when the weather was good, I let him roam. When the weather was bad, I took him into the village with me to be my shop cat. It was a position he both loved and hated. He loved it because he could preen in front of his many admirers. He hated it because I kept stopping him from eating the flowers and plants I was trying to sell.

Hamish didn't like it when I left Ivanhoe to his own devices because the cat was the sworn enemy of Hamish's pet squirrel, Duncan. Mostly Hamish disliked this because Ivanhoe would have enjoyed eating Duncan for breakfast much more than the kibble I fed him.

Ivanhoe purred and wove his thick body in and around my legs as I walked down the hill to the garden. I had to keep watching my feet to keep from falling. He was much happier with me now that he had eaten. "Seriously, you are going to make me fall."

The cat stood still midpurr, and the fur on his back went straight up. He hissed. I blinked. Ivanhoe didn't hiss often. "What's gotten into you?" Then I looked up from my feet and ahead at the garden.

Something was very wrong. I broke into a run. Ivanhoe was right behind me. As I ran, my feet slid on the smooth granite rocks that popped out of the blanket of grass and clover stretching between me and the garden. Usually I took more care when going to the garden because of the slippery stones, but not today.

I tripped and then steadied myself. I reached the wall and placed a hand on the cold stone. "No, no, no, this is not happening. I'm here. I'm here. This cannot happen when the Keeper is in Scotland!" I shouted at the old stone wall of the garden, as if my protests would be enough to stop the garden from dying.

The garden was dying. Again. This was the second time I had seen this happen. The first time had been when Uncle Ian was killed. When there was no Keeper connected to the garden, the garden died. The yellow rose on the menhir shriveled and fell away. The garden had come back when I arrived in Scotland and accepted my role as Keeper. I hadn't known at the time that I was also filling the role as my birthright as his biological daughter.

My breath caught in my chest. The ivy that usually concealed the location of the door had been pushed away. The leaves were bending, turning brown, and falling to the ground. It was just like when I'd first arrived at Duncreigan after my godfather died. The ivy on the garden walls had been dead then, and it was dying now.

I looked over my shoulder, although I didn't know what or who I expected to see behind me. I was alone at Duncreigan except for Ivanhoe. The cat sat at my feet looking as concerned as I felt as he stared at the garden wall.

"What will we find inside?" I whispered the question.

I went to unlock the garden door with my old skeleton key, but when I touched the door, it swung inward. Dread seeped into my body.

I pushed open the door and gasped. When I visited the garden yesterday morning before I left for the concert, it had been the picture of health. Flower beds were bursting with color. The trees were in their autumn glory, with brightly colored leaves. The fox had been waiting for me like he did every day. That wasn't what was in front of me now. I felt my chest tighten. Had the nightmare I'd had come true? Had it in fact been a vision? I scooped up Ivanhoe, as if the cat's warmth would comfort me in some way. Maybe the cat and I would be able to protect ourselves from whatever the garden held.

My shoulders sagged as I stepped deeper in the garden. The grass under my feet crackled and snapped. It was dry and dead. Every crack and snap sounded like a gunshot in my head.

I should have checked on the garden last night before going to bed. It had been late, of course, but what if I could have stopped this?

I set Ivanhoe on my left shoulder, and he made no attempt to jump down. I knew the cat sensed something was off about the garden, too, as he dug his claws into the shoulder of my coat.

I removed my phone from my pocket and called Hamish in his bothy, a tiny cottage half the size of mine just on the edge of Duncreigan. The phone rang and rang, but there was no answer. Most likely Hamish was already making his way to the garden. It wasn't uncommon for him to beat me there in the mornings, no matter what time I awoke.

Even so, I wished the old man carried a cell phone. It would make it so much easier when I needed to get in touch with him—like I did right now—to tell him the garden was in some serious trouble.

I shifted Ivanhoe in my arms, and still the cat didn't fight me. He seemed to understand that this was not the typical visit we made to the garden each and every morning. No, this time was very, very different.

The front of the garden was dead, but I knew the heart of the garden was blocked from my sight by the hedgerow in the middle of the garden. That small hedgerow protected the menhir and its climbing rose from view.

I took a deep breath, came around the side of the hedge, and saw the climbing rose, brown and withered on the stone. Its single yellow blossom was on the ground. A boot print was pressed into its delicate petals. I set Ivanhoe down, and the cat looked up at me with the saddest feline face I had ever seen. I picked up the trampled rose and held it in my hand. Two crushed petals fell from the blossom.

I examined the stem. It wasn't ripped from the plant. It had been cut. Who would do this? I felt sick. There had been one enemy against my garden, but he had died months ago. Who was left that would want to hurt the garden or me in this way?

Then I remembered seeing Carver Finley just for a moment at the concert. Had he come to Duncreigan when he knew I was otherwise occupied? Had he killed Barley McFee to distract me from coming home to the garden?

Now, because the rose was withered, the triskeles—Celtic symbols shaped into triple spirals—etched into the stone stood out more. I place a hand to my throat and felt the triskele necklace my godfather had given me there. Ever since I received the necklace, I hadn't taken it off, not even in the shower. It was my connection to Uncle Ian, but not my only connection. This garden had been the other, and now it was dead? No, it couldn't be dead! Not completely. I was the Keeper. I should be able to bring it back.

I could bring it back, right? Not for the first time, I wished Ian was alive to fully explain the magic of this place and how it worked. I knew I was supposed to have a connection to the garden. Could I save it with the sheer force of my will? I placed my hand on the stone like I had so many times before to receive a vision. Nothing happened. I closed my eyes more tightly. Again, nothing.

I squeezed the stone until my fingers and hand ached from the effort, but still nothing. "Please, please, work," I whispered.

But the menhir and the garden didn't respond. It was utterly silent. No birds sang, and the large willow tree that overlooked the entire garden didn't even move in the wind. There was no sea breeze rolling over the cliffs to Duncreigan. Everything was still. That's when I knew I had a real reason to be frightened for the garden and for myself. What did it mean if I failed as the Keeper? I didn't know. The instructions my godfather had left me about my role had been slim at best. I didn't know what would happen now.

I felt a headache forming in the back of my head from the exertion of trying to force a vision. I should have expected that my gift and connection with the garden could not be forced, no matter how much I needed it to be.

Then there was a sound, and it was like a crack in the stillness. There was a rustling of leaves to my left, and I looked up and stared into the blue eyes of the fox—just like mine, like Uncle Ian's. I wished he could speak to me and tell me he was my godfather like Presha believed. But he said nothing, just watched me. I didn't know if the fox was guarding me or watching over the garden, or both.

I was tempted to hide the blossom behind my back so he couldn't see how badly I had failed his garden. There was no point, and there was no use in doing that. He could see just as well as I could that the garden was dying on my watch.

I placed my hand on the standing stone again. The stone bestowed a gift on each Keeper. Each gift was unique. My gift was visions. My gift wasn't working. Was that my fault or the fault of whoever had done this to the garden? I didn't know.

I saw nothing. Perhaps the stone had lost its magic now that the rose was dead. It couldn't be completely dead, not after all these centuries. One person and a pair of scissors couldn't erase three hundred years of history. I turned to the fox. "Uncle Ian, what do I do?"

He stared at me wordlessly.

I felt a pang in my chest. I should have come early. Maybe I could have caught it before it got this far.

The fox made no effort to move any closer to me.

"Uncle Ian, I'm sorry," I whispered.

I could feel his disappointment from where I stood. A moment later, the fox leaped over the wall and was gone. I felt like I'd lost more than just the sight of the fox. I felt like I'd lost my gift. I didn't know if I could ever bring it back.

If I couldn't receive a vision from the stone, I had to find out who'd done this. I stepped back and took a better look at the boot print. I removed my phone from my pocket and took a picture of it, focusing on the tread. I knew I couldn't be walking around the village asking people to show me the bottoms of their boots, but Chief Inspector Craig could if we narrowed it down to who might have done this. I circled around the stone, looking for other boot prints that might be on the ground. I scanned the area. How had the person who'd done this gotten inside the garden? It was locked. I always kept it locked, and so did Hamish. Would Hamish have forgotten to lock it when he left yesterday? He was the only other person with access to the garden.

I walked around the hedgerow, the rose's blossom still in my hand. Hamish stood in the middle of the garden with his mouth hanging open.

"Oh lass, what has happened here?" Hamish's voice was muffled, like it had become caught in his throat. The old man fought back tears. He spotted the rose in my hand. "What has happened?"

Duncan jumped from Hamish's shoulder to the ground and ran as fast as his tiny legs could carry him to the now-bare willow tree on the other side of the hedgerow. It was his favorite view of the garden.

Ivanhoe began to fight me then, with the squirrel so near. I placed him on the ground, and he ran to the foot of the tree and looked up. For some reason, I was relieved that some normalcy remained, even if it was my cat trying to eat Hamish's squirrel.

"I think someone broke into the garden and cut the rose." I held the blossom out for him to see. "I found it like this." I took a breath. "When you left the garden yesterday, did you lock the door?"

Hamish reared back. "Did I lock the door? How can you even ask me that sort of thing? I have been tending the plants in this garden for over sixty years. Of course I locked the door."

I frowned. "I'm sorry, Hamish. I just don't know how whoever did this got in. I suppose he or she could have climbed the walls. It wouldn't be impossible if the person was physically fit enough."

"Lass," Hamish murmured as he took it all in. "What are you going to do?"

I stared at him. "I was hoping you could tell me what to do."

He shook his head.

I curled my fingers around the yellow blossom. "Okay, then I will just have to figure out how to bring the garden back to life. It's my duty as the Keeper. And I'm going to find out who did this, too."

"You will find a way, lass. I believe in you." His voice wavered. "And you will make whoever did this sorry he or she ever set foot in this garden, too."

I wished I were as confident.

Chapter Thirteen

Hamish promised he would work in the garden, cleaning up the fallen leaves and dead flowers. I appreciated his willingness to do it when I didn't have the heart to.

As much as I wanted to stay in the garden and look for more clues, I needed to get to the village and meet the flower delivery truck. Isla was working at the pub this morning and couldn't open for me. She worked half time for me and half time for Raj at the Twisted Fox. Before I left for the village, I stopped back at the cottage, tucked Ivanhoe inside so he would be out of Hamish's way, and placed the yellow rose blossom in a glass bowl of water on my tiny dining table. The blossom was still vibrantly yellow, and the only way I knew to keep it that way as long as possible was water. I didn't know what condition it would be in when I returned home. I felt sick when I thought of the garden and promised myself I would get back to it as quickly as I could.

In Bellewick, I parked my car in the small community lot just outside the village. The lot was only a quarter full, like it normally was. Things in Bellewick were going back to the way they'd been before the concert—but only to a point, I realized when I walked under the stone arch that led into the village and beyond the foreboding unicorn statue.

The Barley McFee Grannies were out in full force. The women, not the men—they must have bailed—who had stormed into my flower shop the night before were weeping and whispering in front of the small shrine beside the tour bus. I saw Gemma front and center. She cried with the most abandon. Someone played fiddle music from her phone, and I guessed that the performance was one of Barley's.

The flowers I'd sold them were displayed in piles just ten feet from the tour bus. That was as close as the women could be to the bus since crime scene tape, which was attached to pegs in the ground, wrapped around the vehicle.

I blinked when I saw I had been mistaken. There was one man with the group. It was the same man who'd grabbed my arm after Barley died and claimed to be a jilted relative. I glanced around for any sign of a constable to whom I could point the man out. The only officer I saw was Kipling, and no one wanted Kipling questioning a witness. He marched back and forth in front of the bus, his arms swinging like a toy solider. I guessed guard duty was the job Craig had given him to keep him out of the way.

Barley's relative looked over his shoulder and spotted me. His eyes narrowed, and he walked away from the BMGs and started into the village. I followed him. He must have realized I was behind him, because he walked faster, and then he broke into a full-out run.

I ran too. I didn't know why I was chasing him. He had thirty years on me, but the guy was fast.

There was no way I was going to catch him when he had such a big head start, and what did I plan to do or say if I did catch him? Was I going to accuse him of murder and expect him to docilely talk to the police about it? That didn't seem a likely scenario, since he was fleeing.

Now he was so far ahead of me that I lost sight of him when he turned a corner.

I started to slow my pace and removed my phone from my pocket. At least I could tell Craig that the man who claimed to be Barley's relative was still in the village. I couldn't understand why he was still there if Barley was dead.

Even though there wasn't much point to it, I increased my speed, panting as I ran around the corner. I spotted him down the next street. He was still running. A woman opened the gate that led into her postage-stamp yard. It hung over the narrow sidewalk. He must not have seen it, because he ran directly into the gate. He flew backward and landed flat on his back.

I forgot the text I was crafting to Craig and ran up to the man.

The older woman was someone I saw often in the neighborhood. She walked every day to the small Tesco at the end of the road and bought her groceries. She carried all her groceries for the day in one straw bag, and she held that straw bag now. She used it to whack the man on the side of the head.

"Don't you go scaring an old woman like that." *Whack. Whack.* "Didn't your mother teach you better?" Her Scottish accent was thick, and it sounded like she added in some Gaelic chastisements I didn't understand.

She then stepped over him and made her was to the Tesco. She glared at me as she passed. She wasn't happy that an upstart American had moved to Duncreigan. According to Presha, that's what she called me.

The man rubbed the side of his head where she had hit him with the bag. I stood a few feet away, looking down at him. "It could have been worse," I consoled him. "She could have hit you with that bag on her way home from the grocery store when it was full. That would really smart."

He groaned.

I looked down at him. "Are you okay?"

He glared at me. "Do I look okay? I'm not okay in the least. It's your fault that the crazy old bat knocked me to the ground." He sat up and groaned with the effort.

I put my hand out to help him.

He glared at my hand and got up on his own. "Why were you following me?"

"I want to talk to you. I didn't tell you to run into the gate."

He grumbled to himself, but with his thick Scottish accent I couldn't decipher what he was saying. I thought that was probably for the best.

"What do you know about Barley McFee?"

"Nothing," he snapped, and took a step back away from me.

I wouldn't have been the least bit surprised if he bolted again. "You must know something. You said you were a relative of his."

"I shouldn't have told you that. You probably didn't deliver the message to him that I asked you to, either." He glared at me.

"I didn't because he was already dead when you asked me."

"You could have told me that," he said. "It would have saved me a lot of trouble."

"The police hadn't given me permission to do that. I wasn't able to tell anyone."

He crossed his arms.

"Are you going to tell me who you are? What's your name?" I asked.

He studied me for a moment. "What's your name?"

"Fiona Knox. I'm the local florist."

He gaped at me. "Why is a florist chasing me through the village?"

It was a good question, and not one I had a logical answer for, so I moved on. "What's your name?"

"Mick McFee."

"McFee?"

"That's right. I'm Barley's cousin—second cousin, to be clear, but we were friends as lads, as we were close in age. We spent much time together as boys when my family would visit his parents here in Bellewick. I was close enough to him growing up that he should have remembered me later in life," he added bitterly.

"Remembered you how?" I asked.

He narrowed his eyes. "Barley had more money than God. The least he could do was share it with the people who knew him before his great fame. We're the ones who know who the real Barley is. If he wasn't willing to do that . . ."

I shivered, and it was my turn to take a step back. "If he wasn't willing to do what?"

"I was just going to tell the media who he really was and the lives he destroyed on his trip to the top. You don't get to where Barley was in music without a few casualties along the way."

I wished I could text Craig to get here quick. He should have been hearing this, but I couldn't think of a way to text him without Mick seeing me do it.

"What did Barley do on his climb to the top?" I asked.

He laughed. "I'm not telling you that now. There's no point to tell anyone now that he's dead. I will say that he had it coming to him. I'm not surprised that this is the end he came to."

I changed tactics. "It sounds to me like you planned to blackmail Barley."

He shrugged. "I did."

I stared at him.

He laughed. "You didn't think I would come right out and say it like that, did you? But you're right. I was going to blackmail him to get my fair share of what's been owed me for keeping my mouth shut all these years. However, I know what you are getting at, and this conversation should prove to you that I'm innocent."

I took another step back. If I took one more step, I would fall off the sidewalk and into the street. "I don't see how."

"If you thought about it for a moment, you would. What good is Barley dead to me? I won't be seeing any money now. I'm not in the will. I haven't seen him in forty years." He shook his head. "No, I wish he was still alive, because Barley is no good to me dead."

He had a point.

"I guess the question is, who got an advantage when Barley died?" I said.

He looked at me. "I wouldn't know."

I would have bet all of Duncreigan that he was lying.

Chapter Fourteen

I eventually made it to my shop, and I was thrilled to see the flower delivery truck pull up the moment I unlocked the door. The vehicle was plain white and about the size of a UPS truck. By sheer skill, the driver was able to navigate the narrow cobblestone streets around parked cars and bicycles and stop right outside my front door. The thing about delivery people in Scotland, I had found, was that they could fit in the tightest spots. They also drove on the sidewalk when necessary. That would have been a huge no-no back in Nashville.

"Good to see you, Fiona," the driver, Carl, said. He was typically the delivery guy the flower distributor sent me. I was lucky enough to have a flower warehouse so close by. Since Aberdeen was on the North Sea and had so many shipping routes, it had a great selection. It wasn't easy to keep flowers gorgeous from greenhouse to flower shop, so they needed to be moved quickly from point A to point B. Carl was a pro.

"You have a huge order today. What happened? Sheep break into the flower shop and eat everything?" He laughed.

I arched my brow at him. "Sheep?"

He opened the back of the truck, and the sweet scent of lilac and lavender hit me as well as the smell of new leaves. I never tired of any of those smells.

"It's been known to happen," he said. "You know sheep wander free out here. One time I was making a delivery in a neighboring village and saw a whole flock of sheep being chased out of a pub by the owner. He said it was the good music that brought the flock in."

"It wasn't sheep this time," I assured him. "I just had a lot of unexpected sales at the end of the day. I'm so grateful you're able to restock me so quickly."

"You were in luck. A cargo ship pulled in last night, and we were off-loading it when we got your order. I set everything you asked for aside for you, right off the ship."

"You are my hero." I smiled.

"Oh, you are too kind." The tops of his ears turned red. "Being called a hero sounds especially impressive in your accent."

"You like the sound of my voice?"

"'Course I do. I have a soft spot for American country music."

"You're the first one to tell me that since I moved to Scotland."

"There are others." He set a bucket of fresh roses on the sidewalk. "They just don't come right out and say it. It's not the most popular music in the UK overall, you know."

I did know.

Carl and I worked in silence for a while as we off-loaded the truck. Carl was right; it was as huge order. It looked like I'd ordered two of everything as far as the flowers were concerned. Of course, there were the standing orders I always took of sunflowers, daisies, and roses, but I also liked to keep a variety of other more interesting flowers.

The flowers were in water buckets, and I counted a total of forty buckets in all. I had gotten a bit carried away. It was an easy thing to do when flowers were involved. Some women went crazy for sweets, jewelry, or new shoes. My downfall was flowers. It always had been. I wondered now, knowing what I did about Uncle Ian and Duncreigan, if a love of flowers was hardwired into my DNA. Maybe I had no choice but to love them.

He closed the back of his truck, slamming the door shut. "I heard about the concert."

"You did?" My eyebrows went up.

"Of course I did. It was all over the news this morning. I'm surprised you didn't see the reporters."

"There are reporters in Bellewick?" I supposed I should have expected this. The other times there had been a murder in Bellewick, it had involved a local person. In those cases, a short blurb had been run in the Aberdeen paper and on the local news. I couldn't remember any reporters actually coming to the village to check the facts.

This time, things were different because the victim was famous, not just famous but world famous, and a household name in Scotland.

"Where did you see the reporters?" I asked.

"You know I can't get over the bridge that comes into the village with my truck, so I came in the back way behind Thistle House. They were all standing out there. They were speaking to a man with glasses."

It had to be Owen, Barley's manager.

"Were they having a press conference?" I asked.

"That's what it looked like to me. There were police there. Chief Inspector Craig was front and center."

I pressed my lips together, upset Craig hadn't mentioned the press conference to me, not that he should. It wasn't his job to tell his girlfriend what he was up to, but still, he would have known I'd be interested. I didn't think it was an oversight. I knew that much.

Now it made more sense to me that there were no constables by the crime scene and just Kipling standing there looking somewhat official. They would be at the press conference, and that was the last place Craig would have wanted Kipling.

"It's a terrible shame about Barley," Carl went on. "No one played the fiddle quite like him. He could make you cry or tap your toe. It takes a real talent to be able to do both with music."

"Do you think the press conference is still happening?" If it was, I planned to be there.

He shook his head. "It broke up just as I drove by. Chief Inspector Craig said he wasn't taking any questions about the investigation. That sure upset some of the reporters. They seemed to think they could change his mind. Clearly, they had never met the man."

Clearly.

He stretched. "I'd better head out. I have two more deliveries to make before I head back to Aberdeen. You know we have to keep the flowers fresh."

I did know.

Carl left not long after that, and I went back into the shop to organize the flowers. While I worked, my mind wandered between the argument I'd had with my parents and Barley McFee's death. I couldn't get it out of my head that my parents might know more about Barley than they were letting on. What I didn't understand was why they were being secretive about it. That wasn't their way. At least I would have said that a few months ago, before I knew about the bizarre circumstances surrounding my birth, which they'd had no trouble keeping closemouthed about all this time.

My parents had been very close friends with Uncle Ian, and it would have made more sense to me if they'd said they knew Barley—if he really had been a close friend of my godfather.

There was a knock on the shop door, and I looked up from the arrangement I was in the middle of creating. With all these new flowers, I would be at the shop late into the night organizing them. It was certainly the worst day at the flower shop for Isla to be working at the pub. I was considering walking next door to ask if Raj could spare her for an hour or two, just so I could get a handle on all these flowers. I hadn't had so many delivered at one time since before the shop's grand opening.

I set my scissors on the room table and dusted the pollen off my hands. I tried to remember to wear gloves, but it wasn't unusual for me to walk around the village with slightly gold-tinted fingertips from all the pollen I encountered in working with the flowers.

I opened the half door and stepped behind the counter. "May I help you?"

"I believe so." The moment the women spoke, I knew she wasn't from around here. She had a clear English accent. I had lived in Great Britain long enough now that I could recognize the difference between an English and a Scottish accent. When I'd first arrived, I hadn't a clue.

My second clue that she wasn't a Bellewick resident was her outfit. She wore a burgundy pencil-skirted suit, complete with nude pumps that would be a nightmare to walk down the village's cobblestone streets in. The only person who dressed up that much in Bellewick was the local attorney, Cally Beckleberry, but everyone else was more or less dressed for comfort. I looked down at my skinny jeans and oversized sweater. I was no exception.

"I'm looking for Fiona Knox," she said.

"I'm Fiona. Can I help you select some flowers?" Even as I asked, I knew that wasn't why she was here.

She held up her finger and poked her head out the door. "It's her!" She waved whoever was standing there inside. The door opened again and a cameraman entered, wearing a Windbreaker emblazoned with the logo of the local Aberdeen news station.

"We just want to know if we could have a moment of your time to answer a few questions about what happened when you found Barley McFee's body," the female reporter said, pulling a small microphone and a notepad out of her purse.

"Why do you think I was the one who found the body?" I stumbled back.

"It's what everyone in the village is saying." She looked at her notepad. "In fact, we ran into your sister Isla Knox, and she was the one to confirm that you were the person who originally found the body." She studied me. "You two don't look anything alike."

I frowned. I was well aware of my physical differences from my gorgeous younger sister. I didn't need her to point them out. "I'm sorry. I can't help you. The police have asked me not to talk to the press."

"That would be Chief Inspector Craig, who you have a romantic relationship with, then?" She pointed the microphone at me.

Isla! I shouted in my head. I loved my little sister dearly, but her mouth had gotten her and me into trouble more times than I could count. This time was no exception.

"What's your name?" I went on the offensive.

She straightened her shoulders. "Trina Graham, Action News."

"Well, Trina," I began. "I understand that you're just doing your job by coming here to talk to me, but I really can't say anything at all about what happened in the village yesterday. I will have to ask you to leave my shop, unless I could interest you in a bouquet."

She scowled. "Don't you care a man is murdered?"

I blinked. "Of course I care. I care when anyone passes away, especially under such horrible circumstances."

She leaned in. "Tell me about those circumstances. How was he killed? The more descriptive you can be, the better."

The fact that she was asking the question told me Craig hadn't released that information yet, and I sure wasn't going to say a peep about it. He must have a reason to keep the murder weapon a secret.

"I'm happy to talk about flowers. We just had a fresh shipment today, so all the flowers are at their peak. This would be the time to buy."

She gestured at the cameraman to cut filming. He lowered his camera. "We are giving you a chance here to tell the story your way. If you let the gossip magazines at you, your reputation will be ruined."

What was with people in Scotland about reputation? Bernice was worried about the reputation of the village too.

"Thank you for your concern," I said coolly, "but I can't go against the request of the police."

She eyed me. "Do you want it to make it on the news reports that the chief inspector is dating a primary witness? That would get Chief Inspector Craig removed from the case just to start."

My eyes narrowed. "Are you threatening me?"

"This story has the potential for international appeal because of Barley's fame. Don't believe for a second that I will let it fall through the cracks to be picked up by another reporter. This is my story."

"I wouldn't dare," I said, a little more sarcastically than I intended.

"I'll find out what happened to Barley McFee, trust me." She spun on her heel and marched out the door, the cameraman trailing along after her.

I didn't doubt for a second that she would try, but succeeding was a lot different from trying.

Chapter Fifteen

At lunchtime, I put a sign on the front door of the Climbing Rose saying I would be back in an hour and walked next door to the pub for lunch. During the quiet parts of the day, I worried over the state of my garden and the murder in turn. Could the two be connected? They'd happened very close to each other, but that would make me think Barley had a connection to the garden. As far as I knew, that wasn't possible.

I pushed open the heavy wooden door, and my eyes adjusted to the dim light. I didn't know what it was about British pubs, but they all seemed to be intentionally dark, like it was part of their appeal.

Before my vision acclimated, I heard a voice. "There's the American girl. We were wondering when you'd stop by. There's a murderer afoot, so it stands to reason that you would want to know about it."

I immediately recognized the hoarse rasp as Popeye's. Popeye was one of three old sailors who spent their time divided between the Twisted Fox and the village harbor.

I had never seen them go anywhere other than those two places. I knew that if I so much as ran into Popeye at Tesco, I would be shocked.

Isla, who wore ripped jeans, a pink flannel shirt, and a white apron cinched around her waist, set three glasses of ale in front of the sailors. "Why do you call Fiona that American girl? I'm an American girl too. You never call me that."

Popeye smiled at her, and I almost fainted. In all the time I had lived in the village, I had never seen him smile once, but there he was, beaming at my sister.

"Aye, I suppose that you are, but you seem to be more Scottish than she. No one could pour a pint of ale so well and be from the New World."

Isla laughed and then floated back to the bar with her tray. I shook my head. For all her faults, my sister had a way with people that put them at ease; apparently it worked on even the grouchiest of men.

Isla stepped behind the bar and began rinsing glasses. "Raj is in the kitchen grabbing your tikka masala order with the cook."

"How does he know that's what I want?" I asked.

She set the glasses in a drying rack. "It's what you always want."

A moment later, the swinging door between the bar and the kitchen opened and Raj stepped through it, holding a tray of white rice and a steaming brass bowl of tikka masala. It smelled heavenly. It was what I always wanted. Isla was right.

He set it in front of me.

"Thank you. You're a prince."

He smiled. "Be careful. It's hot."

"And spicy?" I asked hopefully.

"So spicy that I'm sure you will break into a sweat."

"That sounds perfect," I said. Before coming to Scotland, I hadn't had much of a taste for spicy food, but with my flower shop being next to a pub that boasted a mix of Indian cuisine and standard pub fare, I now loved anything with a kick.

I dipped my spoon into the bowl. "There was a man who was in the village for the concert by the name of Mick McFee. Does that ring any bells for you?"

"The *McFee* does, since it was Barley's last name," Raj said.

"He claimed to be a second cousin of Barley and said that he visited Barley and his parents here in the village often."

Raj thought about this for a moment. "Could be, but Barley had to have been my age or older. Presha and I didn't come to this village until we were in our twenties. I wouldn't have known Barley as a child. In fact, I believe he had already left the village and begun his career in music before we arrived. We heard of him, but yesterday was the first time I had ever seen him in person."

I nodded, but felt disappointed that Raj couldn't tell me more. I wished there had been someone else in the village I could ask.

I stirred the masala with my spoon in hopes of cooling it to a temperature I could actually put in my mouth.

"I saw a cluster of women by the tour bus," Raj said. "They looked like they were taking it hard."

I nodded. "That's the BMGs."

"BMGs?"

"Barclay McFee Grannies."

"I'm sorry I asked."

I told him about their late visit to the flower shop.

"I wondered why you ordered so many flowers this morning," Isla said, as she came out of the kitchen with a tray of food for one of the tables. It appeared that this set of diners was sticking to traditional British fare in the form of fish and chips and ale.

"Do you have an idea who did him in yet?" Raj leaned in.

I shifted on my seat. "Why on earth would you ask me that?"

"It's a fair question. It comes as no shock to anyone that you will help Chief Inspector Craig with the investigation. I'm sure he is looking forward to your support as well," Raj said. "You two have become quite a team over the last several months."

I tasted my lunch, and it was as spicy and delicious as Raj had promised it would be. Eating also gave me time to control my expression. I didn't think Craig was happy in the least that I might snoop around in the murder investigation, and I didn't know if I even wanted to. I didn't have any skin in the game this time. In the past when I was involved, I'd been the prime suspect both times. This time was very different. No one thought I had killed Barley. I'd had no reason to, and I had an alibi, since I'd been near the stage where everyone could see me at the time of the murder. What I did need to find out was what had happened to my garden. I wondered if it would be wise to close the shop a bit early so I could get home to the garden to investigate the crime that had happened at Duncreigan. Sales had been good yesterday with the last-minute arrival of the BMGs. Could I afford to take the rest of the day off?

The phone under the bar rang, and Raj picked it up. He shook his head. "No, we usually don't deliver, but we can do takeout for you if someone can come and pick it up." There was a pause. "You will pay that much for delivery?" There was another pause. "All right. What will you have?" Raj removed a notebook from his pocket and a pen and began to write furiously. "It will be about thirty to forty minutes . . . No, thank you." He hung up the phone and clapped his hands. "That's one of the biggest orders we've ever had."

I leaned over the bar. "What was it for?"

Instead of answering my question, he asked me one of his own: "Do you want to make a delivery?"

I frowned. "I don't work here. You should send Isla."

"But this is a delivery you would want to make." He smoothed his moustache with his forefinger.

"Since when does it look like I want to make deliveries?" I asked.

"I thought you would want to make the delivery because it's to the Thistle House to Barley McFee's band."

My eyes went wide. "I really shouldn't. Craig wouldn't like it."

Raj chuckled. "But you want to."

I grinned. "Of course I want to go, but I can't leave the flower shop for that long."

He grinned back. "The lunch rush is over. Isla can watch the flower shop for you for a little while—can't you, Isla?"

My sister came back around the bar with a tray full of dirty dishes. "Sure, but I didn't hear—why am I watching the flower shop?"

Raj gave her the quick version.

She shook her head. "I knew you wouldn't be able to leave that murder alone. You always have to snoop. It's part of your DNA."

"No, it's not, and really, this time I have no reason to snoop. I'm sorry Barley is dead, but I don't know him and don't know anyone he's connected to."

Isla smiled. "Then why are you so eager to make the delivery? I could do it, and you could go back to your flower shop."

"Do you want to do it?" I asked reluctantly, because she had a point.

"No way. I just know those people are going to complain about something, and I don't need that kind of negativity in my life. Besides, Mom and Dad are at the Thistle House. I still haven't told them about Seth."

"If you just want to tell them, Isla, do it. I don't like the idea of you being tortured by keeping this secret."

"I'm not being tortured, but Mom keeps dropping hints about me moving back to the farm. I'm not leaving Bellewick. This is where Seth and I want to be. I've fallen in love with him, but I have also fallen in love with this village and the people here. I don't want to leave them or you."

My heart swelled a little to know I was part of the reason my sister wanted to stay in Scotland. I would have been lying if I said I wouldn't be sad if she left. It was nice to have a little piece of home—and family—in the village.

"You will have to tell them eventually, just like I will have to tell them about Craig eventually," I said.

"I know," she agreed. "I'm just thinking of the perfect way. I have some ideas, and I think they will be very impressed if I can pull it off."

That sounded more than a little ominous.

"So you will make the delivery, Fiona?" Without waiting for an answer, Raj went on, "Give me twenty minutes to cook up the order, and you will be out the door. While I'm doing that, finish your own meal. I have a feeling you are going to need that energy."

I did too.

As promised, Raj came back from the kitchen twenty minutes later with a heavy cardboard box.

"Whoa," I said. "Did they order everything on the menu?" I asked.

"Just about," he said. "Delivery is a new venture I had never considered before. It might be a popular way for people to eat. Most Indian restaurants deliver."

"Most restaurants like that are in bigger cities, and so they have more people to deliver to." I stood up from my barstool.

"You always have to innovate to stay in business," Raj said thoughtfully.

I didn't know how food delivery was innovation, but I saw his point.

He pushed the box in my direction. "Now, be off with you. You have a murder to solve and food to deliver before it gets cold."

As I walked out the door, I wondered which of those tasks was more important. I guessed that in Raj's estimation, it was the danger of cold masala.

Chapter Sixteen

"You work as a delivery person and a florist. It must be a hard business selling flowers," Eugenia said as she opened the front door of the guesthouse for me.

I smiled as I carried the heavy box into the room. "I'm just helping Raj out."

She adjusted her glasses on her nose and blushed. "That's so kind of you. Raj is a nice man." She licked her lips. "When you were there, did he say what the specials are tonight? Usually I like to eat at the pub once a week."

I tried to keep my expression neutral, but was I right in suspecting a crush? "He didn't, but I'm sure you could call and find out. It was probably on the menu board at the bar and I didn't notice it."

"Well, maybe I'll just walk down there later to stretch my legs. There are so many people staying at Thistle House right now that it will be nice to slip away for a few minutes."

"I think that's a nice idea," I said, doing my best to hide a smile.

"Raj is a wonderful cook. I don't eat at his pub as much as I like, since I have to cook for all the guests here. It's easier to eat at home. There always seems to be leftovers." She laughed. "I know I make too much. That's what my poor husband used to say."

I didn't know she had been married.

As if she heard my unasked question, she said, "Floyd's been gone for ten years now. He was a good man and was friends with your godfather, Ian MacCallister. Most people in the village were. Everyone liked Ian, and we were so proud of his service for Queen and country."

"Thank you," I murmured. "Is there somewhere I can set this down?" The box was growing heavy in my arms.

"Oh, I'm so sorry. Let me show you to the dining room where they plan to eat." She turned and went back in the direction from which she had come.

I followed her down the hallway and atrium that had been converted into a dining room. It was the perfect place for it, with lots of natural light filling the space. There were six small tables in the room, and each could hold four people. The MacNish brothers sat at one of the tables. Kenda was nowhere to be seen.

"Finally. I'm starved." One of the brothers jumped out of his seat and took the box from me.

The two guys unloaded the box. The takeaway boxes and containers covered two of the tables. The amount of food Raj had been able to fit into the box was impressive. I was also impressed with myself for being able to carry it so far without my arms giving out.

Eugenia backed out of the room. "I should go finish cleaning the guests' rooms so I can walk down to the pub."

"Methi chicken and garlic naan! That's my favorite. We're going to be in a food coma after this," the first brother said.

"It's a good way to be, as long as we are stuck in this village," the second brother said, and then noticed me standing there. "Ugh, are you waiting for a tip or something? Because we told the guy to put it on our credit card."

"No," I said. "I—um—I just wanted to know how you all were with everything that happened. I'm Fiona Knox and a member of the Merchant Society of Bellewick that set up the concert."

The first brother cocked his head. "Les, she's the reason we're here."

If the second brother was Lester, I surmised that the first was Jamie.

"I thought that a concert in Bellewick was Barley's idea."

Lester took a bite of chicken and then shrugged. "I guess it was, but we would never have chosen Bellewick if the village wasn't on board."

"We had no idea that they were being so supportive because they wanted to kill him," Jamie said around a mouthful of food.

I had to look away. "You think the *village* killed Barley?"

Jamie shrugged, and I noted that both men did that a lot.

"Not the whole village," Jamie said. "But someone sure did."

"What makes you think it was someone in the village and not someone with the tour?"

Lester dropped his fork into his Styrofoam takeout box. "You mean like us?"

I nodded.

Lester looked at his brother. "She thinks we killed him."

"That would be stupid," Jamie said. "Now that Barley is dead, we're out of a job. There aren't many high-end acts like this that we can transfer to together. A band might want a guitarist or a bassist, but they rarely want both. They probably have one or the other."

"Yeah," his brother said. "And we like working together. It will be a shame if we have to break up over this." He eyed me. "So we get nothing out of losing Barley. We lost a sweet gig."

"If it makes you feel better," Jamie said, "the police asked us the same questions. I didn't expect them from a pub delivery person, though. This village sure is nosy."

"I'm not the pub delivery person. I was just helping my friend who owns the pub by dropping off this order. He knew I wanted to check on you to make sure you have everything you need, since I am a member of the Merchant Society." For all the times I bemoaned the MS, I sure was milking my involvement with the village group for all it was worth.

"Now that we have food, we are good," Jamie said.

I stood there and pretended I didn't get the blatant hint to leave.

"Is the food here yet?" a husky woman's voice asked from behind me.

I turned around, and Kenda waltzed into the dining room. She certainly didn't look like a woman mourning the death of her former lover.

"You guys didn't call me or tell me everything was ready. You need to keep me in the loop." She turned to me. "Who are you?"

The question was as blunt as it was intended to be.

I repeated the story I had told the brothers about the Merchant Society, and she sized me up. "If it weren't for your *Society*, we wouldn't have come here, and Barley would still be alive." A single tear rolled down her cheek. "Now the police think I killed him. It's so unfair."

The brothers shared a look, seemed to come to some sort of unspoken agreement, and dug into their food.

She took a breath. "I'm not hungry after all." She walked out the side door that led into a garden beside the house. The door slammed against the doorframe as she left.

The brothers weren't looking up from the table as they made their way through the food. They were done talking to me and wanted me to know it. I waited a full second before I followed Kenda out into the garden.

The garden was lovely. It was surround by a low stone wall that came up to my hip. The wall would do nothing to keep any animals out, but it gave a sense of privacy and separateness from the rest of the village beyond. The focal piece of the garden was a small pond, and I watched as a frog jumped from a lily pad into the water. I was surprised that the frog hadn't gone into hibernation for the winter yet. Perhaps he was hoping to catch a few more flies before his long winter's sleep. The tall grasses around the pond were brown and dying away at the end of the growing season. I felt my chest tighten as their demise reminded me of the current state of Duncreigan. That was what I should be doing now, finding out what was happening in my garden instead of spending my time searching for a killer. But what if the two events were related? They had happened on the same day . . .

Kenda sat on the part of the stone wall that faced the pond. She wiped at her face as if she was trying to erase any evidence of—what was it, grief? Grief for the loss of Barley? Or grief over being a suspect in his murder? Having been a murder suspect a couple of times in my life, I understood those mixed emotions.

I stepped on a twig. It snapped in two, and she looked up at me. "What do you want?"

"I told you my name is Fiona, and I want to help you if I may. I know this can be a scary time."

"What do you know about it?" she asked.

"Quite a lot, actually, since I have been accused by the police for murder twice before." I said this as if these events had been as mundane as going to the grocery store.

She stared openmouthed at me. "You don't look like someone who would kill someone."

"I've heard that's what is said about most killers, and it has been true of some I've personally met."

"What happened? How do I know you've really been a murder suspect?"

I gave her the abridged version of the story. I made no mention of my magical garden. There was no reason to muddy the waters with that. "Chief Inspector Craig is a good man. He won't arrest you if he knows you're innocent."

"That's just it. How is he going to know I'm innocent? I was so angry at Barley over, well, *everything* . . . I wasn't thinking clearly. I yelled at Barley a number of times since being in this village, and half a dozen witnesses told the chief inspector that. I even threatened to kill him once. I wouldn't, but I was *so* angry I couldn't control the words coming out of my mouth." She covered her eyes. "I'm in serious trouble."

I didn't correct her because she was right: she was in serious trouble.

"If you have an alibi," I said. "A good alibi is all you really need."

"But I don't. I was in the tour bus with him alone after the first set. The police know. At least five of Barley's Grannies saw me."

"The BMGs?" I asked.

"You know about them?"

I winced. "I'm afraid so."

"Yes, and then I came out and went to the stage just about the time that break was over. When Barley didn't come out, I guessed it was because he was stewing over our fight."

"What happened inside the tour bus?" I asked.

"We argued. It's all we did anymore. There was a time I thought he loved me. By the time we got to Bellewick, I wasn't under that delusion anymore. There were several of those old BMG biddies outside the tour bus, stalking Barley, of course, because they have nothing more interesting to do with their lives."

I winced at the venom in her voice. I didn't think a tone like that would go very far in endearing her to the police— or anyone, really.

"Those old bats told the police I was in the tour bus, and they heard me yelling and things crashing."

"Were you yelling? Were things crashing?"

"Well, yes," she said with a pout. "But that's just how Barley and I were. That's how our relationship was. We had a lot of fire. We were having an argument. He had promised me I would have some solo stage time to show the audience what I could do with a fiddle. Just the day before, he took it away from me. I knew it was out of spite because we broke up."

"If you broke up, why did you stay in his band?" I thought it was a logical question.

She stared at me as if I was the dumbest person she'd ever come across. "Barley was the best fiddle player in the world. Of course I wanted to be on stage with him. It was a great chance for exposure, but he kept pushing me to the background. I think he was afraid I was getting too good, that I was getting good enough that I could really challenge him to a duel. I asked him to duel, but he refused."

I blinked. "Like with swords?"

Was this a Scottish tradition I wasn't aware of?

Again I got the you-must-be-some-kind-of-idiot look. "With our fiddles. It was a way to showcase our talents and show the audience who the better fiddler was. Barley refused to do it, and I know it was because he was afraid I would crush him." She emphasized her point by pounding her fist on the stone wall beside her.

I reminded myself not to mess with Kenda. If she could crush Barley McFee, she could certainly crush me too.

I chewed on my lip. Things didn't sound good for Kenda at all. There was a lot of evidence pointing to her as the most likely killer. Why hadn't Craig arrested her yet? There must be another variable, or perhaps even another suspect. Another suspect would be very good news for Kenda. She needed all the alternative suspects she could find.

"Maybe you can help me, then, since you have had experience with murder. Maybe you can help me deal with the police. The only people I know here are the two MacNish brothers, and from what you saw in the dining room, all they care about is food and family lore. Don't get them talking about their family. It will bore you to tears. They barely even practice their instruments, while I put in hundreds of hours on my fiddle." She said this like it was a major failing on the brothers' part.

"They never practice?" I asked.

"They are just that talented. If they made an effort, they would be able to make names for themselves without Barley, but as of yet, they haven't been able to break away. I suppose they will have to now, just like I will."

"I don't think the police would like me helping you," I said.

"I don't care what they will like or not. I'm not going to spend the rest my life in some prison in northern Scotland."

"I may not be able to help you, but there's a good attorney in the village. Her name is Cally Beckleberry. She would be a good person to talk to about your situation. You can trust her advice."

"I should have thought about getting a barrister before. I should probably look at a few. Do you know any others in the village?"

I made a face. "Cally is it, I'm afraid. The village is under two thousand residents. We are lucky to have someone here at all. She does a lot of work in the city of Aberdeen. There's not enough here to keep her busy. She's sought after in the county, and she helped me when I was in a similar situation."

"All right. I'll talk to her. Do you have her number?"

I nodded and took my phone out of my coat pocket. I scrolled through my address book and rattled off the number while Kenda entered it into her phone.

I put the phone back in my pocket. "I know it might not be my place to ask, but why did you and Barley break up?"

She looked up at me. There were no longer tears in her eyes, but the sadness was still there. Part of me couldn't believe she'd killed anyone. I knew how ridiculous that was. She could be just as sad over the fact that she had murdered Barley. "He was stifling me." She looked up at the bright blue sky. "And I won't be stifled," she said with force. "The police want to pin this on me, but I do have one saving grace that just might be enough to keep me out of prison. I'll be telling Cally about it too."

"What's that?" I asked.

"I know I wasn't the last person to see Barley alive."

I blinked at her. "Why didn't you say that at the beginning?"

She shrugged. "I told the police. That's what's important."

"Who was this other person?"

"It was a man close to Barley's age. He was waiting outside the tour bus as I stormed out. Barley clearly knew him, and from the looks of it, he wasn't all that happy to see him."

"Why do you say that?" I asked.

"Because he said to the man, 'What are you doing here? I told you to leave me alone.'"

This mystery man was sounding more and more like a good suspect. I wondered if it might even be Mick McFee. I wouldn't put it past the churlish man to be lying when he said he hadn't spoken to Barley the day of the concert. Maybe he had even asked me to deliver a message for cover. "Do you know his name?"

"I heard Barley say, 'Hello, Stephen.'"

My stomach dropped to the soles of my shoes.

Chapter Seventeen

"You're sure the name he said was Stephen?" I prayed I had misheard her. This couldn't be happening. Barley couldn't have had a meeting with my father right before he died. It just wasn't possible. Stephen was a common name. It could have been someone else. There had been a lot of people in the village that day.

"I'm certain. I was standing right beside Barley when he said it, and then later I realized the man is staying here at the guesthouse with his wife. The wife is American like you."

This was much worse than I'd first thought, so much worse. I gaped at Kenda because I was at a complete loss for words. I could think of no reason why my father would be talking to Barley McFee after they'd both denied knowing each other.

"Even though Barley clearly didn't want to talk to the man, he let Stephen into the tour bus. Until that happened, I just assumed he was one more of Barley's superfans. In truth, most of his big fans are women, but there are a handful of men. However, when Barley let the man into the bus, I knew

Eugenia was at the front desk and blinked when I walked up to it. "Oh, I didn't realize you were still here."

I smiled. "I wandered into your garden. It's lovely."

"Thank you so much. That means a lot, coming from you, when you have such a way with flowers. You should come back in the summer when the garden is at its height. I would spend all my time out there if I could."

"I can see why." I cleared my throat. "Do you know which room my parents are in? I wanted to stop by and say hello while I was here."

"They are in room ten, but they aren't there now. They left very early this morning, saying they were going to go for a drive today. I don't know where they were headed. It's a lovely fall day for it."

"It is." I said my goodbyes and walked out the door, wondering what to do next.

I texted my mother, but there was no response. I wondered if she had thought to enable international texting on her phone. I knew her phone could do that, but that didn't mean my mother knew that too.

I texted my dad next, with the same results. I scowled at the phone's screen like it was the device's fault. I squeezed the phone in my hand. How could my parents go off the grid like this? Didn't they know there was a murder? And why would they leave the village when my father was connected to it? This wasn't the time for a trip down memory lane.

I took a deep breath. My frustration wouldn't make them come back to the village any more quickly. I started back toward the flower shop and texted Craig. *Why didn't you tell me Dad was a suspect?*

Where did you hear that?

Does that mean he is a suspect?

We shouldn't have this conversation on text.

Agreed. Can you meet me at Duncreigan?

That's a bit out of the way.

I know, but I have a problem there.

What?

Someone vandalized the garden.

What?!

They cut the rose. I had to come to the shop, but I think I'll go back home now and assess the damage.

I can be there in an hour.

I put my phone back into my pocket. I knew Craig was going to ask me why I hadn't reported the crime earlier, but if I had, I would have had police and crime scene techs tramping all over the garden by now. I didn't think that's what the garden wanted or needed.

I jogged the rest of the way back to the flower shop. I had avoided the crisis at Duncreigan way too long. I couldn't find my parents to ask them about Barley McFee, but maybe I could save my garden before it was too late.

Chapter Eighteen

I was relieved when Isla agreed to watch the flower shop for the rest of the day and that Raj was able to spare her. It didn't take much to convince her when I told her about the state of the garden. Things were different here in Scotland. Back home in Tennessee, if there had been talk of magic gardens or psychic stones, I'd have been laughed out of Nashville. Here the folklore was embraced. People didn't wholly believe in the magic, but they didn't dismiss it out of hand, either. Legends had surrounded Duncreigan for many generations.

On the three-mile drive back to Duncreigan, I played a nervous rhythm on my steering wheel with my fingertips. I didn't know what condition I would find the garden in, and I was worried about my parents too. It wasn't like them to go on a drive without telling anyone. If my father was really a suspect, would Craig put a stop on their passports? When I was a murder suspect, he'd taken my passport away.

I parked my car beside the cottage, and there was no sign of Hamish, squirrel, cat, or fox. I hoped that was good news. Maybe they were all making progress in the garden.

My heart sank as I drew closer. The ivy tumbled from the stone walls in dry heaps of dead leaves and withered vines. Nothing had changed. It had only grown worse.

The door to the garden stood wide open. It wasn't the way we usually did things. Typically, the garden was always under lock and key to keep any intruders out. Apparently that precaution was moot, since someone had been able to break into the garden and cause so much damage.

I stepped through the garden door and found Hamish sitting in the middle of the dead grass holding a trowel like he had never seen it before.

"Hamish?" I asked in a low voice.

"Oh, Miss Fiona, I'm so glad you came back. I almost walked to the village to fetch you. I don't know what to do. The garden is worse. It needs you to fix it."

"Why didn't you just call me?" I asked.

"I don't have a mobile phone, as you know, and it was so far to walk back to my bothy, I thought it would be just as well to walk to the village."

His bothy was about a half mile away and the village was three miles away. Between him and Chief Inspector Craig, I didn't think I would ever understand the logic of Scotsmen.

I stepped deeper into the garden, and Hamish followed me. The climbing rose on the standing stone was still withered. I wasn't sure what to do. The rules for being the Keeper that Uncle Ian had left me were vague at best, and none of them said a thing about what happened if the rose was cut from the stone. Perhaps it had never happened before.

I felt my shoulders droop. "Chief Inspector Craig is on his way here. I'm hoping he can help us."

"You can't let anyone see the garden in this state. It will be a black mark on the MacCallister name."

"Hamish, I trust the chief inspector." I sighed. It was a disagreement I'd had with Hamish many times before.

He brushed dirt off his hands. "I know you are sweet on each other, but nothing changes the fact that you are the Keeper and he's not. I don't see how he can help with bringing the garden back to life."

"He can investigate the break-in and might be able to find the person who did this."

"I don't see how," he grumbled. "Or what good that will do when the damage is done. This garden needs to be healed; placing blame on another will not do that."

I suppressed a groan. Hamish wasn't a fan of Craig. When Craig was a teenager, he and another friend—on a dare—tried to break into the garden to steal the menhir. Hamish caught them and never forgave Craig for it.

My proof of that was what he said next. "How do we know Chief Inspector Craig wasn't the one who cut the rose? He has tried to break into the garden before."

"That was a long time ago, and he was just a kid. He's changed," I said.

"I don't think I believe in change, not really. You are who you are, and you can fight it for as long as you have the strength to do it, but you won't change your core."

I bit my tongue to stop from asking him about his grand-nephew Seth. Seth, who had been given every chance to turn his life around, could change, but Craig could not?

"How do you know he is interested in you for the right reasons?" Hamish asked.

"What do you mean?" I gasped.

"He tried to steal the stone before. What if he's just trying to cozy up to you so he can get closer to the magic? It would not be the first time. Master Ian's great-grandfather had the same problem with a fisherwoman."

"That's not what's happening." But even as I said it, just the tiniest kernel of doubt crept into my heart.

I wished I could unhear what Hamish had said. The Craig I knew wouldn't do that, but Hamish was right—he had tried to steal the stone before, and because of what I had told him about my gift from the stone, he might be intrigued by it.

But no, he cared about *me*, not the stone. He never asked me about it. Was it a calculated move that he didn't? Was I having doubts because of bad luck with men in the past? That wasn't fair to Craig or to me.

I stepped around the hedgerow just in time to see Craig come through the garden gate. I was relieved he hadn't arrived two minutes before. If he had, he would have heard our conversation.

"Fiona, the garden," Craig said. He looked absolutely shocked, and all my worries about him using me to get close to the garden faded away.

He hurried over to me and wrapped his arms around me. "Are you all right?"

It was a fair question. Craig knew how important the garden was to me, but I couldn't answer because he pressed my face into his thick chest.

"What happened?" Craig asked as he released me and held me at arm's length.

"The rose," I said. "Someone cut it from the menhir, and the rest of the garden died."

He followed me around the hedgerow. "Can you fix it?"

I stared at the withered vines and leaves around us. "I don't know how."

"There has to be way. This can't be the end of your garden."

I wished I could believe he was right. However, this very much felt like the end of the garden. I felt worse about that now than I had when I'd first made my discovery. Perhaps it was because the reality of what happened had finally settled in.

"Who could have done this?" Craig asked.

"I was hoping you would help with that part."

"We need the techs to process the scene," Craig said.

I frowned. I saw his point, but the fewer the people who knew about the condition of the garden, the better. I didn't want the village to know the garden was in jeopardy. It would be proof to them that Ian MacCallister had picked the wrong person to inherit the garden when he died. The villagers didn't know about my personal connection to Uncle Ian. They only thought he'd left a Scottish treasure to an upstart American. There were some who would like to take that treasure away from me and some who would have gloated in its death as proof of my shortcomings.

Craig sighed. "Do you have any idea who could have done this? Have you seen anyone around Duncreigan? The cottage and garden are out of the way from any main roads. I don't think you often have visitors."

I nodded. "We don't. The only people we see way out here are an occasional hiker. Now that it's getting colder and the weather grows more unpredictable, we've seen fewer of those than we did in the summer."

"That reminds me," Hamish said. "There was a hiker here a couple of days ago. He said he heard there was a beautiful garden at Duncreigan and he wanted to see it."

I spun around and looked at Hamish. "Why didn't you mention that before?"

"I didn't remember it until just now when you told the chief inspector about the hikers that come through Duncreigan." He frowned. "He said he was a hiker, but he didn't look the part, and his backpack and boots were all wrong for a long day traveling up and down mountain trails. I pegged him as a tourist because of his poor gear."

"He spoke to you?" Craig asked.

"Oh, yes," Hamish said. "We had a nice long chat. He said he was visiting the area and had spent some time here in the summer. He mentioned that he met you then, Miss Fiona, and that the two of you have many of the same interests."

I frowned. "What interests are those?"

"Celtic symbols and history? He said he knew of your legacy. I thought it was odd and asked him what legacy he meant, but he would not answer that."

"Does this nonhiker have a name?" Craig asked.

Hamish frowned and moved Duncan from his pocket to his shoulder. "He said his name was Carver." Hamish looked at me. "He said you knew him."

I did indeed.

Chapter Nineteen

Carver Finley. I hadn't wanted to place the blame on him right when I saw the garden in disarray, but that was because I felt biased in thinking it was him. However, what Hamish said made it clear to me that I was giving the historian too much benefit of the doubt.

Craig knew my history with Carver. Carver and I had been at odds with one another since the murder of local village minister who had been spearheading the historic chapel ruins project last summer. At the time, I had even thought Carver was the killer. It turned out he was innocent.

"Carver Finley is back in Bellewick. I thought he was done with the village when he finished assessing the chapel ruins," Craig said.

"He might be done with the village, but I don't think he's done with me. He's been interested in the garden since we met at the chapel ruins last summer."

Craig raised his brow. "You never told me that."

"I didn't think it mattered. I hoped he would leave the village and never come back after he was done assessing the stability of the chapel."

"Is this the first you've heard of him being back?" Craig asked me.

I shook my head. "I saw him too," I said.

"Near the garden?" Craig asked.

I shook my head. "No, I saw him yesterday at the concert."

"You didn't mention that to me either." Craig squinted at me.

"I didn't think to. There were a lot of people in the village for the concert. There was no reason Carver couldn't have been there for the concert too."

He nodded. "True," he said, but he didn't sound happy that I hadn't told him about Carver being in the village.

"And honestly, when I found Barley in the tour bus, Carver slipped my mind."

"Do you think he could have a connection to the vandalism in the garden and to Barley's murder?"

I shook my head. "I don't know. He could be involved in Barley's murder, I supposed. They were both from the area and might know each other, but Carver was at least twenty years Barley's junior. What could Carver gain from Barley's death? However, he could have something to do with the state of the garden. No one else has shown the same kind of interest in the garden as he has. Most of the villagers just accept the garden's magical properties as fact and don't think much more about it. Or they don't say anything to me about it. Carver told me he wants to understand it and study the menhir."

"We need to find Carver, then, and find out what he knows," Craig said.

Hamish patted Duncan on his shoulder. "If you don't need anything else from me, Miss Fiona, I'm going to head back to my bothy for my midday meal. I've been here all morning and into the afternoon and have made no progress on bringing the garden back. It's enough to drive poor Duncan to tears." Tears gathered in Hamish's eyes as he looked up at the squirrel.

I patted Hamish on his other shoulder. "Go home and relax, Hamish. There is no more that you can do here."

He nodded. "We can't lose the garden, Miss Fiona. It's the only constant in my life."

"We won't," I promised him. "I'll find a way to bring it back."

His wrinkled face cleared. "I know you will. That I do. Master Ian would not have left this garden to you if he didn't think you could care for it just as well as he could. I have all my confidence in you."

As he walked out of the garden, I prayed his confidence wasn't misplaced.

After Hamish was gone, Craig turned back to me. "Are you sure you don't want my crime scene techs in here?"

I nodded. "I'm sure. Maybe it's the wrong decision, but I don't think the techs would find anything more than what we see here."

"I should get back to the station. I'm not sure what more I can do for you here."

"Before you go, there is something I found that I want to show you," I said.

He raised his brow.

I walked around the hedgerow and pointed to the boot print I found near the stone. "Proof that someone was in here and did this."

Craig bent over and stared at the print. "Someone with a larger foot than you or Hamish, too." He removed his phone from the pocket of his jacket and took a picture just like I had. "Even if you don't want crime scene techs in the garden, we need to preserve this print. It's our best hope of finding its owner. I have plaster of Paris in my car. Let me make a cast of it."

"You can do that?" I asked.

He eyed me. "I'm more than just a chief inspector, Fiona."

I nodded and waited while he went back to his SUV to collect the supplies he needed. He wasn't gone long, and I watched with fascination as he made the cast.

While the cast dried, I asked Craig, "Why didn't you tell me my father was a suspect in Barley McFee's murder?"

"I was hoping you would forget that."

I made a face. "Like I could."

"Where did you hear that?"

"Does it matter, if it's true?"

"Yes," he said slowly. "You should focus on whatever has happened to your garden, not on my murder investigation."

"Neil, you know I can't leave it alone now that I know my dad is involved."

He sighed. "I was afraid you were going to say that. I knew you'd be upset."

"So you didn't tell me because you were afraid I would be upset? Of course I'm upset. I'm more upset that you didn't tell me."

"No. I mean, yes, I knew you would be upset and I wasn't looking forward to that, but I didn't tell you yet because I didn't have all the facts. I wanted to hear your father's side of the story before I told you."

"And what's his side of the story?" I asked.

"I don't know. I haven't been able to talk to your father about it yet. It seems he and your mother left Thistle House very early this morning and haven't been back." He frowned.

"I can tell from your face that you think that's a bad sign and you wonder if he's running away from the scene of the crime."

Craig smiled down at me. "You can read all that in my face."

"Most of it," I said.

He laughed.

"I'm worried about them. Eugenia mentioned to me that they went for a drive, and I know it's nothing more than that. They are on vacation, after all, but I've tried to text them both. Both messages said they were undelivered." I paused. "And to answer your question from before, Kenda told me that Dad was a suspect. She didn't know he was my father when she told me."

"You spoke to Kenda?"

I shrugged. "I was helping Raj by delivering food to the band."

"I didn't know the Twisted Fox did takeaway."

"It doesn't, but Raj is looking to expand in that direction."

He frowned as if he found this all very suspect. "Why did he ask you to deliver it and not someone who worked at the pub?"

"Will you forget about the takeout and focus?" I let out a breath. "I'm sure there is some sort of simple explanation as to why Dad would have spoken with Barley. There has to be. Maybe he just wanted Barley's autograph."

Craig arched his brow. "Did your father collect celebrity autographs?"

"No, but I can't think of any reason he would be there. He and Barley claimed they didn't know each other. I know that because I asked both of them separately when I found out that Uncle Ian was their mutual friend."

Craig pressed his lips together, and I knew things were very bad for my father. I had to find him before the chief inspector did. I trusted Craig, but he was still a cop. If my father said too much or too little when Craig interviewed him, he could be in some serious trouble. As a former murder suspect, I would be a good coach.

"That's not all," I said.

His broad shoulders drooped. "You have more?"

"Not about my dad, but a reporter by the name of Trina Graham from Action News out of Aberdeen came to the flower shop today."

"I know reporters are in the village because of Barley's murder. It's a big story, but why was she interested in you?"

"She heard from Isla, I'm sorry to say, that I was the one who found Barley's body."

Craig rubbed his forehead. "With all these reporters in the village, I have to be extra careful with this case. One mistake and it's going to end up on the news."

"Trina knew that we are dating."

"*Great*," he muttered, and I felt like he'd donkey-kicked me in the chest. He must have seen the look on my face. "Don't take it that way, Fiona. I don't regret being with you. I just don't want that to confuse the investigation."

"I know," I said quietly.

He sighed as if he knew I didn't completely understand. Maybe I didn't. I didn't want to be a hindrance to Craig in any way, neither in the investigation nor in anything else.

He touched my cheek. "Please believe me. This will be fine. What you and I are to each other has no bearing on the investigation. I'm sure Trina brought it up just to see if it would get you to talk or react. That's her job. I've dealt with her before in cases that have involved the city of Aberdeen. She can be a real bulldog. I'm not happy she's here." He opened and closed his mouth as if he was going to say more, then snapped it closed.

I wished I knew what he had been about to say.

The accusations Hamish had spouted off about Craig not that long ago came into my head. *He's only interested in you so he can learn more about the magic. He tried to steal the stone before.*

"Fiona?" Craig asked. "Where did you go for a moment there? Did you have a vision?"

I licked my lips. "No, I can't have a vision now that the rose is dead."

He studied me. "How do you know that? You've told me before that you don't know exactly how the magic works. Maybe if you tried to have a vision, you could have the answers you seek."

I frowned at him. "I can't just try to have a vision. It's not like television and I press a button and turn it on."

"I wasn't saying that it was, but you won't know if you don't try."

My frowned deepened. What did he know about it? What did anyone, even Hamish, know what it was like to be the Keeper? Trying to have a vision. That sounded to me like Craig thought I was some sort of magician with a hat trick. There was no hat trick here. The magic was gone, and it was my fault because I hadn't been here to protect the garden. After three hundred years, the garden was dead, and it was my fault. Why did everyone think I had the ability to bring it back?

Craig looked down. "The cast is dry."

It had dried much more quickly than I would have expected it to. He squatted next to the boot print and carefully removed it from the ground. He showed the print to me and stood up. "I can at least have the lab find the type of boot that made this print. We will find out who did this to the garden, Fiona, and who killed Barley too."

He sounded so confident that it was hard not to believe him.

Chapter Twenty

Before he left, I showed Craig the yellow rose in the bowl of water in my cottage. It was still as vibrantly yellow as ever. Seeing it gave me hope, but not more clues as to who'd cut it from the menhir. Shortly after that, the station called Craig to come back about another pending case, and he and I parted ways. As he drove away from Duncreigan, I tried to shake off the uneasy feeling that hovered just above my head. Nothing seemed to be going right. Barley was dead, my father was a suspect, and I might not be able to bring the garden back.

Among all those things that were wrong, the second was the only one I could do something about at the moment. I might have a shot at clearing my father's name if I could just find him. I stopped at the cottage to check on Ivanhoe. The cat was asleep on his cat bed on the hearth.

Now that I knew Craig did suspect my father of the murder, it became more urgent to find him. I texted both my parents, again with no response. I would just have to go back to the village and wait until they returned. I knew they would. They had to.

A little while later, when I walked into the Climbing Rose, Isla was miffed. She put her hands on her hips as she stood in front of the sales counter. "You never told me you were going to be gone this long. My shift at the pub ended a half hour ago. I was supposed to meet Seth at the harbor. He has some big news to tell me!"

"What's the big news?" I asked as I removed my coat.

She threw up her hands. "I don't know. He hasn't told me yet. Honestly, Fi, I think sometimes you don't listen to a word I say."

I frowned. "I'm sorry I was late. Craig came out to Duncreigan to look at the garden."

"Does he know who did it?" she asked.

"Nothing certain." I was hesitant to tell my sister about Carver Finley. Isla wasn't the best at keeping secrets, and I didn't want Carver to hear we suspected him before Craig was sure enough to make an arrest.

She sighed. "Well, I'm sure Seth will understand that you made me late. He's such a caring guy. He knows I have to take care of my family. He has a lot of responsibility too, being the janitor at the school and also with all his charity work."

Seth's charity work was picketing for environmental causes. I saw nothing wrong with that. I agreed with him on most points, but the fact that he didn't actually pitch in and clean up the stony beach at the harbor or volunteer to plant trees or anything of the sort made me skeptical of his commitment to the cause. I thought he more liked to picket and be photographed doing it. He even had an Instagram page for his pickets. Not that I had ever seen it. I didn't want to. Isla kept me up-to-date on his every movement.

"Have you heard from Mom and Dad?" I asked.

"Not a peep. I feel like they are in less contact with us now than they are when they're home," Isla said.

"That's probably because Mom doesn't know she can use her cell phone in this country."

She shook her head. "I gave up trying to teach our parents technology a long time ago. It's too headache inducing." She hopped back and forth on her feet.

"You don't have to break into a jig. You can go," I said. "The shop closes in an hour. I can handle it from here. Thanks for staying so long."

She nodded and pulled on her coat, which was lying across the sales counter, and grabbed her purse from the same spot. It was clear she had been itching to leave for some time now.

"What are you going to do after you close up?" Isla asked at the door.

"Find Mom and Dad. I'm starting to worry."

Isla cocked her head. "You're worried because you're a worrier, Fi. I'm sure they are fine. I bet Dad wanted to see some of the countryside that he missed. You overthink things too much."

It was an old argument from my sister, and maybe there was some truth to it. I did worry about a good many things because I knew so many things could go wrong. Isla, on the other hand, ran headlong toward whatever she might want. It could be a relationship, a job, or even just a new outfit from the mall. She went for it without weighing all the pros and cons like I did. I envied her ability to do that. I thought we both might do better if I worried less and she worried a little more.

But I couldn't tell her the reason for my worries—that Dad was a suspect in Barley's murder. She was still my little sister and I wanted to protect her as much as possible. Presha would have scolded me for that.

Isla left the shop, and I set to work finishing putting away the shipment of flowers I had received. I was happy to see that Isla had organized a quarter of them. My sister had a good eye for color and pattern. I thought she would make a good florist if she wanted to, other than the fact that she spent as much time as possible with her boyfriend.

It had always been different for me. I'd known what I wanted to do from the start. When I first set foot in Uncle Ian's garden as a child, I knew I wanted to work with flowers. I knew now that it was my connection to the garden that had caused that feeling. I hoped that connection wasn't lost now that the garden was in danger.

I placed a large bundle of canna lilies inside a green bucket of water and set it on the floor. I had ordered only a dozen canna lilies. They were popular for spring and summer weddings but not as popular in the fall. People tended to pick their flowers seasonally. For one, you rarely saw tulips at a December wedding. It was possible, but the cost was prohibitive when buying flowers out of season.

The front door of the flower shop opened and the morning glory–shaped bell that hung from the door rang. Presha walked into the shop.

I smiled. "It's so good to see you."

"It is good to see you as well, Fiona. I stopped by to check on you. You had quite a shock. I have taken it upon myself to make sure you are all right. Ian would have liked that."

"He would, and you're right. I have had a shock. The problem is, I have no idea how to bring the garden back to life."

"The garden? What is this about the garden?" She wrapped her colorful shawl more closely around her shoulders. "I was talking about the murder."

I shook my head. "Right. Right, the murder."

"What's wrong with the garden?" She sat at the little white wrought-iron table and chairs I had placed in front of one of the two windows. I'd bought the set at a street sale during the summer and painted them white. I'd found, after the shop was open for a few weeks, that customers liked to sit when placing large flower orders. The table was just big enough for the three matching chairs around it.

I sat across from her and told her what had happened.

"Oh." She folded her hands in front of her as if in prayer. Her shawl draped over her arms, giving her an even more penitent appearance. "I sensed that something was wrong, but I never expected it to be this."

"You sensed it? Presha, do you have magic too?"

She smiled. "No. Just a woman's intuition. I have learned to trust it in my many years. There is something mystical in a woman's way of knowing."

Maybe for Presha.

"How is the garden?" she asked.

I told her the current state of Duncreigan, but she only nodded as if she waited to hear something more, maybe even something worse. She listened patiently as I cataloged everything that was wrong.

"You don't seem to be that upset about it." I paused. "I mean it's not your garden, but it's important to me and Uncle Ian's legacy."

"This is true." She wrapped her shawl a little closer around her body. I kept the shop at a lower temperature than other shops in the village might have because it was better for the flowers. The cooler air helped the plants to stay fresh longer. "All will be well with the garden. I have faith in you."

"How?"

"I am not concerned, because I know you will be able to fix it. If Ian MacCallister chose you to be the next Keeper of the garden, he thought you were up for the job. The garden has died many times before. The Keeper has always been able to bring it back to life. I have faith that you will be able to do that too."

I blinked at her. "The garden has died before?"

"Of course it has. Gardens are living and breathing entities, and all living and breathing things have a life cycle. All life ends and is reborn in a new and different way. Where is that not more evident than in a garden, where the weather and the seasons dictate what will live and what will die?"

I didn't want to argue with Presha over the Hindu belief in reincarnation. I didn't know if she was right or wrong. I didn't know if what I'd been taught in my church back in Tennessee was right or wrong. What I did know was that the garden was as dead as I had ever seen it. It was farther gone than when I'd first arrived at Duncreigan after Uncle Ian's death, but Presha's words gave me hope. I had to find a way to bring the garden back to life. It was my legacy, and I needed to use my gift to help others. That was the most important part.

"There is always life. It might be deep under the surface, but you will think of a way to bring it back." She smiled.

"Do you have any ideas about how I can do that? Because that would be a big help." My voice wavered. "To be honest, I don't know what to do."

She shook her head. "Even if I did, I shouldn't share them with you. It is your challenge to bring the garden back, not mine. My challenges are different. The challenges of every person are different from the next." She patted my cheek. "I have great faith in you, Fiona Knox, just as your godfather did."

Before I could respond, Presha went on, "And you've done it before. When you first arrived in Scotland, the garden was dead, and you brought it back to life."

I knew she was trying to help, but it didn't feel like help at all. "But that time the rose was still living. This time the rose is dead."

She leaned closer to me and took my face in her cool hands. "The magic is not dead. All you need is that to bring the flowers and plants back."

"Where's the magic?" I asked.

She pressed her hands together. "The magic is from Duncreigan earth, is it not? It's where the stone stands and from which the rose grew."

"That doesn't tell me how to bring the garden back, though." I sighed. "The dead garden and the dead body aren't the only problems I am having. My parents are missing too. They left early this morning to go for a scenic drive, according to Eugenia at Thistle House, and still haven't come back."

"Your parents aren't missing, then. They are just sightseeing." She shook her head as if it was the craziest thing she had ever heard.

"Maybe they aren't officially missing, but Isla and I are worried sick. Mom and Dad aren't using their mobile phones."

"You shouldn't be worried. I saw both of them this morning, and they were fine. Your parents came very early to my tea shop," Presha said. "They were cheerful and seemed to be enjoying their break from home."

"What time was this?" I asked.

She thought about it for a moment. "It was before I even opened, and I open at seven. Six thirty, I would say. It was still dark out."

"What did they want?"

She smiled. "What do you think they wanted, child? It was scones and tea. Your father raved over the scones I'd sent to Duncreigan for their arrival. Thankfully, I had just pulled a tray of orange and another tray of blueberry out of the oven. I packed up a takeaway basket with the scones and a thermos of chai."

"Did they say where they were going?" I asked.

"Your mother said they wanted to go for a drive through the countryside, visit some of the castles, and be a tourist for a day." She cocked her head. "Is something wrong with that?"

"No, I just wish they would have told me their plans. They can't just pick up and go wherever and whenever they like without telling Isla and me."

She put her hands on her hips. "Who is the child and who is the parent here?"

My face flushed red, and Presha, like she did many times, made me see how ridiculous I was being.

"I saw Isla a little while ago, and she didn't mention it at all," Presha said.

"Well, okay, I've been worried about it. Isla is Isla, and she is preoccupied with Seth at the moment."

She nodded. "Young love will do that," she said, as if she spoke from experience. Presha and her brother had lived in Scotland for over forty years, and neither of them had ever married. Presha never mentioned men or women in that way, now that I thought about it. I wondered if she'd had a romance in her life when she was younger. The question was on the tip of my tongue, but I held it back. She would tell me if she wanted to.

"Your parents will return this evening. Don't fret about it so much," she advised.

"Well, you have put me at ease about one thing. Now I just have to bring the garden back to life and solve a murder.

Considering the scale of my worries, having one thing off my plate is better than nothing."

"You're investigating, then. You want to help Kenda?"

I trusted Presha one hundred percent, but I didn't say my true reason for wanting to investigate the murder was because my father was a suspect too.

"I don't believe Kenda did it," Presha said, when I didn't say anything.

"Why do you say that? Do you know her?" I asked.

She shook her head. "No, I just met her this weekend, but I still don't think she did it. She's not the type to get her hands dirty."

I frowned.

"Murder is a messy business, and Kenda is the sort of woman who wants others to take care of the messes in life, especially in her life. She's a blamer. She blames others for where she is and where she isn't. Sometimes," Presha said, "others might be to blame for these things, but not always. A way to foster humility is to accept your part in your own life. Choice plays a great role. I don't know that Kenda would believe me if I told her that. Even so, it is something she needs to hear when she is ready to take it to heart."

"Could she have hired someone to kill him, then?" I shivered at the very idea. A scene from a mob movie flashed in my head. Was there even a Scottish mob?

"I suppose, but who else was seen around the tour bus?"

I knew one person who had been seen at the tour bus: my father.

Presha shook her head. "To hire a hit man would take a lot of planning. Does Kenda strike you as a person who would plan so well a murder in advance?"

When she put it that way, I had no idea. I had no idea what Kenda or any of Barley's friends or fans were capable of. All I knew was that one of them had committed murder.

Chapter
Twenty-One

E ven though I still didn't know exactly where my parents were, Presha's words comforted me. I knew I had been overreacting to think they were missing. They had gone for a drive. There was nothing illegal in that. I also knew it would be a most welcome break for them. In running the farm, they rarely had a moment to travel, even to downtown Nashville. And downtown Nashville was lovely. The music and foodie scene thrived, with local bars and five-star restaurants. All of which boasted live music. But at the farm, there was always something that needed mending, planting, feeding, or harvesting, which was why I'd known from an early age that it wasn't the life for me.

Neither Isla nor I wanted the kind of life where we were tethered to the land to such a degree that leaving would cause so much strain. Then I laughed at myself as a thought crossed my mind: wasn't that the situation I was in now with the garden at Duncreigan?

Part of me wanted to camp out at Thistle House and wait until Mom and Dad returned. But I scrapped that idea.

Eugenia would get suspicious, and Barley's bandmates would wonder why I was there. I didn't think it was a great idea to reveal to Kenda that the man she'd seen go into Barley's trailer after her was my father.

Instead, I decided to go back to the scene of the crime.

But when I got to where the tour bus had been parked, the scene of the crime was gone. The bus was missing from the other side of the troll bridge, and I wasn't the only one who'd noticed.

Kenda and the MacNish brothers stood in the spot where the bus had been with their mouths hanging open.

Kenda threw up her hands. "Now what are we supposed to do? Stay here forever?"

"We had gear in there. The cops can't take our gear," Jamie complained.

"Who cares about your gear?" Kenda asked. "What about our ride? We need to get out of this village!"

"Call an Uber," Lester joked.

"No Uber would come all the way to this little village," Kenda snapped, not picking up on his humor.

That wasn't entirely true. Kipling was starting a new business of giving people rides. It was a side business he was running with mixed results, considering that his mode of transportation was his motorbike. I had seen a handful of villagers on the back of his bike, but only out of sheer desperation.

"Hey," Jamie said. "It's the delivery girl."

Kenda and Lester spun around to see me standing at the end of the troll bridge. I gave them a little wave.

"We didn't order any more food," Lester said.

Kenda shook her head. "She's not a delivery girl, she's a detective, and she's looking into Barley's murder."

The brothers' heads snapped in my direction.

I walked over to them. "I'm not a detective," I said. The last thing I wanted was for it to reach Chief Inspector Craig's ears that I was impersonating a police officer.

Kenda flipped her red braids over her shoulder. "You said you have dealt with murder investigations before."

I shifted back and forth on my feet. "I have."

"And you need to help me, so I can leave this village and never come back."

I sighed. The MacNish brothers watched me with renewed interest. I forced a laugh. "Kenda and I spoke earlier, and I told her I'd had my own trouble with the police."

"What troubles?" Lester asked.

I waved away his question. "It's not important." I cleared my throat. "What happened to the tour bus?"

"What does it look like?" Lester frowned. "The cops took it."

"With all our gear," Jamie said. "We need that back. Some of those instruments cost more than those cops make in a year."

"Yeah," Lester said. "It takes a lifetime to find just the right guitar. We're going to need everything back."

"You will have to talk to the chief inspector about that," I said.

The brothers scowled at me.

Lester shook his head. "It just seems one thing after another goes wrong."

"Les," Jamie said.

Lester shook his head and stomped away. Without a word, Jamie went after him.

"What did he mean when he said that?" I asked Kenda, who was still staring at the patch of grass where the tour bus had once been.

"I never know what they're talking about." She folded her arms, and fiery braids fell back over her shoulder. "Have you found the man who was talking to Barley after I left the bus?"

I shook my head. "Not yet."

"You had better find him, because he's the one who did this. I promise you. When you find him, you tell me, because he single-handedly ruined my life. I mean to ruin his." She stomped away.

I watched her go as the gas lampposts in the village began to flicker on. It was before six in the evening, but darkness came early to Scotland in November. It wouldn't be long before the sky was completely dark.

Even though Presha had made me feel more secure about my parents just an hour ago, my confidence evaporated with Kenda's words. I knew she wasn't going to let go of the idea that the man she saw, my father, was guilty, and now on top of that, I had to worry about her ruining his life. I wasn't sure what a fiddler player would do to a farmer, but I didn't want to find out either. Kenda had made a serious threat.

I removed my phone from my pocket and turned on the flashlight app. The light was weak, but I still shined it on the grass where the tour bus had been. I knew I wouldn't find anything. Craig and his officers would have combed the area before and after moving the bus.

I turned the phone off and walked over the troll bridge. When I was halfway across the bridge, I heard a scrapping under my feet. Maybe I had been right all along and there was a troll under that bridge. I bolted to the other side and peered under it. I couldn't see a thing in the dark.

When I straightened up again, I saw a figure walk under one of the lampposts on the main village street. It was Carver Finley. My breath caught when I saw him. I hadn't expected to run into him so soon.

He moved at a brisk pace down the street. I hesitated for half a second before I followed him. As I walked a few paces behind him, I wondered if I should just make myself known and ask him what he'd done to the garden. I held myself back. My best guess was he was headed to the Twisted Fox for dinner, and that would be a good place to confront him because I would have backup there.

To my surprise, he walked by the Twisted Fox without as much as a backward glance. He did the same going by my flower shop, and at the end of the road he turned left in the direction of the harbor.

I frowned. What interest could Carver have in the harbor? Of course I followed him.

I'd expected the harbor to be deserted at this time of night, but I was wrong. Several fishing vessels had just pulled into the dock and were unloading the fish they had caught in the North Sea with giant nets into giant holding tanks.

From there the fish would be divided and shipped all over the country, if not the world.

The air smelled of salt and fish. My skin was instantly dewy the moment I stepped onto the dock. In the commotion of the fishermen and boats, I lost sight of Carver. There were so many places to hide in and around the harbor, I didn't know how I could find him.

"Are you looking for your pip of a sister, lass?" a scratchy voice called from the dock.

On the other side of the diving gear shed were two overturned oil barrels. An old man sat on each barrel, and a third elderly man, who had only one leg, sat in a wheelchair. The one-legged man was the one who spoke to me.

I walked over to the three men. The old gents were a constant fixture at the docks. It seemed that day or night, rain or shine, I would see them sitting in the same spot swapping stories about the good old days when they were at sea.

"Hello, Old Milton." I nodded to the one-legged man.

"Your sister and that string bean of a lad, Seth MacGregor, were just here a moment ago. Is that who you're looking for?"

It wasn't, but I wasn't going to tell the men that.

"Isla told me she was meeting Seth at the harbor," I said.

Old Milton patted his stump of a leg. He told visitors to the village that he'd lost the leg to a great white shark. In truth, he'd lost it in a car accident, but there was silent agreement among the villagers to let Old Milton have his fish story.

"Aye, they were here. They had a right long conversation with Ferris Brown."

My eyebrows went up. I knew Ferris from the Merchant Society of Bellewick, of course, but I had no idea why my sister and Seth would have a chat with him.

Ewan, one of the men on the oil barrels, spoke up. "They were having a long conversation with Ferris. It seemed to me that everyone was happy at the end of it. They were too far off to hear what they were saying," he said with a sigh. "Had we known you'd be coming alone, we would have been sure to tell you. We know that you like a good snoop."

I knew that to be true. The fishermen were as bad as the ladies back in my home church in Tennessee when it came to gossip.

"I would never ask you to spy on my sister."

Ewan laughed. "Sure you wouldn't, lass. If you were worried about her enough, you would."

I frowned and then proved them right by asking, "Was it just chitchat?"

"Looked to me like they were hatching a plan," Old Milton said.

"Aye," Ewan said. "They had their heads together."

"Seeing your sister at the harbor is unusual, that's for certain," Old Milton said. "Seth comes around now and again."

"He's looking for something to complain about. Always trying to see it the boats are leaking oil. That sort of thing," Ewan agreed. "'Course Ferris is down here each and every day. He owns half the fleet."

"He's working on getting the other half too," the one-eyed man grumped.

"Is that a problem?" I asked. I couldn't help but be curious. I didn't know Ferris well, but he was always pleasant to be around during out Merchant Society meetings, meetings that had the tendency to drag on painfully long.

"If you ask me," Old Milton said, "I never think it's a good thing for one man to own all the businesses, but I can't fault Ferris. He pays a fair wage and his sailors always speak highly of him. Whoever comes after him might not be as good. That's the trouble with one man ruling all. The man who rose to power might be grand, but the men that come after him, who inherit his power by right or birth, they might be a horror."

"Sounds to me that you are preaching against the monarchy," Ewan said.

"Nay, the British monarchy is all show now," Old Milton replied. "The rich businessmen hungry for power, those are the ones to keep both eyes on." He nodded. "Or just one, if that's all you have."

The one-eyed man grunted.

"He won't be working on buying any more boats, if you ask me," Ewan said. "Nay, all his money now is going into the manor. That will be a money pit and could destroy his fortune. I hope he doesn't take it too far in the restoration."

I frowned. The manor? "What manor are you talking about?"

Old Milton's mouth fell open. "You have been in Aberdeenshire all this time and don't know about Winthrope

Manor? I'm not sure you can call yourself a Scotswoman. The manor is one of the most famous landmarks in County Aberdeen."

"I've been kind of busy," I said. Since coming to Scotland, I had opened a new business, learned how to deal with my magical gift, and gotten a new boyfriend, not to mention solved a couple of murders. There wasn't much time to wander around the remote manors of Scotland.

"Aye, you will want to see the Winthrope Manor, lass," Ewan said. "It's a grand, crumbling place. Ferris hopes to bring it back to its former glory."

"He has more money than God, so if anyone can do it, it is he," Old Milton said.

"Has he been working on it for a long time?" I asked.

"Nay," Ewan said. "He's wanted it for a long time, that's for certain. My, I can remember him talking about wanting to buy that old crumbling place when he was just a boat hand. I think he worked so hard to build his company just so he would have the money to buy the manor. It took him decades, and he just settled on buying it last week. There seemed to be another claim to it, but like Old Milton here said, Ferris has the money to make problems like that go away."

I raised my brow and wondered what Ferris could have to say to my sister or Seth. Neither, as far as I knew, was interested in fishing or in old buildings. I couldn't help but think that Seth was up to yet another scheme. I prayed he didn't drag Isla into it this time.

"I'll check the manor out," I promised. "Did you happen to see which direction my sister went?"

"Aye," Old Milton said. "They went in the direction of the stony beach. Watch your step while on the beach, lass. You don't want to take a tumble into the sea."

I took the old sailor's warning to heart.

Chapter Twenty-Two

I walked back down to the dock and turned north. Fifty yards in front of me, the dock ended abruptly at the edge of the stony beach. There was no soft white sand on the shores of County Aberdeen. Instead, rocks that ranged from the size of my fist to pebbles made up a wobbly beach.

I stopped for a moment at the end of the dock. In the middle of the beach, Seth and Ferris were shaking hands, and then Ferris walked to a waiting scooter on the water. He climbed on and waved to Isla and Seth as the small boat pulled away. It headed for one of the fishing boats anchored just outside the harbor.

I waited for a moment and wondered if I should just leave and give my sister and her boyfriend a private moment. However, my curiosity won yet again, and I carefully stepped onto the beach.

When I was about thirty feet away, Seth picked my sister up and twirled her in the air like they were in the middle of a movie dance number. He set her on the rocks again, and she laughed. When she saw me, she gripped Seth's arm. "Fi, what are you doing down here?"

I pressed my lips together. "I was out for a walk, and Ewan and the others told me you were here."

Isla shook her head. "Those old coots need to mind their own business. All they do all day is sit and talk about people." She sniffed.

Seth wrapped a protective arm around her shoulders. "It's all right, babe. They don't mean any harm."

She looked up at him adoringly. "You're just the sweetest man who ever took a breath of life."

Seth beamed back down at her.

Isla shook her head. "I'm glad you're here, because you're the first one that we want to tell our big news!"

I braced myself. The last time she'd made an announcement like this, it was to tell me she and Seth were engaged after knowing each other only two weeks. Thankfully, they'd changed their minds and decided to be promised to be engaged instead of actually engaged. If she wanted to marry Seth, there wasn't anything I could do to stop her, but I was relieved they'd decided to wait. I didn't think anyone could or should make a decision about marriage after just two weeks.

What surprised me most was that their feelings for each other hadn't changed. Isla had been with Seth for several months now, and she was living with him full-time and still got a dreamy look in her eyes anytime she spoke of him. I no longer saw their relationship as a passing fling. All evidence pointed to a real engagement right around the corner.

"Is this about the two of you?" I asked, trying to sound as upbeat as I could.

She twirled, and Seth had to grab her by the waist before she fell over in the rocks.

"Please be careful. You don't want to twist an ankle," I warned.

"You worry too much, Fi." She beamed up at her beloved. "Can I tell her?"

He nodded.

"Seth got a new job!" she practically shouted.

I raised my eyebrows at Seth. "But I thought you liked being the janitor at the village school." I liked it for him because it was full-time and the position paid well. All I really wanted for Isla was happiness and stability. Was that too much for a big sister to ask?

"He likes working at the school," Isla answered for him. "But he's always looking for a new path. He was going to be a doctor, you know."

Was being the operative work in that sentence. I didn't doubt for a minute that Seth was smart enough to be a doctor. He'd gotten into medical school, after all, but he didn't have the motivation to be a doctor. I steeled myself to hear what his latest life plan was. In the time I had known him, there had been many.

"Are you going back into medicine?" I asked.

Seth shook his head. "That life isn't meant for me."

Isla nodded. "He can't. It's just too much for him emotionally. There is so much pain in medicine."

I felt proud of myself for not making a smart remark.

"I would do it if you wanted me too, babe," Seth said. "I'd do anything for you. Even work a job I loathed. You're that important to me."

This *babe* stuff was starting to get on my nerves.

She wrapped her arms around his side. "No, I don't want to ever be the kind of wife who pushes her husband into a job he doesn't like. I think that's just wrong. Everyone should choose his or her own path."

I felt an eye twitch coming on. If Seth didn't want to be a doctor, that was fine. I only wished he had discovered that before wasting thousands of dollars of Hamish's money on an education, then throwing it away without a second thought.

"What's he going to do, then?" I asked.

"Do you know about Winthrope Manor?" Seth asked.

I frowned. "I've just heard of it from Ewan and his pals. They said Ferris Brown bought it. He plans to restore it, too."

"That's right." Isla hopped in place. "And it's a massive undertaking. He needs the very best workers to bring the house back to life. He just hired Seth to work on the construction team. Isn't that wonderful?"

"Construction? Have you worked construction before?" I asked Seth.

"No, but I'm willing to learn. Ferris is willing to give me a shot. I think this could really be my calling. I mean, what man doesn't want to say he can work with his hands? I want to be able to make a home one day." He held out his hands, looking at them, and smiled at my sister. "I would never have been able to do it if it weren't for Isla, who is always telling me to follow my heart."

"But what about the job at the school?" I squeaked. I knew being a janitor might not have the glory Seth craved, but it was solid, reliable work.

He shook his head. "I quit that a week ago. I just wasn't enjoying it. I can't work at a job I don't enjoy. Life is too short for that."

I bit my tongue, because what I wanted to say was work wasn't always about enjoyment. Sometimes it was about making money to feed yourself and, in his case, his someday wife.

I bit down just a little harder on my tongue and reminded myself of something Presha had said to me several times since Isla moved to Scotland. "Isla is an adult and has to make her own life. You aren't her mother." I had never been her mother, of course, but at times if had felt like I was. I was older than her by eight years, and because our parents had been occupied with the business of running a working farm, a lot of Isla's upbringing had been left up to me. I was the one who'd taught her to ride a bike, tie her shoes, and read, so I was more than a little protective of my younger sister. I wished I could put her in a bubble to save her from making any mistakes that could hurt her chances of a perfectly happy life, but I knew a perfectly happy life wasn't possible for anyone and life in a bubble would be no life at all.

I took a breath. "I'm happy for you, Seth, that you found work you're finally excited about doing. I hope you enjoy working with Ferris. I know him from the Merchant Society of Bellewick, and he is a good man."

"Thank you, Fiona. That means a lot." By the way he said it, I gathered that he knew I wasn't his number-one fan. Maybe Seth was more observant than I'd given him credit for.

"I'm proud of him too!" Isla said.

Seth smiled at her and looked back to me. "I want to work with my hands. If all goes well, I will go into construction full-time. I just have to try it out to see if I have a connection to the work, and I know there are greener ways of building and remodeling. I really think this is the field I should be in."

"Connection?" I asked.

"You have to be connected to your work to find joy in it," he said. "You have that with your flowers."

"So you don't know if you will continue with it. I mean, there is no guarantee you will have a connection when you get started." Despite my wish to let Isla live her own life, the words popped out of my mouth. I was taking Presha's advice to heart, but, it seemed, only in little bits at a time.

Isla rolled her eyes. "Fiona, if it were up to you, everything would come with a guarantee."

"I just think it's not a bad idea to be cautious."

Isla snorted. "Like running after murderers is cautious."

Her words stung because I knew they were true.

"Seth has made a great choice, and I want him to finally meet Mom and Dad."

"When?" I asked.

She rubbed her hands together as if she had been waiting for me to ask all day. "You will bring Mom and Dad to the Winthrope Manor just like you are showing them around Aberdeen. Seth and I will already be there. Seth can show us around and tell us the plans for the estate. It will be perfect, because they will get to see what a hard worker he is. You know how much hard work means to Mom and Dad." She rolled her eyes. "Must be all that farming."

It was true that working hard was at the top of our parents' list of must-haves in other people.

Isla jumped up and down. "This will be perfect. Mom and Dad will get to meet Seth at this beautiful house, and they will love him. I just know it."

"Are you sure you want me to go? Maybe it would be better if the four of you did this alone," I said.

Isla was still unaware of the tension between me and our parents, and I was going to do my best to keep it that way until things were more settled. Then I would have a heart-to-heart with my sister about it all.

She put her hands on her hips. "But you're my sister, and I need your support."

I nodded. I couldn't argue with her when she put it like that. "I'll do it."

Seth smiled at her. "And if they are anything like you, babe, I know I will love them too."

Isla grinned from ear to ear.

Chapter Twenty-Three

Isla and Seth seemed in no hurry to leave the beach, and feeling like the third wheel that I was, I slipped away, muttering something about needing to get home. Not that they heard me; they were intertwined in a tight embrace.

I thought I would make one last attempt to see if my parents had returned to Thistle House. I figured stopping in to see if they were back made sense, as the guesthouse was on my way to the small community lot where I'd parked my car.

I huddled down into my coat as I walked back through Bellewick's cobblestone streets. On a cold evening like this, it was easy to imagine myself as a character in a Dickens novel as I walked by the two-hundred-year-old and sometimes even older buildings on my way to the village entrance. Thistle House's garden was lit up with white twinkle lights that had been strung from the young trees in the small space. It gave the quiet garden an ethereal glow. As far as I knew, this tiny garden wasn't magical, but it certainly looked like it had the potential to be.

Unsurprisingly, due to the chill in the air, the garden was empty. I hurried around the front of the stone guesthouse and came around the corner just in time to see a woman leave through the front door. I froze. It was the reporter Trina Graham. I ducked behind the corner of the building before she could see me. I didn't want to answer any more of her intrusive questions about the murder.

I peeked around the side as Trina dug through her purse. Maybe she was looking for her car keys, I guessed. She was alone. The cameraman was nowhere around, as far as I could see.

She yanked the keys out of the depths of her bag just as the front door opened. A man stepped out, and he was holding a scarf. "You forgot this." He held it out to her.

She smiled and took the scarf from his hand. "Thank you, Jamie, and thank you and your brother for taking the time to interview with me."

"Anytime. Barley's death deserves your coverage, and as members of his band, we were a big part of his life."

I could see Trina clearly in the light by the guesthouse door, but Jamie was in the shadows.

"Can I ask you a question off the record, since you refused to answer it on the record?" Trina asked.

"Shoot," Jamie said.

"Do you think Kenda Bay is capable of murder?"

I saw Jamie's shadow move in a shrug. "Maybe. She and Barley had a difficult relationship. My brother and I had many sleepless nights listening to them scream at each other after a concert."

"Thank you. I appreciate your honest answer, even though I promise not to use it in my reporting."

His shadow shrugged again. "Anytime."

I had a feeling Kenda wouldn't be too happy with her bandmate when it got back to her that Jamie thought she was capable of murder, and I had no illusions that it wouldn't get back to her. I guessed Trina might not quote Jamie about this detail of her interviews, but what he said would work its way into the case one way or another.

Trina said goodbye and then walked at a fast pace toward the community lot. Jamie went back inside the guesthouse. I hesitated and wondered if now was really a good time to ask after my parents.

I removed my phone from my pocket and texted them again.

"If I knew you were coming here anyway, I would have had you deliver our order."

I yelped, and the phone flew out of my hands into the bushes beside the guesthouse. I spun around to find the second MacNish brother, Lester, standing just behind me. He held a takeaway bag from the Twisted Fox. Indian spices wafted from the bag.

He held up his free hand. "Steady there. I didn't mean to scare you. Everyone is so jumpy in this village."

His comment made me wonder who else he had scared half to death.

"Are you here delivering more food? I wouldn't put it past my brother to order extra. We might be the same size, but that guy can eat me out of the water."

For what felt like the fiftieth time, I said, "I don't deliver food for the Twisted Fox."

"But you did." He cocked his head.

"I was doing my friend Raj a favor."

He shrugged.

I had a feeling that the MacNish brothers shrugged a lot. It was difficult for me to believe they were passionate about anything, including Barley's murder.

"I guess it's for the best that I went down there myself." He moved the food bag to his other hand. "I ran into some old sailor, and they were able to tell me a lot about my family history. I can't wait to tell Jamie."

"Are you from Aberdeenshire?" I asked, surprised.

He shook his head. "Not personally, but my mother's family lived here until about sixty years ago. The old sailor was able to tell me quite a bit about my mother's clan. He gave me advice to find out even more, too."

"Was the old sailor Popeye?" I asked.

"Now that you mention it, one of them looked a whole lot like Popeye. Is that his real name?"

I shook my head. "And I wouldn't call him that to his face, if I were you. I have a feeling it wouldn't go well."

He nodded. "Duly noted. I don't want to do anything that might dry up a valuable source of information." He shifted his stance.

I nodded. To me, Lester and Jamie seemed awfully young to be so interested in their family history, but I supposed that, with all the genetic DNA testing now available for finding out one's heritage, genealogy was trendy. "What other advice did Popeye give you?"

"He told me to look up a county historian. He said the man knows everything there is to know about the history and people of Aberdeenshire."

I swallowed. There was only one man I knew who fit that description. "Carver Finley?"

He perked up. "Do you know him?"

"I do."

"Oh wow, can you introduce us to him?" he asked excitedly.

"I don't think that's a great idea. You'd be much better off if Popeye or even Raj makes the introduction."

"All right," he said, sounding confused.

I didn't say anything.

"Did I see that reporter leaving the guesthouse just when I arrived?"

I nodded. "She was talking to your brother."

He sucked in a breath. "My brother was talking to a reporter about Barley?"

I stepped back. His mood had shifted so dramatically that I didn't know what he might do. I mentally adjusted my assumption that the MacNish brothers weren't passionate.

"He shouldn't be talking to the press. It's bad for—it's bad for our careers. We need to know if the record label will keep us on without Barley. Jamie shouldn't say anything that could jeopardize that."

"You want to branch out without Barley?"

"'Course we do. Any musician worth his salt wants to make his own name. If he tells you otherwise, he is lying." He paused. "And we have no choice but to branch out now, considering . . ."

This was interesting, as I remembered what Kenda had said about the brothers not caring about their music and barely practicing. I wondered which of them was telling the truth and why it was worth lying about at all.

"Good night," Lester said. "I need to get this food in before Jamie calls me."

I stepped back and watched him go. I dug my cell phone out of the bushes just as it beeped, telling me I had an incoming text. It was to both Isla and me.

We are back at the Thistle House. All is well. Your father and I had a lovely tour of the countryside. Will see you girls tomorrow. We are off to bed. Love, Mom.

I smiled. Anytime my mother sent a text, she had the need to sign it *Love, Mom*, and I knew despite everything that it was true and that she did love Isla and me.

Another text message appeared in the conversation, Isla telling our parents about the visit to Winthrope Manor the next day and that I would be taking them there. I frowned at the screen.

That would be perfectly lovely. We will be there. Love, Mom.

It looked like there was no way I was getting out of my sister's plan now.

Even though I hadn't seen Mom and Dad with my own eyes, I considered my reason for stopping by the Thistle House tonight as mission accomplished. They were safe. That's all that mattered. My father being a murder suspect could wait until tomorrow. It was time to return to Duncreigan and to the garden yet to be saved.

Chapter Twenty-Four

When I woke up the next morning, I realized Isla's plan for a little outing with our parents wasn't a bad idea. I couldn't remember the last time the four of us had been together on a day off even when we all lived within a thirty-minute drive from each other. Between our busy lives and my parents' farm, there hadn't been much time for family bonding, and it had never been a priority with my parents that I could remember.

Ivanhoe followed me out of my bedroom in the cottage, and I stopped and looked at the rose in the water bowl. It was still bright yellow. I touch it with the tip of my index finger, and it bobbed in the water. As I did, a view of the garden, green, alive, and blooming, flashed across my mind. I pulled my hand away, and the vision was gone. Was it a vision or wishful thinking?

I touched the rose again, but this time nothing happened. I scooped it out of the water and held it in my hand. "Come on, work. Please work."

Nothing.

Maybe it hadn't been a vision at all, but I had to know for sure. As much as it pained me to see the garden dead, I put on my puddle boots and walked out of the cottage and down the hill toward the garden. I was yards away when I saw that the garden was still in trouble. The ivy on the walls was withered and dry. The vision or whatever it had been when I touched the rose wasn't showing me the current state of the garden.

Ivanhoe, who was walking with me to the garden, bolted ahead of me.

"Ivanhoe, wait!"

He didn't stop. The garden door was open, and he dashed inside. I ran after him. The soles of my boots slipped on the smooth rocks poking out of the earth. I came to the garden door and held on to the frame.

I looked down at the cat. What had made him run? He was crouched down a few feet from the open door. I scanned the garden for a bird or animal that Ivanhoe would want to catch. The only thing I saw was my poor dead garden.

I bent down to pick up Ivanhoe, and he hissed. I retracted my hand.

He looked up at me, the fur on his back settled down, and he mewed as if seeing me for the very first time.

"Ivanhoe?"

He mewed again, and I picked up the cat and held him to my chest. He snuggled against me. His little heart was beating out of his chest. Something had frightened him, but I had no idea what.

I stepped farther into the garden, and he started to shake. His claws came out and dug into my coat.

"Okay, okay," I whispered, and backed out of the garden with the cat still in my arms.

After his little episode, I couldn't leave Ivanhoe at Duncreigan alone, and I knew Hamish wasn't going to care for him because of Duncan. I packed up his food, cat bed, and favorite toys, and took those and the cat into the village with me.

Presha was standing outside the front door of the Climbing Rose when I carried Ivanhoe and his possessions to the shop from the village lot.

She folded her arms when she saw the cat. "What is he doing here?"

Presha had agreed to watch the flower shop for me while one of her workers minded her tea shop so that Isla and I could have our little outing to the manor with our parents. As usual, she wouldn't let me pay her. I would have to figure out a way to compensate her for everything she had done for me over the last few months. She and her brother Raj always refused to take money from me, and I ate at one or the other's place at least four times a week. I gave them flowers all the time, but there had to be something else I could do for them. In many ways, they were now my Scottish family. It wasn't lost on me that they were Indian. Perhaps they were my modern Scottish family as the United Kingdom, like the United States, became increasingly more diverse.

"What is that puff of fur doing here?" she asked again as I unlocked the door with one hand. It was no easy feat, considering I had Ivanhoe and all his possessions in the other arm.

I let the three of us into the shop and set the cat and his bag on the floor. Ivanhoe immediately began to nose around the shop, stopping to smell all the new blooms.

I told her about Ivanhoe's odd behavior that morning.

"I'd say that's good, child."

I looked at her. "Good."

"The magic is fighting to come back."

I wondered over what Presha had said as I walked to the Thistle House to collect my parents.

When I approached Thistle House, Kenda was sitting outside the guesthouse smoking a cigarette. She held it up to me. "I bet you are thinking that no one smokes these anymore. I guess I'm living proof that's not true." She took another drag and blew smoke out the side of her mouth. "And before you say anything like they are bad for me, I have been under a lot of strain. The man I loved is dead and I'm a suspect in his murder. My career is probably over, and I can't leave this too-perfect little Scottish village until the police let me go."

"Are you under house arrest?" I asked.

"No, but the chief inspector said in no uncertain terms that the MacNish brothers and I weren't to leave the area. It's maddening. I have nothing to do."

"I suppose you can practice your fiddle."

"Even the best instrumentalist can't practice twelve hours a day, every day," she said, and took another puff. "Did you find out who killed Barley yet, so we all can go back to our normal lives—or what may be left of them? Granted, for me, it's not much of a life."

"I'm afraid nothing has changed since I saw you last evening."

"Bullocks," she swore. "I'm going to have to walk to the Tesco for another pack of cigs at this rate."

"There she is!" a woman cried.

I turned around just in time to see Gemma lead a charge of six other members of the BMGs.

"She's the one that killed our Barley!" one of the BMGs cried. I didn't think it was Gemma.

Kenda jumped to her feet. "Omigawd, it's like a scene out of *Games of Thrones*." She tossed her cigarette into the grass, jumped behind me, and used my body as a human shield. "Keep those crazy old bats away from me."

Gemma jammed her fists into her hips. "Who are you calling a crazy old bat, you floozy?"

"You are deranged," Kenda shouted over my shoulder. "Go get your own life instead of dreaming that you had mine."

Gemma made like she was going to lunge forward.

"Stop! Stop!" I cried.

Gemma pulled back and glared at me. The ladies behind her did their best to look fierce, but they had a little trouble pulling it off in their flower-printed blouses and cardigans. I noted that the number of BMGs present had dwindled by two-thirds since I saw them yesterday morning by the tour bus, and all the men were gone. I supposed it was just the diehards left.

"She's the flower lady," one of the women in the group said to me.

Gemma scowled. "You're friends with this murderess?"

"No." I tried to step away from Kenda, but she grabbed my shoulders and pulled me back. I was her cover, after all.

"I mean," I said. "I don't know that she killed anyone, but we only just met. I don't know her well. I don't know any of you well."

"Then step aside. You have no reason to protect her. It's time she gets what she deserves." Gemma held her fist in the air.

My eyes widened. Kenda had a point. I wondered if these women were George R. R. Martin fans.

"I think we all need to take a breath and calm down," I said. "I know everyone is upset over Barley's death, and rightly so, but you have to remember, you all and Kenda cared about Barley. Your affection for him should bring you together, not tear you apart."

"We care for him," Gemma said. "She tossed him aside when she didn't get her way. Barley told me that you broke it off with him because he thought it was unwise for you to play a solo for one of his performances. No one comes to Barley McFee's concerts to hear an amateur like you."

"Amateur?" Kenda shouted directly into my ear. "You nasty old—"

"Let's not call each other names," I said, feeling like an elementary school teacher on the playground. I wouldn't want to be the teacher for any one of these women.

The back door of Thistle House opened, and my parents came out. Dad was holding a giant SLR camera, and Mom carried a tote bag and large thermos. It appeared that they were more than ready for their family day out.

Dad waved at me.

"If you are looking for the killer," Kenda cried. "Look no farther than at him! He was the last person to see Barley alive. He killed him!"

Dad's mouth fell open as the BMGs circled him.

Chapter Twenty-Five

My mother stood in front of my father. "Fiona, what on earth is going on?"

Kenda stepped away from me. "You know these people?"

My mother sniffed and gripped her thermos. "We're her parents."

Kenda stared at me as if I had betrayed her in some way. "You used me."

I blinked at her. "No, I didn't."

She stepped back. "And to think I trusted you. I told you about Barley and me, and all this time you were just trying to help me because you wanted to protect your father."

Mom shook her thermos. "What's going on here?"

"He's the one you should be chasing," Kenda told Gemma and her cronies. "Not me. He was the last person to see Barley alive. He went into the tour bus after I left."

"How can we believe you?" Gemma asked. "We know you've lied before."

"Ask him," Kenda said.

Gemma turned to my father, who stepped out from behind my mother. "Did you see Barley alive on the tour bus?"

Dad glanced at me before answering. "I did."

"Get him!" one of the BMGs shouted.

The others raised their fists, ready to charge. Not that I knew what they planned to do to my father other than maybe wallop him with their patent-leather pocketbooks.

"What is going on?" a strong, deep voice asked.

Everyone turned in the direction of the voice. Chief Inspector Craig stood at the corner of Thistle House with his hands on his hips. The sun was at his back and made him look even larger that his six-five height. His broad shoulders appeared to be a mile wide. The BMGs dropped their hands and stared. If I was being totally honest, I stared too. He was an impressive figure.

"I asked a question," Craig said when no one spoke.

Gemma cleared her throat. "Kenda said this man killed Barley. The BMGs want justice!"

Craig studied her and everyone standing behind the guesthouse. He briefly met my gaze before moving on to the next person with his penetrating stare. "I am the lead investigator on this case, and I have already spoken to Mr. Knox about why he was in the tour bus with Mr. McFee." Craig spoke in a measured voice. "Please know that my constables and I are taking this investigation very seriously. At this time, we are not ready to make an arrest. I would advise all of you that harassing others is a good way to find yourselves in lockup for a few hours."

Gemma scowled at him and then turned to her friends. "Come on, ladies, we need to get ready for our prayer vigil tonight." She walked away, her small band of loyal followers behind her.

Kenda folded her arms and rocked back on her heels. "I hope you consider every suspect the same."

"I do, Ms. Bay," Craig said.

She glared at me. "Stay away from me." She stalked off, leaving me standing there with Craig and my parents.

My mother put a hand to her chest. "My word, the women in Scotland are much more confrontational than the women we're used to back in Nashville. And that Kenda woman needs to get a bit of etiquette schooling, if you ask me. Her behavior is just shameful."

Craig raised his thick eyebrows at me.

I glanced from him to my parents and back again. "You all met?"

Mom nodded. "Yes, Chief Inspector Craig had a few minor questions for your father, and we cleared up a little confusion. Didn't we, Stephen?"

Dad nodded.

"I'm glad," I said. "The inspector is . . . umm . . . a good friend of mine." For whatever reason, I couldn't just come out and say that Craig and I were dating, not when my father was still a murder suspect.

Craig smiled, and his white teeth flashed out from behind his dark beard. It was as if he could read my mind.

"Well, I am glad that you have made a few friends here in Bellewick," my mother said. "Your father and I met Presha Kapoor yesterday, and she was lovely. She had so many nice things to say about you and Isla. It made me blush as your mother." She turned to Craig. "Thank you for the rescue from the crowd, Chief Inspector."

"It was my pleasure," Craig said. To my father, he added, "Thank you for taking the time to answer my questions. I know this must be a difficult time for you, having lost an old friend."

Old friend? What did he mean by that?

My father nodded.

"Now," my mother said. "Where's Isla? I thought we were supposed to be on a family outing."

"We are. Isla is already at the manor house. I'll take you to her."

"I do love old houses," my father said. "The homes back in the U.S. are just not the same level of old as the ones we have here in Scotland. It has been good to be back in my home country."

Craig stepped back. "I will leave you all to it."

"Mom, Dad, my car is over in the community lot just across the troll bridge. Why don't you two walk over there? I just need to speak to the chief inspector for a moment."

My parents shared a look, but then did as I asked. When they reached the bridge and I knew they could no longer hear me, I turned to Craig.

He smiled down at me. "I'm your . . . good friend?"

"You *are* my friend," I said defensively.

"And that's all there is to it?"

"No, you know that it's more than that."

"Then why didn't you tell your parents?" he asked.

I held my hands aloft. "I chickened out."

He grabbed my hands. "I appreciate your honesty."

I looked over my shoulder to see if Mom and Dad could see us.

"They are on the other side of the village arch. They can't see us."

"I wasn't worried about that," I said.

"Sure." He chuckled.

"I will tell them about us," I said. "I promise. It just didn't seem like the right time right after you questioned my father about murder."

"I suppose that's fair."

"What did Dad say about Barley?" I asked.

"I think you should ask him." His eyes creased with concern.

"You won't just tell me?" I asked, unable to keep the hurt out of my voice.

He sighed. "It goes back to college days, and I think it's something you need to hear from them."

College days. That's when my biological father, Uncle Ian, had decided to give me away. I knew this must be the reason Craig wanted me to hear it directly from my father.

He lifted my chin with his finger. "Everything will be all right. I don't think your father killed anyone."

"That's a relief," I said, but it wasn't like I was going to let the investigation go now that Craig didn't seriously suspect my father. I was in too deep. I had to see it through to the end. I knew better than to say any of this to Craig.

He laughed.

I sighed. "I had better head over to the car. If I'm here much longer, Mom will send Dad to fetch me. I don't think he should be alone in Bellewick with the BMGs out to get him."

He kissed me lightly on the mouth. "I'll be here when you get back."

I knew he would.

When I reached my Astra, my mother tapped her foot on the gravel lot. "What did you have to speak to the inspector about? Were you asking him about your father?"

I sighed. "We had better get going. We don't want to be late."

My mother pressed her lips together, but without another word climbed into the car. My dad was already in the back seat. I could already tell this would be a fun drive to Winthrope Manor.

I drove away from the village, and my mother settled back in her seat. "I'm looking forward to Isla moving back home."

I bit my lip to hold back the words on the tip of my tongue.

"You know that nice Peterson boy at the neighboring farm? He's always had his eye on Isla. I think he's still interested. The sooner she gets home, the sooner she can meet up with him again."

My father was quiet, but my mother continued to prattle on about Isla's return to Tennessee. My shoulders deflated the more she talked about it. I wanted to talk to my dad about Barley McFee but decided this wasn't the right time. It was best to speak to my father about that when Mom wasn't around. She would be too tempted to answer for him.

Mom went on to tell us about how great the Peterson boy was. For my mother, I thought the real draw was that he was a farmer and lived in the same community as my parents. I had one guess how this meeting with Seth was going to go. It wasn't good.

Guilt flooded me. I should stop my mom. Give her a hint that her machinations and planning weren't going to go her way. But the words wouldn't leave my mouth. Goodness, it was awkward. But I just didn't want to be the one to burst my mother's dream of her daughter's return. Besides, I consoled myself, what if Mom was right and she somehow managed to convince Isla to go home? Stranger things had indeed happened.

The manor house, which was about ten miles outside Bellewick, came into view. It was on a beautiful spot in full view of the craggy rock cliff above the North Sea. The building itself was lovely in an old, crumbling way. It was a flat-faced tan brick affair that rose three stories high. Above the very top floor was a widow's walk with some of the fencing missing. From the front, the house appeared tall and narrow, but as we came along the side of it, it stretched out the length of a basketball court.

The driveway from the road that had once been gravel had mostly been retaken by the mountain, and my little Astra bounced and hopped over the tufts of grass that had fought and won their way through the stones.

"Please do be careful, Fiona. You're going to give your father a concussion if he bounces off the roof of this car one last time. We should have brought the rental."

"I don't know the way to the manor house," Dad said from the back seat.

"Fiona could have driven the rental," my mother said reasonably.

"No," Dad said. "The car rental place was very clear that I was to be the only driver of that car."

"Stephen, we would have followed GPS," she huffed.

I shifted the car into park in front of the manor. Seth and Isla stood in the front doorway like the lord and lady welcoming us to their home. She had her arm linked through his, and he was wearing a hard hat that I guess was supposed to give him authenticity in his new career choice. The hat was a little too large for his head, so it sat lower than it normally would and made his ears bend down, giving him a Dumbo-like effect.

"Who is that young man that Isla is touching?" Mom wanted to know.

By the way my mother said *touching*, you'd have thought Isla and Seth were making out right in front of her instead of standing there as prim and proper as statues.

As I had thought before, this wasn't going to go well . . . at all.

I climbed out of the car without a word.

"Mom, Dad." Isla beamed at them. "I'm so glad you're here." She stepped off the stoop and pulled Seth forward with her. "This is the love of my life, Seth MacGregor, and we are getting married."

My mother fainted on the spot.

Chapter Twenty-Six

"Mom?" Isla asked in a high-pitched voice.

Dad and I knelt beside my mother's prostrate body. She lay on her side and had her left arm flung over her face. She moaned, "What happened?"

Dad helped her sit up. "You took a spill."

Mom shook her head and winced. "I've had the most terrible dream that my baby girl was marrying a Scottish man."

"It's not a dream, Mom," Isla said.

My mother put her hand over her chest again. "I'm feeling faint again."

Isla and I shared a look while our father helped her to her feet.

Seth clasped his hands in front of him and appeared to be at risk of fainting too.

My mother turned to me. "Did you know about this? Why didn't you tell me? If you had told me, we could have done something about this before it got so out of hand."

"It's Isla's life," I said. "It wasn't my place to tell you, and nothing is out of hand. Isla and Seth do love each other."

Mom shook her head. "Love is not enough. We know nothing about this man. How do I know he's the right fit for my youngest daughter?" She turned to me. "I never thought Ethan was right for you."

I winced when she mentioned my ex-fiancé.

"I never thought he was right for you," she went on. "But you didn't listen to me. If you had, you could have saved yourself a lot of heartbreak."

"Hello," Isla said. "Seth and I are right here. We can hear everything you say."

"I'm glad you can," Mom said. "It will show you how unhappy I am with everything. Isla, you promised you would come back to the farm." She pointed to Seth. "Are you moving with her back to Nashville?"

Seth blinked as if he didn't know how to answer that.

"Mom," Isla said. "I asked Fi to bring you here so that Seth and I could show you his work. I know you worry, but you will see Seth has a good head on his shoulders."

No comment.

Before my mother could argue more, Dad stepped in. "Let's hear them out. Seth, what is it that you do here?"

Seth blinked a few times as if he was trying to gather his thoughts. Isla elbowed him in the side.

"A local fishing merchant, Ferris Brown, bought the manor about a month ago," Seth blurted out.

"I know that name," Dad said. "Ferris owns half the boats in the harbor."

Seth nodded. "And he has always wanted to buy and restore Winthrope Manor. He hired me to be part of the construction crew."

Mom narrowed her eyes. "Do you have experience in construction?"

"Unconventional, but yes." Seth swallowed hard.

Mom looked like she wanted to ask what unconventional construction experience was, and I was curious to hear that answer too, but just then Ferris and Carver Finley came around the side of the manor house. I had expected to see Ferris there, but Carver was a surprise.

"Well, hello," Ferris said in his jovial voice. "Look at all these visitors. Are they all here to see you, Seth?"

Seth nodded and made introductions. As he spoke, I felt Carver watching me.

"It's very nice to meet you. I just brought Seth on board earlier this week, and we are looking forward to setting to work just as soon as Carver finishes his report."

"Report?" Mom asked.

Ferris stood a little straighter. "Winthrope Manor is nearly two hundred and fifty years old. It's a historic estate, and as such, I need to take that history into account during the restoration." He clapped Carver on the shoulder. "This man is the foremost authority on Aberdeenshire history, so of course, I hire the best. Isn't that right, Carver?"

Carver's lips curved into a smile. "You're too kind," he said, but he said it in such a way that gave the impression he didn't think Ferris too kind at all. "It's essential that we study and learn from the old buildings and monuments in the area in order to preserve history. Ferris had been very kind in letting me do that." He glanced at me. "Others have not been that open."

I frowned at him and wondered if I was looking into the eyes of the man who'd killed my garden. Was it fair of me to suspect him just because he'd expressed interest in the garden in the past?

"It's nice to see you again, Carver," I said.

He smiled as if he knew I was lying.

"Do you know each other?" Ferris asked.

"Why yes," Carver said. "Fiona visited me while I was working on the chapel restoration project in the summer. She had many questions about it."

He didn't say I'd had many questions because he was a suspect for murder at the same time I was. I thought it best if my parents never found out I had been a murder suspect . . . twice.

"That's nice to hear. I didn't know about your interest in history, Fiona," Ferris said. "We must grab a pint at the pub sometime to chat about this." He turned to Seth. "Why don't you and I show your friends around?"

"I should be off," Carver said. "I'll begin working on that report. I'll be in and out of the manor while I'm drafting it."

Ferris shook his hand. "I appreciate all the time you're spending on it. I want to do this right."

Carver nodded and walked toward a blue sedan parked a few yards from the manor.

Ferris clapped his hands. "Now, let's go inside, and Seth and I will show you all the fabulous things about this estate." He opened the large door, and it creaked. Seth, my sister, and my parents followed him inside.

I turned and followed Carver.

Carver leaned against his car as I approached. "I had a feeling you would want to talk to me, Miss Knox."

I frowned.

"What can I help you with?"

One of the most difficult things about Carver Finley was that he was distractedly handsome. He was well-built in a thin, academic way and had green piercing eyes, perfect hair, and just enough stubble on his face to look like he wasn't trying too hard.

I stared at him. Did I just come right out and ask if he'd hurt my garden? That seemed to be a little too direct, but maybe being direct was what I needed to get some answers from him.

He opened the driver's side door to his car. "If you have nothing to say to me, I will be on my way."

"My caretaker Hamish said you visited Duncreigan and asked to see the garden."

He closed the car door. "I did. The old man said no."

"As he should have," I replied. "You need my permission to go into the garden."

"Something as of yet that I haven't obtained. You can't judge a man for trying another tactic to get what he wants."

"And what is it that you want with Duncreigan?"

He leaned in close to me, so close that his nose was just inches from my face. I refused to step back.

"What I want is to understand the history of County Aberdeen. It's all I have ever wanted. Yet for reasons I can't understand, you refuse to give me access to a vital piece of that history, your garden."

I didn't say anything.

He stepped back. "What do you think I would do if you let me into the garden?"

"I don't know," I said. "What have you already done?"

"What do you mean by that?" He leaned on the car again.

"Have you been inside the garden?"

"How would I do that when you haven't given permission?"

"That's not exactly a no," I said.

"Are you accusing me of something?"

I was quiet for a moment and then said, "Should I be?"

He laughed and opened his car door again. "This conversation is going nowhere. Just remember, Miss Knox, I get what I want." He climbed in his car and drove away.

Chapter Twenty-Seven

I watched Carver speed away, knowing I hadn't handled that well at all. Maybe I should have come right out and asked him if he had been in the garden. I sighed and turned back to the manor. I thought I saw movement on the widow's walk, but when I cranked my neck back to look up to the third story, no one was there.

I shook off the eerie feeling that the shadow I'd seen or thought I'd seen gave me. I walked to the front door and pushed it inward. The door was made of heavy wood, and a willow tree had been carved into the front of it with three birds on its limbs.

Inside, the building was dark except for the light that fought through the dusty windows. The manor's door opened into a great entry. A chandelier hung from the ceiling thirty feet above my head. I saw that the base of the chandelier was no longer affixed to the ceiling; the giant piece hung precariously from its electrical wires. One more gust of wind and it was coming down.

To my left was a massive dining room with a table that could have easily sat twenty people in its heyday. There weren't any chairs around the table. Behind it was a marble fireplace with a hearth large enough for me to stand inside. The rug was worn, and the wallpaper was water-stained. To my right was a drawing room, and it was completely empty. The wallpaper was a faded peacock pattern that I imagined had once been startlingly lifelike. I stepped into the drawing room for a better look at the wallpaper.

I peered at the paper, and there was a creak behind me. I spun around just in time to see the giant front door slam shut. I hurried over to the door, and it took all my strength and both hands to throw it open. When I finally did, whoever had been there was gone. I frowned.

The only people who should be at the manor now were the construction workers, my family, and Ferris. What reason would any of them have to run away from me?

I looked down at the stone steps that led to the driveway. There was a dusty footprint on one of them, leaving the house. It could have been there a while. If could have belonged to any of the men working in the manor, but I suspected it was a footprint left behind by whoever had fled the house.

"The manor was built in 1772 by an English gentleman who wanted to get away from busy London life. He'd made his wealth in the shipping industry and came here with his family to retire. The descendants of that man owned the home until 1960, when it was foreclosed on and taken by the banks. By that time, the home was in disrepair, and the bank could not sell it until I came along." Ferris's voice floated to me.

I stepped back into the manor and let the door close with a thud. My parents, Isla, Seth, and Ferris were in the dining room. They all seemed to be listening to Ferris's tale with interest. My mother no longer had a scowl on her face, so perhaps she was warming up to the idea of Isla having a Scottish almost-fiancé.

"The bank was more than happy to unload that manor on me. I got it at a higher price than I first thought I would have to pay because there was another party bidding against me. I supposed, since I could up my bid and pay in cash, there was little chance of them taking it."

"Do you know who the other party was?" Isla asked.

Ferris shook his head as I joined the group. "No idea. I know it wasn't anyone from Bellewick. I would have heard the gossip from that. My guess it was another Londoner looking to make a summer vacation home in Scotland, just like the Queen." He chuckled.

"How long do you think it will take for the restoration?" Mom asked.

Ferris rubbed his chin. "A year at least, but I'm budgeting time for two years. If there is one thing I have learned in business, it's that everything takes longer than you think it will. That goes for fishing and construction."

"Isn't that the truth," Dad said.

Ferris glanced at the watch on his wrist. "I would love to stay here longer and show you more, but I have a meeting at the harbor with one of my boat captains. The fishing never stops. Will you show them out, Seth?"

Seth promised he would.

After Ferris left, my mother turned to me. "Fiona, where have you been all this time? You didn't go with us on the tour."

"I—I walked around outside the manor."

Mom pressed her lips together as if she didn't believe me. I didn't blame her. It was a lame lie, with a poor delivery to boot. "Well, Isla," Mom said. "I still am concerned about your vision, but it seems to me that Seth has some stable work for the next couple of years. In this economy, you can't ask for much more than that. Even so, I do wish that you would come home to the farm."

"You never ask Fiona to come home to the farm anymore," Isla whined. "It's only me. She could take care of the farm as much as I could, probably better, since she is so good with plants."

"Fiona's responsibility is Duncreigan. It was always going to be Duncreigan," my father said. "That was part of the agreement."

I shivered, feeling like a bargaining chip. What he said made the cottage and garden feel more like a sentence than a gift.

Isla wrinkled her small nose. "What agreement?"

Mom, Dad, and I didn't look at each other. The answer to Isla's question was a loaded one, and I didn't think any one of us wanted to get into it with her when we hadn't even dealt with it ourselves.

"I know something is going on, and I will find out what it is," Isla said. "Come on, Seth." She took her boyfriend by the hand and led him out of the manor.

I glanced at my parents. "Do you want to talk about it now?"

"Talk about what?" my mother challenged. "I think it's time for us to go back to the village." She took my dad's hand. "Stephen?"

Dad followed her out the door.

I sighed and went outside, where I found my parents already waiting in my car. We drove back to Bellewick in silence. When we reached Thistle House, my mother jumped out of the car and stomped inside. My dad watched her from the back seat.

He reached forward and placed a hand on my shoulder. "It's hard for her, being back here. You have to understand that. She loves me. I know this, but she also loved Ian." Dad's voice shook as if that was difficult to say. "She took his death much harder than either one of us thought she would. She's dealing with a lot, including missing you girls."

I gripped the steering wheel, unable to speak. There were so many questions I wanted to ask him now that I had his undivided attention. But I couldn't seem to formulate them.

Dad opened the door to the car, and I knew I had lost my chance. "Just know," he said in a quiet voice, "I did what I thought was best for you and your mother. Maybe we handled it wrong as you grew up, but we just wanted to keep you safe from hurt."

Before I could say anything, he got out of the car and followed my mother's path into Thistle House.

Chapter Twenty-Eight

I knew I should go back to the flower shop and relieve Presha of her post. She had been so kind to watch the shop while Isla and I were gone, but I realized there was another murder suspect I hadn't considered: Owen Masters, Barley's manager. I was reminded of him when, a few seconds after my parents went over the troll bridge to Thistle House, he stomped over the bridge toward the community lot carrying a briefcase.

This was an opportunity not to be missed. I jumped out of my car. He walked under the village arch in the direction of an expensive-looking sports car. He had told me the day Barley died that he was a rich and powerful man. It seemed he wanted his car to show that too.

"Mr. Masters," I called, and stepped between him and the car.

He pulled up short and blinked at me. It was clear he hadn't noticed me standing there until I spoke. "Aren't you the flower girl?"

"Fiona Knox. I'm a member of the Merchant Society of Bellewick," I said in my most official voice.

He groaned. "What do you want? I'm in a hurry."

Oh-kay. I had a suspicion that music manager Owen Masters was always in a hurry.

"I just wanted to talk to you about Barley for a moment," I said.

He stared at me. "Why would I talk to you about Barley?"

I tried to keep my face neutral, but internally I winced. It was a fair question. "Well, the Merchant Society feels just awful over what happened, and—"

"As you should! Do you even know how much money Barley's homecoming concert to Bellewick is going to cost me?"

I blinked at him.

"Millions of dollars. Millions! Barley could have been on the stage for another twenty years, playing sold-out concerts. He had the potential for even bigger and better record deals. It didn't matter that he was a man pushing seventy; the kind of music he played didn't have an age limit. It's not pop!" He waved his briefcase in the air for emphasis.

I took two big steps back so that I was out of range of the swinging briefcase. "I would have thought you would be more upset over Barley's death than the money lost."

He stopped swinging his briefcase as if he'd just realized how awful and selfish he sounded. "Yes." He coughed. "Yes, of course, I'm upset Barley is dead. He meant a lot to me. I was his manager for over a decade."

I folded my arms. "He meant a lot to you because of who he was, or because he made you a lot of money? I'm thinking the latter."

Owen narrowed his eyes at me. "Listen to me, florist, you have no idea—no idea—how cutthroat and tough the music industry really is. Even in a genre of music like Barley McFee's. Musicians like Barley will do anything to stay at the top. They will hold others back if necessary."

"Like Kenda?" I asked. "Did he hold her back?"

He relaxed his shoulders. "Let's just say that he recognized her talent and that it was a threat to him."

I took that as a yes.

"Did he ever hold you back?" I asked.

He laughed. "He made my life hell. He was a demanding client, but like I said, he made me rich too. I would crawl through the mud to make that man happy because he made my bank account happy."

"So you had no reason to kill him."

He laughed again. "Have you listened to a single word I've said? No, I would never have killed Barley, no more than I would cut off my own foot. And if that's not enough for you, I have an alibi. Ask anyone on the stage crew. I was on the stage all through intermission sweating bullets because Barley was gone so long. You even saw me there too."

He was right. I had.

"Now I'm leaving this village with no plans to come back. I was just at the guesthouse trying to talk some sense into Kenda about her future career, but apparently she has chosen not to sign me as her manager. That's her loss. She will need all the luck in the world to find a manager who can make her half the money I would have been able to make her."

But I bet she would have an easier time finding a kinder manager who's a much better human being, I thought. I liked Kenda Bay a little bit better for the choice she'd made about her career.

He stepped around me just as a high-pitched voice called, "Mr. Masters, I'm so glad I caught you." Bernice half jogged, half walked toward us.

"Dear Lord, will I ever be able to get out of this village?" Owen complained.

Bernice caught her breath. "I'm so glad I caught you," she repeated. She glanced at me. "Well, hello, Fiona."

I nodded.

Bernice shook her head as if she didn't have time to ask me why I was standing there with Barley's manager. She turned back to Owen. "I know you not only lost a friend but an important client. I was hoping to hear that you can make a go of it with Kenda and the MacNish brothers. I do love fiddler and folk music like they play. They all seem to be very good musicians."

I winced. Bernice hadn't been here when Owen went on a rant about Kenda turning down his offer to be her manager.

Bernice gave Owen a hopeful smile. It was clear to me that Bernice would do anything to put a positive spin on what had happened. I couldn't say I blamed her. I knew she felt responsible for what had gone wrong at the homecoming concert, even though she wasn't responsible for Barley's death.

He scowled at her. "That's not an option."

She sighed. "I am sorry to hear that. I just want to say, Mr. Masters, just how sorry everyone in the village is over what happened." She paused. "We hope that the village won't be shone in a poor light after what happened."

Owen looked down at her like he was a scientist examining a speck of mold. "You can trust me when I say that I will never send an act to Bellewick again."

I personally didn't think that was much of a loss. Bellewick had been fine before Barley's concert, and there weren't any other famous musicians I knew of who might want to host a homecoming concert in the little fishing village.

"Oh, I do know how upsetting this must have been for you, and we understand your decision. But we would greatly appreciate that there not be any bad press about the village. As you know, what happened to Barley could have happened anywhere. He's a famous man, and I'm sure there are many crazy fans that are so delusional that murder pops into their heads." She smiled brightly, like she was talking about a beautiful spring day.

I inwardly groaned.

"You see," Bernice went on, "there are reporters in the village, and I'm sure, since you were such an important figure in Barley's life, that they would want to talk to you about the murder. We would very much appreciate it if—"

"If I only said nice things about Bellewick," Owen offered with a smile.

I knew the smile wasn't genuine. I knew it was just a warning.

But Bernice did not know it, and she beamed up at him. "Yes, that's exactly it. We would appreciate it so much."

"I'm afraid it's too late for that," Owen said. "I have spoken with Trina Graham from Action News and told her what an awful and disgraceful village this is. In fact, I told her she should tell her viewers never to come here."

Bernice gasped. "Well, I never . . ."

"If that's all, I must be going." Without waiting for our answer, Owen stomped to his car, threw the briefcase in, jumped inside, and drove away. His tires spit gravel in our direction.

Bernice's mouth hung open. "What a terrible man."

I couldn't have agreed more.

She stared at me. "Can you believe what he said about the village? It's just horrible." She sniffled. "This is all my fault. I can't believe this is happening. The reputation of the village in the county, if not all of Scotland, is ruined." She started to cry.

I gave her a hug. "Oh, Bernice, don't cry. This will all blow over. Trust me. It won't hurt the village. Bellewick is a fishing town. We were never going to become a tourist hot spot."

She sniffled and stepped back. "I suppose you are right." She took a moment to remove a tissue from her purse and wipe her eyes. Some of her eye makeup smeared onto her cheek. "I must look a fright."

"You look fine. Just stop at the bathroom before you go back onto the floor of the jewelry store. It's nothing that a little makeup can't mend," I said, and patted her arm.

"Thank you, Fiona. You have been very kind." She took a breath. "And I must say that you and your business have been a lovely addition to the village. Like a lot of the villagers, I had my reservations about an American coming to Bellewick, and even more so one taking over Duncreigan, but you have done a wonderful job of it. Your godfather Ian would have been so proud of the job you are doing and how involved you have become in the village. I know he wasn't here often as an adult because of his service in the army, but he loved this village and always meant to do right by it."

I swallowed as the image of the dead garden at Duncreigan came back to me. I didn't know how proud Uncle Ian would have been about that. If fact, all evidence pointed to the fact that I had failed in the mission he had left me to complete.

"Do you still have the triskele necklace he had me fix for you?" she asked.

When I moved back to the village, Bernice had given me a necklace that Uncle Ian had held for me at her shop. It was in the shape of a triskele, just like those etched on the menhir in the garden and the ones Carver Finley was so desperate to study.

I touch the triskele at my neck. "I wear it every day."

She nodded. "Good. Ian would have liked that."

I nodded, unable to speak.

She clicked her tongue. "As for Owen Masters." She shook her head. "He is one angry man."

I silently agreed with her. Owen Masters was an angry man, maybe even one capable of murder, but sadly his alibi was airtight, which left me with the suspects I'd had before the music manager showed his true colors.

Chapter Twenty-Nine

I smelled the smoke before I saw the flames. That wasn't all I smelled. I caught the scent of seawater too. I couldn't see a thing. Was I trapped in the fire and blinded by smoke? I touched my arms. Nothing hurt. I wasn't in the fire, only near it.

Slowly I could see bits in front of me. It came in fragments. A burning boat mast. Fiery pieces of line falling to the deck below. Ewan and his friends staring openmouthed at a scene I could not fully appreciate. It was like I was caught in a dream within a dream, and part of my vision was taken from me.

There was a splash. Something was in the water. More splashes. Someone was in the water.

I sat up in bed and sent poor Ivanhoe flying. My T-shirt was soaked with sweat, and I was freezing cold. It was a dream, just a dream. Or a vision of something yet to come? The visions I had experienced in the past had either come when I touched the menhir in the garden or in dreams like this. However, those visions had been so much clearer. I saw everything, felt everything, smelled everything. It was all there. This was in fragments. Was it fragmented because the garden was dead? Perhaps it wasn't dead completely if I could receive any vision at all.

I threw back the blankets from the bed and put my feet on the floor. I winced when they hit the cold hardwood. The cottage was freezing. The fire I'd had going before I went to bed must have gone out. I had propane-powered heating as well, but I didn't like to run it until it was absolutely necessary because of the cost. It seemed that the time had come that I could no longer avoid it. Honestly, I should have started using it at the end of October, but I was stubborn that way. Isla would have said cheap.

I shoved my feet into a pair of slippers. The heel of one of the slippers was missing. Ivanhoe had chewed it off one day when I was away from home too long for his liking. In many ways he was more like a dog than a cat.

I hobbled on the mangled slipper into the main room of the cottage. A beam of moonlight came in from the side window and hit the glass bowl with the still-yellow rose blossom inside it. The flower was as bright and yellow as it had ever been on the menhir. Somehow, without its stem and roots, it was still alive. I had no idea how long that would last. Logic told me flowers could not survive so long on water alone. Well, maybe some varieties, but not roses.

Ivanhoe rubbed against my legs and mewed. He then walked over to his empty food bowl in the tiny kitchen. He mewed again. I looked at the clock on the small microwave on the counter. It was three thirty in the morning.

"Ivanhoe, it's not time for breakfast yet. It's still the middle of the night."

He lowered himself on his haunches and mewed again.

I rolled my eyes, and he flipped over on his back and waved his paws. I sighed and took the two steps into the kitchen.

Knowing he had won, the cat jumped to his feet and purred.

I fed the cat and went back to the bedroom. I lay on the bed and stared at the ceiling, unable to sleep.

When it was first light out, I went outside and headed to the garden. This time I left Ivanhoe in the cottage. I bribed him with a second breakfast. The best way to distract Ivanhoe was always through his stomach.

I didn't run or hurry to the garden this time. I walked slowly because I carried the glass bowl with the rose blossom inside it. I took care not to spill a single drop of water. I went into the garden through the open door. The ivy on the garden wall was still dead, and the garden was withered too. There was no amount of sun or water that could bring it back. I knew the menhir was the answer. I just didn't know how. I walked around the brown hedgerow. The menhir was just like I had left it. The climbing rose's vine and stem were wilted to the ground. I could clearly see all the etched triskeles in the stone. This was what Carver Finley wanted to see. He wanted to study these markings. He found them particularly interesting because they were rare in Scotland. It was a more common Celtic symbol in Ireland. Would he cut the rose for a closer look at them? I thought he might.

I touched the stone and closed my eyes. Nothing happened. No visions came. Frowning, I stepped back from the stone to see the fox, standing just a few feet away from me. I held the bowl in my hand, not touching the stone. Gently I set it on the ground next to the standing stone. The fox gave the slightest of nods, so slight that I might have imagined it.

"Should I leave the blossom here?" I asked the fox.

As usual, he said nothing, only stared.

"I really wish you could talk. It would make things much easier for me." I studied him. "But you are here."

He cocked his head.

"That must mean there is still magic in this place." I pointed at the bowl. "In this stone and in this flower. You couldn't still be here if the magic was gone."

He straightened his head and stared at me with those bright blue eyes.

I left the rose there. I didn't know if that was the right thing to do or not, but it felt right. With the garden in such a state, it was all I had to go on.

* * *

In the Climbing Rose a few house later, Isla draped herself over the sales counter. "It was a rocky start, but I think Mom and Dad meeting Seth went well overall. I think they can see that he really has drive."

I was in the back room of the shop making flower baskets for a birthday party order. "Drive? That's the word you are going to use for Seth?"

She opened her mouth to protest, and I held up my hand. "You're right. I'm sorry. I shouldn't have said that. I'm happy Mom and Dad weren't too upset. I mean, after Mom fainted, everything seemed to go swimmingly."

She stood up and said, "I think so too."

I added a bow to the arrangement and stepped back. I was proud of how it had turned out. It was for an eightieth birthday party being held at Presha's Teas this afternoon. The guest of honor was Maggie Grig. Presha had put in the order for the flowers because she wanted everything to be perfect for the party. I'd put extra effort into the arrangement because of everything Presha had done for me.

I patted the purple satin bow on the front. "Perfect," I said. "Do you want to take this order over to the tea shop or stay here and watch the shop?"

"I'll stay back at the store, if it's all the same to you. Seth needs to come into the village to pick up construction supplies at the harbor and said he would swing by for a visit on his way back to the manor."

Yep, drive was what Seth MacGregor had, all right. Wisely, I kept my thoughts to myself.

I put on my coat and picked up the heavy basket. I didn't mind at all that my sister wanted to stay back. I loved any excuse to go see Presha, and I knew she would give me a scone or tea cake when I made the delivery. It was well worth the walk, even carrying a thirty-pound arrangement.

I took care as I strolled the cobblestone streets to Presha's Teas. Presha's shop wasn't on the same road as the Twisted

Fox and my flower shop. It was one street over. When the tea shop came into view, I gave a sigh of relief—the basket really was heavy.

When I opened the door to the shop, the welcome scent of baked goods, caramel, and chai hit me full in the face. I could have stood there all day just taking it in.

"Fiona, that is lovely!" Presha floated toward me. One of her bejeweled scarves flowed behind her like a cape. "You really outdid yourself with the arrangement." She took it from my hands. "Maggie, happy birthday."

A woman in a blue dress, stockings, and orthopedic shoes turned around. Her white hair was styled in pin curls, and there was a tiny silver barrette over her left ear.

I blinked. Maggie Grig, the guest of honor, was the Tesco lady. She was the older woman I saw each morning making her daily walk to Tesco.

She recognized me too and frowned. I had always thought, from the moment I came to the village, that the woman didn't care for me. What she said next proved it. "You bought me flowers from the American?"

"Now, now, Maggie. Fiona does beautiful work, and besides, hers is the only flower shop in town."

The door opened behind me, and six or seven more elderly ladies came inside. Each of them carried a wrapped box or gift bag and stopped to hug Maggie and tell her happy birthday.

She smiled at them, and her whole face transformed. She was no longer the sad, sometimes bedraggled Tesco lady I saw each morning shuffling down the street. She was happy and loved, and I felt that even though I had never said more than hello to her, I owed her an apology for misjudging her.

"Who brought the flowers?" one of the women asked. "They are gorgeous." She leaned forward to inhale the flowers' scent. "Lovely."

"They are from her." Maggie pointed at me with a light-pink-polished fingernail.

"You're the girl from the flower shop. Your father is the one who killed Barley," the woman who had smelled my flowers said.

A hush fell on the tea shop, and every set of eyes turned to me.

"Who are you?" I asked, trying to avoid their stares. I knew I should leave, but Presha hadn't given me a scone yet. I wasn't leaving without one. I had priorities.

"Gertrude Bully. I'm a member of the BMGs. I'm the only local member we have. You would think there would be more in the village, since Barley was from here. People seem to forget the history of the village so easily."

"The BMGs are a bunch of women who have lost their minds," Maggie said. "They waste their time and money going to all of Barley's concerts in the UK and some even on the Continent. There are certainly better uses for their money and time."

Presha clapped her hands. "Everyone is here now. Please, ladies, take your seats, and we can start our tea to celebrate Maggie's birthday."

"Are you staying?" Gertrude asked.

"Why would she stay when you accused her father of murder?" one of the women at the table asked.

It was a fair question, I thought.

"I don't think her father did it," Gertrude said.

"Who, then?" another woman said as she poured herself a cup of tea.

"It was Kenda."

"Jealousy of a pretty, young, talented woman is not a flattering attribute," Maggie said.

"I'm not jealous, but Gemma certainly was."

"Jealous enough to kill?" another woman asked.

"Maybe," Gertrude replied.

Chapter Thirty

"We are supposed to be celebrating Maggie's birthday, not discussing murder," a woman at the table with straight silver hair said.

"Talking about murder," Maggie said, "is much more interesting than talk about my birthday. It's my eightieth one. I know how birthdays go by now."

I inched toward the door.

"Where are you going?" Maggie asked.

"I—I was just going to leave you to your party. I'm not going to barge in on your special day."

"You already have," Maggie said. "Now, sit yourself down. It's my birthday, which means you have to do what I say."

Silently, Presha added another chair to the table and winked at me. I sat. Presha went back to the kitchen, leaving me with the group of six women. I watched her go and did my best not to whimper.

"Maggie, are you going to open your gifts?"

Maggie waved her question away and folded her hands on the table. "We will get to that. Gertrude, why do you think Kenda did it, other than that's what Gemma wants to have happened?"

Gertrude gasped. "You think Gemma wants Kenda to be the killer?"

"Of course she does. Then she will feel better about the fact that Barley never showed any interest in her. I've seen it before. Barley McFee may have been a small man, but he was handsome and charming. He was very popular with the young and old women in Bellewick when he was a lad."

The kitchen door opened, and Presha came out with a tray of tea sandwiches and cakes on two three-tiered plates. My mouth watered when I saw them. She set a small dessert plate in front of each person, including me.

Several ladies reached for cakes and sandwiches. Since I was stuck there until I knew why Maggie wanted me to stay, I did the same.

"You knew Barley when he was young?" I asked.

"Oh my, yes, I knew him. I have lived in this village for eighty years as of today. There is little I don't know about." She sipped her tea and looked at me appraisingly. "People think all I do is walk to the grocery each morning, but I do much more than that. I see things, and I know all the happenings in the village." She looked over her teacup at me as if she wanted that statement to sink in to me in particular.

I glanced over my shoulder just to make sure there wasn't someone else she could be giving the beady look to. Nope, there was no one there. I was most definitely on the receiving end of that stare.

Gertrude clapped her hands. "Now, why haven't you told me you knew Barley when he lived here? You know how much I love his music."

"Did you know him?" I asked Gertrude. She looked like she would be closer to Maggie's age than Barley's, but I was smart enough not to say that.

She shook her head. "I moved to Bellewick as an adult after I married my late husband. He worked in the ship-yards. God rest his soul. He was a good man, and he loved a cheerful fiddle concert as much as any man did. We went to two or three every summer, but of course, Barley was the very best there was."

"Aye," another woman at the table agreed. "That's true." She nodded to me. "I enjoyed his music but am not one for joining groups like the BMGs. I never was one for organized sports neither."

I nodded as if the comparison made sense.

"I did not tell you," Maggie said, addressing Gertrude's question, "because it never came up. I can't possibly know everything that you want to know."

Gertrude huffed and sat back in her chair.

"Have a scone," the silver-haired woman said. "It will make you feel better." She held out the plate to Gertrude.

Gertrude hesitated and then took two.

I approved of her choice. I had always thought that two scones could cure what ailed any person.

"Can you tell me about Barley McFee and his family?" I asked.

Maggie looked at me through eyes so wrinkled I could barely see the blue of her irises. "Are you asking because you are helping the chief inspector again?"

I pressed my lips together. "I was the one who found Barley. I want to know what happened." I didn't mention that my father's involvement had brought me into the investigation at the beginning. I hoped I would get to hear what she had to say about Barley before bringing my father into it.

She studied me, and just when I thought she wasn't going to talk about it, she said, "The McFees are an old family in the village. Though they no longer live here. They are dead or moved away, some farther than others."

"Barley has more relatives in the area."

"Not many, but you met one," Maggie said. "You were there when I walloped him with my grocery sack. I don't like young men running. It's not proper, and I did my best to show him that."

"Mick McFee?" I asked.

She nodded. "I was trying to teach him some etiquette."

I thought I would pay attention to Maggie's etiquette lessons too if I was knocked on the head four or five times with a grocery bag. Again, Mick had been lucky the sack was empty. If Maggie had been going the other way, it would not have been.

"Mick seemed to have been very upset with Barley. It seemed that Mick thought Barley owed him something."

"He may have," Maggie said. "But Mick is the type of lad who always believes someone owes him something. The

243

family was as poor as church mice. I suppose when Barley was so successful, Mick felt that Barley should help the family."

"Did he?"

She shrugged. "Not that I ever heard."

Gertrude seemed to have recovered from the insult from before, and she leaned forward. "What made Barley leave Bellewick and never come back until this concert? It's a question he received often in interviews but never seemed to answer."

"Oh," Maggie said. "That's an easy answer. His band with Ian MacCallister broke up."

A piece of cucumber got caught in my throat. One of the women, the silver-haired one, I thought, shoved a teacup into my hand. "Here. Drink!"

I did as I was ordered and sputtered as I forced the cucumber down. It felt like the inside of my throat was raw.

"Are you all right?" one of the women at the table asked.

I pressed a hand to my cheek. I was hot from embarrassment and nearly dying. It wasn't a great combo.

Presha set a glass of water in front of me and patted my back.

I smiled at her and coughed. Then I looked back at Maggie. "Did you say that my godfather was in a band?"

"Aye, he was. He and Barley were in it together. They started the band as boys when they were in boarding school with another boy they met there."

I folded my hands in front of me so tightly that the knuckles turned white. "Do you know the name of the other boy?"

She tapped her cheek with her index finger as she thought. "I do. He was a close friend of Ian more than Barley. I always thought there was some jealousy there between Barley and the third boy." She snapped her fingers. "I have it. His name was Stephen. I don't remember his last name, I'm afraid."

I felt an instant headache between my eyes. She didn't need to tell me the third boy's surname because I already knew it. It was Knox, just like mine. My father had been in a band with Uncle Ian and Barley McFee? It was a little too much to process. Dad had never shown any interest in music. Even when I was engaged to Ethan, a struggling musician in Nashville, Dad had never mentioned that he had been a musician himself. What could have happened that he would keep this secret the rest of his life? What could have happened that Mom would keep the secret too? She had to have known, right? She'd met my godfather and father at university.

Presha squeezed my shoulder. Of anyone in the tea shop, she was the most astute, and would know why this information came as a great surprise.

"Why did the band break up?" Gertrude asked.

I was grateful that she asked the question. It was one I wanted an answer to too, but my mind was spinning far too much to ask.

I picked up my teacup from the table and sipped from it. The spicy chai was just what I needed to wake up my senses. I needed to focus. I felt like I was on the cusp of learning something important. The teacup was a beautiful, delicate piece with orange and purple chrysanthemums painted around the rim.

"From what I hear, it was over a girl."

I dropped the teacup on the table. It shattered into a thousand tiny shards, and hot chai splashed across the linen tablecloth and onto my shirt.

Chapter
Thirty-One

The ladies jumped back from the table. I stood up too. "I'm so sorry." I glanced back at Presha. "I'm so sorry about the teacup. I will happily pay for it, and that tablecloth too, if it's stained."

Presha handed me a damp cloth. "For your shirt."

I took the cloth and dabbed at my clothes. "I hope you ladies are all okay."

"Everyone is fine, Fiona," Presha said in a calming voice.

With the help of the other women, she quickly cleared the food and moved it to another table. "Here, sit here. I can clean up that mess," Presha said.

"I can," I said. "It's my fault."

She placed a hand on my shoulder. "No, Fiona, you need to talk to the ladies."

Maggie and her friends settled at the new table. I was happy to see that none of the scones had been drenched with my tea.

"My, you gave us a start," Gertrude said. "I nearly jumped right out of my skin."

"I'm sorry. I can't believe I was so clumsy," I said, even though I knew clumsiness had nothing to do with it. It was shock, plain and simple, that had caused me to drop the teacup. I was shocked because I knew the girl Maggie mentioned had to be my mother. She was the only girl who had ever been in Uncle Ian's and my father's life. If the band broke up over my mother, had it in a way actually broken up over me? I didn't know how to ask Maggie this without revealing too much about my own story, a story I didn't really know.

"Who was the girl?" the silver-haired woman asked.

Maggie shook her head. "I don't know. It was someone they met at university."

Maggie's statement was just more confirmation that it was my mother who'd broken up the band. I was relieved that Maggie didn't seem to know my connection to her or the band, though.

I stood up. I had a lot to think about after this birthday party, and I had a few more questions for my parents. I wondered what other secrets they were keeping from Isla and me. I also wondered why they didn't tell us. What was their goal? Did they even have one?

"Thank you for inviting me to join your party," I said. "But I really must go. My sister will be wondering why it is taking me so long to deliver the flowers." I looked to Presha. "And I am sorry about the mess."

She waved the end of her bright scarf at me. "Forget it, my friend."

"Happy birthday, Maggie," I said, as I inched toward the door. I had to get out of there and go over in my head everything I had learned about Barley, my parents, and in a strange way, myself.

Maggie nodded at me. "If you want to find Mick McFee, go no farther than the harbor."

I stopped at the front door of the tea shop with my hand on the handle. "He said he doesn't live in Bellewick."

She pointed her teaspoon at me. "He might not live here, but he still works here every day of the week except for Sundays, as they are the Lord's day and no one should be working on those days."

"He works at the harbor?" I asked.

"The shipyard," Gertrude answered for Maggie. "That's where my husband worked, too, until he retired. It's hard, backbreaking work."

I could imagine that it was.

When I stepped out of Presha's Teas, I was torn. Did I go to Thistle House to talk to my parents? To the harbor to look for Mick McFee? Or back to the Climbing Rose, so my sister didn't throw a fit about me being away so long?

I started walking. I really didn't have a choice. I had to ask the questions that were most on my heart. As I hurried to Thistle House, I texted Isla that I had been caught up with something and would be back to the flower shop just as soon as I could. She texted back a string of annoyed emojis. I knew she would be fine, especially if Seth was there. But that didn't stop me from feeling guilty.

The Thistle House garden was quiet. An English robin sat on a limb and twittered, and a rabbit nibbled on the grass. There wasn't a person about. I didn't know my parents' plans for the day, so it was very likely they were out sight-seeing again. My father had mentioned that he wanted to go to Aberdeen to walk around the old part of the city.

"You made a mistake, and like always, it's left up to me to fix it," an angry voice said from the front of the house.

"I'm not asking you to fix anything. I'm asking you to ignore what happened. It's all any of us can do," another, much calmer voice said.

I crept along the side of the stone building. I couldn't help myself. My inner nosiness and need to know always seemed to have the upper hand with me.

However, when I came around to the front of Thistle House, no one was there. I walked back and forth in the yard. I even looked up in the large ash tree that stood in front of the guesthouse. There was no one. Whoever had been speaking appeared to have vanished into thin air.

"What are you doing back here? Are you following me?"

I pulled my eyes away from the tree and saw Kenda standing in the doorway of Thistle House with her hands on her hips.

"I—I, no, I was looking for my parents, actually."

She leaned on the doorframe. "You mean your father, the killer."

"He didn't kill anyone," I said, as calmly as possible.

"I don't know how you are going to prove that," she said.

I didn't know either.

"Your mom and dad aren't here," she said. "I heard them tell Eugenia they were headed to the pub."

I took a step back. The pub—great, that was just by the Climbing Rose. I would talk to them about everything there. I didn't really want to have this conversation with my parents in a public place like the Twisted Fox, but if this was the only way I could have the conversation, I was going to do it.

I started to walk away.

"Hey," Kenda called after me.

I turned around.

"Do you think I did it?" Her voice wavered.

I shook my head no.

"Do you think your father did it?"

Again, I shook my head no.

"Then who?"

"I haven't the faintest idea," I said, and walked away.

Back in the main part of the village, I hurried down along the cobblestones, reciting in my head over and over again the script I had rehearsed in order to convince my parents to tell me what was going on. Each time in my head, they refused to talk.

As luck would have it, as I was within a few yards of the pub's front door, my parents walked out arm in arm. They chatted and smiled at each other. To me, they had always been in love, so much so that at times Isla and I had been left to our own devices because our parents were so concerned with each other.

It was startling, after a lifetime of believing that, to think it might not always have been the case.

Dad looked up first and saw me standing in the middle of the street. He stopped and caught my mother's attention. She stopped as well.

My mother said something to Dad and kissed him on the cheek. He nodded and went back inside the pub, while Mom walked toward me.

"Let's go for a walk, Fiona," she said.

I nodded and led her down the street in the direction of St. Thomas Church. There was a bench just outside the church gate. From there I could see most of the graveyard, with its moss-covered Celtic crosses and centuries-old English oak trees. To my left, I could see the village school where Seth had worked as a janitor until his sudden change in career this past week. It was a new, modern building that stuck out in Bellewick, with lots of sharp angles and glass.

I sat, and my mother sat next to me. We sat there quietly for a few minutes. I wondered if my mother knew that Uncle Ian was buried in the graveyard beside us. I decided not to mention it.

"When your father and I decided to come to Scotland, I had thought it was to convince Isla to move back home. I had been getting the feeling that she was considering staying here permanently. I know you are both adults, but I hate the idea of both of my girls so far away."

I opened my mouth to say something, but she went on before I could. "However," Mom said, "I realized that we really came because I needed to have this conversation with you about Ian and your father."

"Just tell me what happened. Please," I whispered.

She sighed and folded her hands in her lap. "I have always loved your father, from the moment I first met him while I was spending that year studying abroad at St. Andrews. We fell in love right away, and were inseparable. You don't know this, but your father and Ian were in a band."

"I know," I said. "With Barley McFee."

"How?" She shook her head. "Never mind, you always seem to be able to get the facts."

I almost laughed. That couldn't have been further from the truth. I'd had no idea Ethan was cheating on me with our wedding cake decorator or that my father wasn't my biological father, so me being able to "get the facts" was as far from the truth as possible.

"It wasn't long before I was set to return home to Tennessee. I wanted your father to come with me, or at least move to Nashville when he finished school. He was torn. He wanted to, but the band was doing so well that they were on the brink of a record deal. If he left, that would all fall apart. I was young and a bit of a wild card—I know Isla gets that from me—and I broke up with your father. I had no interest in a long-distance relationship."

She sighed. "I had always known that Ian also had a crush on me, but I never gave it much thought. He was a popular guy on campus, with many girlfriends. He never seemed to be in need of a date." She shook her head. "One night I cried on his shoulder over your father." She paused.

I held up my hand. "You don't need to paint the picture; I can guess what happened next."

She nodded. "We were young and stupid and made one mistake." She shook her head. "The next day, your father came back to me. He said he'd changed his mind, that I was more important than the band and he would come to Nashville with me." She closed her eyes. "Even though I didn't know it yet, by that time I was pregnant with you. When the truth came to light weeks later, it was awful. As you can imagine, your father was devastated. Ian and I were horrified with what we had done. We both loved your father and didn't want to hurt him."

I bristled.

She took my hand, and I let her. "I never once considered not having you. I planned to go home alone and raise you on the farm myself. Even though it didn't happen the way I would have liked, I was so happy I'd be a mother. It's something I had always wanted."

I nodded for her to go on.

"After many nights of arguments and tears, Stephen finally accepted our apology and took me back. He loved me, and I loved him. What had happened was undeniable proof that nothing could change that."

"So Uncle Ian just pretended that I wasn't his child," I murmured.

She moved a strand of hair behind my ear, just as she had when I was a little girl. "Ian loved you. As far as I know, you were the only person he ever really loved. But at that time, he wasn't in the place to be a dad. He was going off to the army.

It was something he'd been thinking about for a long time. He'd postponed it because of the band, but since the band was breaking up anyway with Stephen moving to the U.S., he decided to go. He asked Stephen to take you as his own daughter; he begged for it. He didn't want you to agonize over having a father at war."

I tried to process everything she was telling me. "So you were never going to tell me."

She shook her head. "We wanted to. We planned to. Time just got away from us." She gripped my hand. "I know we didn't handle our decision well with you. It's something we should have sat down and told you many years ago. Your father and I had a plan to tell you when you were eleven. We thought by then it would be information you could handle." She took a breath. "But then eleven became thirteen, then eighteen, then never. It seemed the longer and longer we put it off, the harder and harder it would be to tell you. We knew you would be upset. Ian wanted to tell you as you grew older. I think he was impatient at times, but he respected our wishes. I believe he thought he had to because it was his idea to tell you that you were Stephen's daughter in the first place."

I didn't know what to say. The face that came to mind was Isla's. How was I—were they—going to tell Isla all of this? She had been lied to, too.

Mom removed a handkerchief from her pocket. My mother was a true southern farmer's wife and always carried such a thing in her pocket, even if she was helping in the fields or milking the cows. "You have a little smudge on your cheek."

She wiped off the smudge, and I wanted to pull away from her. I forced myself to remain still. I knew it would hurt her if I pulled back. Even though I was hurt, I didn't want to hurt her in return. It would solve nothing and close off any way to resolution.

She dropped her hand and shook her head as if she was dissatisfied with how well she was able to clean my face. "Ian warned us that you would find out someday because of the garden and your connection to it."

The dead garden now.

"Where does Barley McFee fit into all of this?" I asked.

"Barley never forgave the three of us for what happened. He thought the band was destined for great things, and the situation we were in ruined it. Of the three of them in the band, he was the most ambitious. He wanted it the most. He would let nothing get in his way to reach his dreams. Because Stephen went to America and Ian went into the army, the record deal the band was on the cusp of signing fell apart. Barley was furious."

"He's the most famous fiddler in the world," I said. "And he was still angry about it?"

She shrugged. "Perhaps if Ian and your father had stayed in the band, Barley would have become famous much more quickly. All I know is, Ian and your father never heard from him again. He broke all contact. Of course we heard when he hit the big time, but so much time had passed that your father decided not to reach out to him. He didn't want it to seem that he wanted to talk to Barley now simply because Barley was famous."

I could understand that. "Was that why Dad was on the tour bus with Barley at intermission?"

She nodded. "Your father went into that tour bus to make amends."

"When he was there, was Barley still alive?" I asked.

She nodded again. "And I think your father and Barley came to terms with what happened all those years ago. Stephen said it was a good conversation, and he and Barley made plans to meet again before Barley left the village." She shook her head. "As you know, that didn't happen."

No, it had not.

Chapter Thirty-Two

I went with my mother back to the Twisted Fox, and my dad was pacing outside the pub. I walked over to him and gave him a hug. "I love you, Dad."

Tears welled in his eyes. "I love you, too. You are my daughter and always will be."

I nodded, unable to speak.

"I'm sorry," he added.

I smiled. "It's over now, but"—I glanced at the Climbing Rose—"someone needs to tell Isla. She should know."

Dad straightened his shoulders. "I'll tell her. Your mom did the hard work by explaining it all to you. The least I can do is tell Isla."

Mom squeezed my father's hand. "Knowing how our youngest girl reacts to things, I don't think you got the easier job at all."

Dad smiled, kissed her on the cheek, and marched into the flower shop. He looked like a man off to war.

"Phew," Mom said. "I'm going back into the pub for a pint. Want to come with me?"

"I do, but there's something I need to check into first."

She frowned and looked like she was going to ask me what that was, but then she thought better of it and nodded.

After Mom entered the pub, I turned and hurried toward the harbor. I wanted to see if I could catch up with Mick McFee before he left for the day. It was already late afternoon, and I knew the shipyard workers usually called it quits around four if there weren't any night boats coming into Bellewick Harbor.

As always when I entered the harbor, the smell of sea and fish hit me full in the face. The waters were choppy this afternoon. There were more whitecaps on the sea than there had been the other day. I'd been in Scotland long enough now to recognize a North Sea squall coming in. I hoped it would pass by Bellewick and Duncreigan. It was always hard to tell where the storm would touch down.

Waves hit the dock hard.

"Don't look so worried, lass," Ewan said. "The storm is going to the south of us. It will give Dunnottar Castle a wallop, I daresay."

Ewan was on the oil barrels with his two friends, right where I'd left them the last time I visited the harbor.

"Aye," Old Milton agreed. "But the castle has stood there for hundreds of years. It will last a hundred more, I wager."

The man with the one eye nodded in agreement.

"What can we help you with, lass?" Ewan asked.

"Why do you think I need help?"

He laughed. "Because you only come down to the docks when you are looking for someone or something."

He had a point.

"I heard that Mick McFee worked in the shipyard. I came down to see if he was still here."

"Aye, he does," Ewan said. "You want to talk to him, I bet because of the death of his cousin Barley. You're not the first."

"The police have been here too?" I asked.

"Chief Inspector Craig was here last morning, and a reporter woman was here too."

That had to be Trina Graham. It was interesting to hear that she was still in the village. She must really be desperate for this story.

"Did they talk to Mick?"

"Don't know," Old Milton said. "We just told them where they could find him, just like we will tell you. He's in the warehouse next to the beach. That's where a lot of the shipyard workers wait for boats to come in."

"Thank you. You've been a big help." I turned to go.

"Wait, lass," Ewan called. "Keep your wits about you when you're down there. It's no place for a pretty young thing such as yourself. The men are as gentle as a leather strap."

I nodded and took his advice to heart. I was certain that the warehouse was not a place Chief Inspector Craig would like me to go, but I had to find Mick McFee to hear what he might know about his cousin's murder. Besides Trina Graham had gone to the warehouse and spoken with him—or at least tried to; she hadn't been dressed for that rough crowd, I was sure. But if her cameraman was with her, she hadn't been alone either. I shoved that last thought into the back of my mind.

Following the directions from the old men, I walked toward the warehouse. It was up on giant concrete pilings, so it seemed to hover over the harbor. I knew it was so high up for the times the tide came in unnaturally high or high waves were brought in by one of the North Sea's furious storms. I had lived through a couple of those storms now since moving to Scotland, and they were nothing to trifle with.

The giant garage door that led into the warehouse stood open. A clean-shaven man in tan coveralls was folding a giant fishing net in the doorway. He looked up at me. "Are you lost?"

"I'm looking for Mick McFee. Ewan at the docks told me I could find him here." I didn't think it could hurt to make it known that someone knew where I was, even if that someone was only Ewan and his friends.

The man looked over his shoulder and shouted back into the warehouse. "McFee, you have another visitor."

"Who is it?"

The man looked me up and down. "It's a girl."

I scowled. Somehow the way he said *girl* sounded like an insult.

"She's American," the man with the net added.

Somehow he made that sound even worse than being a girl.

Mick McFee came out of the shadows of the warehouse. He wore the same tan coveralls as the first man and removed a pair of gray work gloves. The gloves' fingers were stained with a brick-colored substance. I was afraid to ask what it was.

"You again? Don't you have anything better to do than follow me around?"

"I just have a few more questions about Barley," I said.

The other man watched our exchange with interest.

Mick threw his gloves on the dirty concrete floor of the warehouse. "When will I be rid of that man?"

"Mick, why don't you and your lady friend go for a little walk and chat?" his coworker suggested. "I can watch to see when the boss comes back."

"And who's the boss?" I asked.

"Ferris Brown. He owns more of the harbor than God," the other man said.

Mick scowled, but then he said, "If Brown comes back, tell him I'm taking my fifteen."

The other man nodded.

To my relief, instead of walking deeper into the warehouse, Mick came out. I wasn't about to follow him into those dark aisles of shipping containers.

I followed him to the edge of the rock-covered beach. He stopped and crossed his arms over his coveralls.

I thought it was best to get right to the point. "Why do you think Barley owed you something?"

He glared at me. "Because I'm family. Family takes care of family. That's the way it's supposed to be. It goes back to the time of the clans here in Scotland. You're American. You wouldn't understand legacy or any of that."

I didn't say that I certainly did understand legacy. I was living with it every day at Duncreigan.

"And that's what you wanted to tell him," I said.

"Yes, it was, but I never got to speak to him. I could never get close enough. He was either with his band or surrounded by those old-lady groupies all the time." He scowled at me. "I know you think I killed him, but as you can see, the police haven't arrest me. I bet you wonder why."

"Why?" I asked.

"Because I didn't do it, and I have witnesses to prove it. I was at the pub's booth grabbing a pint when he was being murdered. I needed a little alcohol to build up my strength to talk to him."

"Oh," I said, wishing he'd told me this sooner so I wouldn't have walked down to the creepy warehouse to find him.

"Both the Indian man who owns the pub and Seth MacGregor told the police they were helping me. I was memorable because I made quite a fuss over the ales they had. I didn't like the selection and didn't think I should have to walk all the way down to the Twisted Fox to get the drink I wanted. They were there selling beer and ale and should have had what I liked."

I nodded as if I was agreeing with him, which I wasn't. Mostly I was just making a mental note to ask Raj if what he told me was the truth.

"If that's all, I need to get back to work. I don't have Barley's money, and I still have to make a living." He stalked away in the direction of the warehouse.

His last comment sparked a new question in my mind. Who had gotten Barley's money?

Chapter
Thirty-Three

When I walked into the Climbing Rose a few minutes later, Isla was *fit to be tied*, as my maternal grand-mother used to say.

She paced back in forth in the middle of my shop. "When were you going to tell me we are only half sisters?"

Seth was also in the shop. I wondered if Ferris Brown knew how long Seth's delivery to the village was taking. I had a feeling that his career in construction would be short-lived if he didn't focus a little less on my sister and a little more on work.

I winced. If she was this angry at me over the great family secret, I could only guess how well she'd taken it when our father told her.

I removed my coat and hung it on the coat-tree by the door. "I haven't known that long, and I only got the full story today right before Dad came in here and told you."

"And that makes it okay?" she asked. "You should have told me the moment you thought something strange was going on with them."

"I knew you would get upset, like you are, and I wanted all the facts beforehand, so we could discuss it calmly."

"I can't believe our mother had a one-night stand with Uncle Ian. It's so disgusting."

I frowned at her. "Let's not go over the particulars, okay? What's done is done. I'm your sister, your only sister. That's all that matters."

"It was a pretty crazy story," Seth said.

I shot him a look. He really shouldn't get in the middle of this conversation. "Don't you have somewhere you are supposed to be?" I asked.

"Not really. Winthrope Manor is waiting for permits, so there's not much I can do. Ferris told me to take my time. He's a great boss."

I frowned at him. "Isla, I'm sorry if you're hurt. Honestly, I was hurt too."

"You should be hurt." She crossed her arm. "You're not who you always thought you were. I would be in the middle of a full-blown identity crisis."

Her assessment didn't make me feel any better.

I couldn't think of anything to say in reply to that, so I turned to Seth. "Since you're here, Seth, I have a question for you."

His eyes went wide. Seth knew I was watching him and constantly assessing if he was the right guy for my little sister, so I supposed there were a whole host of questions he didn't want to answer about himself.

"I was just talking to Mick McFee. He said you and Raj supplied him an alibi for the time of the murder because he was complaining about the ale choices you had at the booth. Is that true?" I asked.

"Oh yeah," Seth said, relieved. "He was a real pain in the—"

I held up my hand. "We get the idea."

There went another suspect off my list. Kenda was still at the top, but Dad had seen Barley alive after she spoke with him. Could she have circled back after Dad made amends with Barley? I supposed it was possible. She would have been hanging with the backstage crew and musicians waiting to go back on. The MacNish brothers would be the ones who could vouch for her. I added them to my list of people to talk to again.

"Can I leave now?" Isla asked. "My shift here technically ended an hour ago, and I'm working at the pub tonight. I could use a break." She looked up at Seth. "And we need some time together. Now that Seth is working so many hours, I hardly ever see him more than six hours a day."

I nodded absent-mindedly. My thoughts were all jumbled together—my parents, Barley's murder, the dead garden. I could use some time alone too. When Isla was in the shop, she talked nonstop. Sometimes I liked the company of her chatter, but there were other times, like this, when I needed quiet to think.

Isla grabbed her purse and coat from the workroom, and as she walked to the front door, she grabbed Seth's hand and dragged him along behind her. He willingly went. There might be quite a few things about Seth that I worried about in respect to my sister, but I never doubted for a moment his devotion to her.

"Bye Fi," she chirped as the front door closed.

I sighed and went into the workroom. I had only a couple of hours left until the store closed for the evening. This late in the year when the store closed at five, it would be almost dark outside.

I checked my online account and saw that a new flower order had come in while I was out. I smiled, happy for the distraction. I was so engrossed in this new arrangement, which was for a retirement party the next day, that I didn't hear the rose-shaped bell on the front door ring.

Someone cleared their throat.

I yelped and threw the bunch of eucalyptus leaves I had been holding into the air.

Craig held up his hands. "I didn't mean to scare you. You were just so focused on your task that I couldn't seem to get your attention."

With a pounding heart, I gathered up the leaves.

"Are you all right?" he asked.

I set the leaves on my worktable in a makeshift pile and removed my gardening gloves. "No, I'm fine. You just shortened my life-span by one year."

He came into the workroom. "What is this arrangement for? It's beautiful."

"Are you trying to flatter me, Chief Inspector, to make up for scaring me half to death?"

He smiled. "Is it working?"

I rolled my eyes. "The arrangement is for a retirement party."

"I would think flowers that beautiful would be better suited for a wedding," he said.

I stepped away from him and tried not to read too much into that comment. I didn't know if I liked or disliked the fact that Craig was thinking about wedding flowers. After my disastrous engagement, weddings were still a sore spot for me.

"I was just having a chat with Mick McFee, and he told me that you were down at the harbor warehouse." Craig raised his brow.

"I wasn't just there. It's been a few hours."

He rolled his eyes. "You shouldn't be wandering around alone at the shipping docks. A lot of the men down there aren't the good kind. What if something happened and no one knew where you were?"

"Ewan and his pals knew I was there."

He frowned. "And how is that makeshift group of old gents supposed to save you if someone is about to knock you over the head?"

"No one threatened to knock me over the head," I said.

"Yet," he muttered. He rubbed his eyes, and I realized for the first time how tired he must be. This murder investigation wasn't like the others. He was dealing with the press too, which reminded me of Trina.

"Ewan said Trina Graham had been down to the warehouse as well," I said.

He rubbed the back of his neck. "I am aware how Trina is thoroughly investigating the case. I have five voice mails from her on my phone right now."

"Oh! Did she learn anything new?" I asked.

He shook his head. "She just wants an update on the investigation, which I plan to avoid giving her for as long as possible."

I nodded and changed the subject. "I had a conversation with my parents about Uncle Ian." I began to finish the arrangement as we talked.

His brow drooped in concern. "How did that go?"

"It went well." I gave him the short version, including the part about how my father knew Barley.

Craig nodded. "When I interviewed him, he told me he was in a band with Barley when they were at university. It surprised me that you never mentioned it."

"I didn't know."

"Clearly." He nodded and sat on a stool. "If you don't mind, I'm just going to sit here for a moment and watch you work. I need to head back to the station in Aberdeen, but I think a little rest is in order. I like watching you in your element."

It was my turn to raise an eyebrow at him. "Why?"

"Because I'm tired, and because you look so happy anytime you are working with plants. You get this little serene smile on your face. I love to see it."

I blushed and focused on the flowers in front of me. I worked quietly for a few minutes. There were so many questions I wanted to ask him, but he looked so exhausted that

I held my tongue. When I looked up from my arrangement again, I saw that his right cheek rested on his arms on the table and he was fast asleep.

I put the finishing bow on the arrangement and tucked it into the refrigerated case in the back room. After I cleaned up the worktable, I knew it was time to close up the store, but Craig looked so peaceful sleeping there that I didn't have the heart to wake him.

I tucked a stray hair behind his ear, just as my mother had done to me earlier in the day. He sighed in his sleep.

His cell phone, which was sitting by his hand on the worktable, rang. Craig jumped up on his stool, wide awake. "Chief Inspector Craig," he barked into the phone. "What? All right . . . all right . . . I'm still in the village . . . I'll be right there." He ended the call and hopped off the stool.

"What is it?" I asked.

"That was Kipling. I have to go to the harbor." His voice was tense.

"Why? What happened?" I felt panic grip my chest. I knew whatever he was about to tell me was bad.

"A shipping boat is on fire." He ran out of the flower shop.

Chapter Thirty-Four

As soon as I reached the harbor, I could smell the smoke. It mingled with the scent of the sea.

"You must be looking for the chief inspector, lass," Old Milton said. "He just ran by here toward the fire."

His two companions agreed. All three men's faces were tense with strain.

"Where's the . . ." I trailed off then, because there was no need for me to ask. There was a fishing boat anchored a hundred yards from the dock's end just on this side of the breakwater. In the fading light of day, orange flames ran up the boat's mast and ate away its ropes.

"Aye, lass, you see it, don't you. That's the *Mourning Star*, a boat in Ferris Brown's mighty fleet. In all my days working the seas, I have never once seen a boat ablaze like that," Ewan said.

"Aye, the same for me," the one-eyed man agreed. "I never saw such a sight even when I had two good eyes to see with."

As I watched the flames engulf the deck of the boat, fear gripped me. Where was Craig? He couldn't have possibly climbed onto that boat. It would be madness.

"Where's the chief inspector? You said he went to the fire," I said, not even attempting to cover the fear that laced my voice.

"Aye, lass, that's right. He jumped on a dinghy with Kipling," Old Milton said, as if he was sorry to tell me this.

"With Kipling?" It was worse than I thought. I would have felt better if I'd known Craig was tackling the fire alone. Kipling was clumsy at best and quite forgetful. Craig would have to worry about the volunteer police chief and himself in the middle of that blaze. "What was Craig thinking when he went to the fire before the fire department arrived? He doesn't have a water hose. What kind of backup is Kipling?"

"We saw someone on the deck," Ewan said. "The chief inspector could not wait. It is his duty to save another person whenever possible."

I knew what he said was true, but it didn't make me worry any less.

"Someone on the deck?" I gasped. At the moment, the deck appeared to be completely engulfed in flames. Would Craig climb onto that boat to see if a person was trapped there? I knew he would. He would make any attempt to save another person's life, even if it cost him his own. My hands began to shake. I couldn't lose him.

"The volunteer fire department will be here soon," Old Milton said. "They just have to get to the water boats. The boats are always filled and ready for such a crisis."

As if he'd beckoned them, two fireboats with lights flashing and sirens wailing flew around the end of the harbor. They approached the fire at top speed. The two boats stopped on either side of the burning ship and trained their firehoses on the blaze.

I wrapped my arms around myself. I was at a loss. There was nothing I could do to help Craig. The fire crew was already there, and they sprayed the ship with gallons of water. I turned back and faced the village. Maybe I would be more help if I called Aberdeen's fire department. I was sure they must have been alerted, but it could not hurt to call again.

I started to walk away, back in the direction of the village, when there was a loud bang, so loud that it made my ears ring, and a flash of heat on my back. I fell forward onto my hands and knees. A piece of charred wood landed just inches from my right hand. There was still a small flame on it.

I struggled to my feet and stamped the small flame with my boot.

Only an explosion could have knocked me to the ground like that and thrown the piece of smoldering wood so far. I spun around. The mast of the fishing boat had fallen into the sea, and there was a black hole in the side of the boat. The fireboats backed off from the scene, as if to stay clear of any flying debris. The fire workers moved around the decks of their boats and retrained their hoses onto the flames from a safer distance away. There still was no sign of Craig or Kipling.

The three old sailors were frozen in shock. All three lay on the dock. In a moment of horror, I thought they were dead, but then Ewan groaned and sat up. The one-eyed sailor did the same. I let out a sigh of relief. Old Milton was thrown from his wheelchair and lay facedown on the dock. I ran to him. "Are you all right?"

"Aye, help me up, will you," he grunted. He wasn't even able to lift himself up on his elbows, he was so weak.

Ewan was at my side, and the two of us lifted Old Milton into his chair. All the time, all I could think about was Craig. Had he been on the boat during the explosion? Was he alive?

Behind us the boat continued to blaze, and there were more pops and snaps as windows broke and doors to the lower decks cracked from the heat of the flames.

I removed my phone from my pocket and called emergency services. I didn't know if any more help could be there in time to save what was left of the vessel or if it was a lost cause. As I did that, my dream or vision from the night before came back to me like a wave crashing against the break wall. This was what the vision had been trying to show. This was the piece of the future it had revealed. Despite everything, relief flooded through me. If that was true, if I was right, that meant the garden wasn't really dead. It was dormant but not lost. I could and I would bring it back from the brink.

The relief was short-lived, because I still didn't know where the chief inspector was.

I stared at the fire. "Maybe we should step back from the dock in case there is another explosion."

"There is no fear of that," Old Milton said. "The fire is too far away from us to hurt us."

I noted that this was said by the man who'd been knocked out of his wheelchair by the initial blast.

The smell of burning wood and gasoline permeated the air. It was now much stronger than the sea. It took everything in me not to steal a boat and go look for Craig in the sea and fire myself, but I knew that was the last thing he would have wanted me to do. I shook my head. I needed to concentrate on keeping the three old sailors safe.

"I really think we should step back," I said "A lot of these boats, if not all of them, are filled with gasoline. We don't want to be anywhere close if a flame catches a gas tank."

"That's a good point," the one-eyed sailor said. "I've already lost one eye in my time; I don't want to lose another."

Ewan was at the end of the dock, squinting at the boat ablaze. "Ferris Brown will lament the loss of the *Mourning Star*."

Old Milton nodded his head. "Aye, won't he be hot under the collar when he sees that. You know he hates to lose money, and now he must save every penny he has to bring the crumbling old manor back to life."

"I don't much care for him or any man with so much wealth," Ewan said. "But the men working on that boat will be out of work."

"Won't the crew be able to save the boat?" I asked.

Old Milton shook his head. "Nay, there is no way to do it. The *Mourning Star* has met her sad end."

What did that mean for Craig and Kipling, who were on a small dinghy looking for someone on that ship? I felt ill.

The flames tickled the gray sky and rushed up the smaller mast of the boat, since the first and larger one had fallen.

A bell somewhere in the village tolled. It sounded like the bell of St. Thomas Church on Sunday morning, but the ring was much more frantic.

"Aye, the sexton at the church has sounded the alarm," Old Milton said. "It's a little too late for that now. The fire is already dying back."

I looked closer and saw that he was right. The firemen on the two boats, both of which were a third of the size of the massive fishing boat, were finally making some headway with the flames.

I stared hard at the boat and was shocked when I saw something fly from the bow. No, it didn't fly off, it jumped. It was a person.

"Craig!" I cried, but my voice was eaten up by the sound of the fire before it could ever reach the burning ship.

A police officer from Craig's department ran into the harbor. I grabbed him by one arm.

"Get back!" he cried.

I didn't let go of him. "Someone jumped off the ship, and Kipling and Chief Inspector Craig are somewhere on a tiny boat in the water."

"I said get back," he cried.

I let go of his shirt sleeve. That's when I realized it wasn't just the three old fishermen and me on the docks any longer.

Half the village was there, watching the proceedings with their mouths hanging open. Kenda Bay was among them. Her orange- and red-tipped braids glowed in the firelight and looked like flames of their own.

One of the fireboats came into the dock. "Medic! We need a medic!"

I spun around. On the deck of the fireboat, one of the crew leaned over a prostrate man. I gasped. It was Craig.

I ignored the shouts and warnings from the police officers and ran to the end of the dock. An EMT walked passed me and climbed onto the fireboat. She knelt next to Craig, checking his vitals, while another EMT placed an oxygen mask over his face.

Craig grabbed the mask and removed it. "Where's Kipling?"

"Here, sir." Kipling stood in the shadow of one of the massive water guns that had attempted to put the fire out on the *Mourning Star*. It had failed. While the other fireboat gallantly tried to put out the blaze, piece by piece, the fishing boat sunk to the bottom of the harbor.

"Are you all right?" Craig rasped.

"Fine, sir," Kipling answered, and he did look fine. He looked a whole lot better than Craig did.

The female EMT forced the oxygen mask back onto Craig's face. "Keep this on. Stop trying to be a hero."

"Tell me, what is it like seeing your boyfriend in so much peril?" Someone shoved a microphone into my face.

I jerked back and found Trina and her cameraman eagerly awaiting my comment. "Leave me alone."

"Miss Knox seems too distraught to give us a message," Trina said into the camera.

I had a message for her, but it wasn't suitable for repeating. I hurried to the fireboat. "Let me on."

A fireman pushed me back. "No civilians."

Craig removed the mask again and coughed. "Let her on the boat."

The fireman frowned but stepped back, allowing me onto the boat deck. I knelt next to Craig. His face and clothes were covered in soot.

"We are going to transfer you to Aberdeen to the hospital, Chief Inspector."

"No," he said. "I'm fine."

"Sir," she said. "I strongly suggest that you agree to be transferred to the hospital. It is for the best."

"I'm fine. It's just a little smoke inhalation," Craig said with a cough. "All I need is a ride home and rest."

I grabbed his hand and squeezed it in both of mine. "No," I said with force.

Craig tried to prop himself up on his elbow.

I pushed him back down. "No. If you're not going to the hospital, you're coming to Duncreigan with me."

"All right," he agreed, and there was a faint smile on his face as he replaced the oxygen mask and laid the side of his face on my knee.

Chapter
Thirty-Five

I sat up in bed and was drenched in sweat. Ivanhoe wasn't at the foot of my bed where he usually slept. I fell back onto my pillow. "It was just a dream," I whispered to myself. A dream of what, I didn't know. The moment I sat up, the scenes my imagination conjured in my sleep had vanished, but the feeling of fear remained.

Rain pattered on the windows and the old roof of the cottage. It was one of the few times I still wished Isla lived in the cottage with me. I hated tripping over her shoes and clothes or having the bathroom counter buried under her makeup, but to know she was there and safe made me feel so much more at ease. I supposed knowing that all those I loved were safe was what I wanted most in this world. It was also completely out of my control.

There was a *tap, tap, tap* on my window. It was a tap from a hand. It was not the sound of rain. I knew the difference.

"Someone is out there," I whispered, and wriggled further down under the covers.

Tap, tap, tap came again.

Guilt started to eat at me. What if a hiker was lost in the rain and looking for a place to dry off for the night?

Tap, tap, tap. Whoever it was couldn't get inside. I had to see who or what was there. The cottage bedroom was small, and I could reach the tiny window in the corner of the room without setting a foot on the floor.

I pulled the curtain back and saw the fox. There was just enough break in the clouds amid the rain to see him clearly in the moonlight. He stared at me and slapped his brown paw on the glass. Startled, I fell off the bed. When I got up, I found the fox had jumped back twenty feet from the window. He hadn't expected my reaction. Neither had I, to be honest.

The fox turned and dashed away.

I rubbed my forehead. There was no hope now of me falling back to sleep. In my bare feet, I crept into the main room of the cottage. Craig lay on his side on the couch. His arms were wrapped around Ivanhoe like he was squeezing a teddy bear in his sleep. Ivanhoe stared at me with his round amber-colored eyes as if to say *help me.*

I tried to insist that Craig sleep in my bed and I take the couch, but he wouldn't hear of it. Even after battling a fire and suffering smoke inhalation, he was a gentleman to the end.

I tiptoed to the kitchenette, hoping to get a glass of water without waking Craig. I thought I was moving silently.

Craig shot upright on the couch, and Ivanhoe hissed as he went flying through the air. Craig grabbed his gun from under the couch. It was still in its holster.

I held up my hands. "It's Fiona. Don't shoot."

Craig dropped the gun into his lap. "Fiona, what the . . ."

I could see his face in the moonlight streaming into the cottage through a crack in the curtains. The rain had stopped. Craig was confused, but then his face cleared, as if he remembered where he was and why he was there.

His shoulders relaxed. "Fiona."

"That's my name," I said. "I was going to get a drink of water. You should have one too. I imagine your throat is sore after the fire."

He rubbed his neck. "Aye, it is. Thank you."

I filled two glasses of water at the faucet and handed one to the chief inspector. His feet were on the floor. It was the first time I had seen his bare feet. I didn't know why that struck me as odd. Northern Scotland wasn't really a place where someone owned multiple pairs of sandals. I perched next to him. "How did you sleep?"

"All right. This couch is not exactly built for a man my size, but not many are."

"I told you that you could sleep on my bed."

He touched my cheek and smiled. "Your little double bed isn't big enough for me either, so I saw no reason to make us both uncomfortable by having you sleep on the couch."

I frowned but then smiled. "You and Ivanhoe looked pretty cozy."

"Was he sleeping next to me?"

"You were holding him like a teddy bear." I chuckled.

Craig laughed. Ivanhoe, who was curled up in his cat bed on the hearth, hissed softly.

"Why are you awake?" Craig asked.

I told him about the fox. I shook my head. "It's like the fox wanted to wake me, but I don't know why. Maybe it was to check on you. You really should have gone to the hospital last night."

He coughed and sipped his water.

I gave him a look, as if to put emphasis on my point.

"I know," he said. "I will go this morning when I go back to Aberdeen. I'll get checked out. Maybe it was stupid of me not to go last night, but I just—" He paused. "I just wanted to be with you."

"I would have gone to the hospital with you."

He touched my cheek. "I know. And I promise to go see a doctor."

"Thank you," I said, looking down at my glass of water.

He grabbed my hand and held it on his thigh. "Thank you for worrying about me. I haven't had someone worry about me in a very long time."

I swallowed. "There was someone on the *Mourning Star*," I said abruptly. "I saw whoever it was jump off the boat and into the water."

He smiled as if he understood my need to change the subject, but he didn't release my hand. I was happy for that.

"I did too," Craig said. "That's why I was on the boat. I thought, stupidly, that I could save the person. Little did I know when I climbed aboard that he didn't need to be saved. He was the one setting the fire."

"What?" I almost dropped my glass and set it on the floor.

Craig nodded. "Kipling and I saw a man running around the deck, so I climbed on. Kipling wanted to go, but I wouldn't let him." He set his glass on the floor next to mine. "What a disaster that would have been. When I was on the boat, I saw the man, and he was splashing gasoline on the deck."

I covered my mouth. "Arson?"

"Clearly."

"Who was it?"

He shook his head. "I couldn't see in the smoke, but it was a man. I'm almost certain."

I shivered and squeezed his hand hard. "You're lucky to be alive."

"You have Kipling to thank for that. I jumped off the back of the boat just before the explosion, and he came and yanked me out of the water."

"Now Kipling has saved both of us once," I said. "Maybe he is a better police officer than anyone thinks."

"I wouldn't say that," Craig said. "But he means well and has a good heart. That holds a lot of value in my book."

"Mine too," I said.

Tap, tap, tap sounded on the window. Craig dropped my hand and grabbed his gun.

I placed a hand over the gun. "That must be the fox again, like I told you." I stood up and went to the window. When I pulled back the curtain, I didn't see the fox. Instead, a dark figure moved across the moor down the hill toward the garden. I knew it wasn't the fox because he was carrying a flashlight.

I told Craig what I saw.

"You're not going with me," Craig said as he quickly pulled on his boots.

"Yes, I am." I stood at the door. I already had my wellies on and my coat over my pajamas.

He walked to the door, and I didn't move.

"Fine," he said. "But I go first."

I stepped away from the door. "Deal. Besides, you're the one with the gun, so you should go first."

We went out the front door and walked toward the garden. I had a small flashlight in my hand, but the moonlight was bright, and I knew my way to the garden well enough that I didn't need it.

The grass was slippery from the overnight rains, and Craig and I took care to avoid the many smooth boulders poking up out of the earth.

Just when the top of the garden wall came into view, a man screamed. Craig broke into a run, and I followed suit. I began to slip on the rocks, so I had to slow my pace out of fear of turning my ankle. Craig was far ahead of me now. When I came up to him, he stood over a man writhing in the grass and swearing so colorfully that he could have worked at the shipyard.

I clicked on my flash and shone the light in his face. Carver Finley.

He held up his hand to block the light. "Turn that off! Are you trying to blind me?" Beads of sweat gathered on his forehead.

I lowered the light to his left leg, which was bent at an odd angle. "It looks like his leg is broken."

Carver swore again. "Yes, it's broken." He winced. "I will have to have it grafted together at this point."

"You don't know it's that bad," Craig said. "In any case, we need to get him to the hospital. It would take too long for an ambulance to come all the way out here." He frowned. "Do you think you could make the ride to Aberdeen?" he asked Carver.

"I don't think I have much choice, do I?" Carver snapped.

"I'll carry him back to the cottage," Craig said to me.

"You can't carry me," Carver said through teeth clenched in pain.

"Of course I can," the large chief inspector replied. "Now grit your teeth. It's going to hurt like hell when I pick you up."

Carver nodded, and Craig picked him up like he was a baby. Carver screamed. The sound was made that much more horrible by the fog rolling in on the moor. The cry carried for miles, and I wondered if it might have scared Hamish and Duncan awake in Hamish's bothy.

I walked behind Craig as he carried Carver like he was a swooning maiden. Craig glanced over his shoulder. "Fiona, run ahead of me, grab my car keys from the cottage, start the SUV, and open the doors to the back seat so I can set him inside."

I took off without a word. When I reached the cottage, I flew through the door and found Craig's key on the small dining table by the window. I did everything as he asked and waited while I saw him struggle up the slippery hillside with Carver in his arms.

I glanced behind me toward the three pine trees that stood beside the cottage to break the wind that came off the sea half a mile away. The fox sat under the trees, watching me. "Thank you," I whispered. I knew he had woken me because Carver was sneaking around Duncreigan. I also knew Carver was there because of my garden.

Craig crested the hill and walked with Carver to the SUV. As carefully as he could, he put the man in the back seat.

Some of the swear words Carver was saying I had never heard before.

When Carver was in as best as could be hoped, Craig stepped back. He was covered in sweat from the exertion. "You did well, Fiona."

"All I did was get the car ready. You carried Carver over the moor like Superman."

He shrugged. "It would have been a lot more difficult if you weren't here. You make my life easier every day."

From the car, Carver yelled, "This would never have happened if you'd just let me study your menhir, but no. It's your fault that the garden is dead."

I gasped. "You cut the rose."

"Of course I did," he snapped. "I needed a closer look at the stone and triskeles carved into its sides. I couldn't see them with that plant covering them up. I just needed to move that flower. I didn't know it would shrivel up and die. Maybe if you would have been a little more generous with your garden, you wouldn't be in this place."

"You have no idea what havoc you've caused," I said. "The garden may never come back."

"Then I could have plenty of access to the stone, which is all I want. I don't care a bit about your flowers. Plants die. Stone and history live forever."

I glared at him. "I can't believe you did this."

He shrugged. "I had to cut the rose away so I could make a rubbing of the etching in the stone. Perhaps I would have behaved differently if you had given me access to the garden."

"You can't do that without my permission." I held out my hand. "Where are the rubbings of the stone?"

He laughed and then winced in pain. "I don't have them on me, and even if I did, I wouldn't give them to you. The etchings on that stone in your garden are much more interesting than I first believed. There are triskeles there, which are unusual for this part of Scotland. What I need to know is how they got here and how your stone does what it does."

And just what exactly does he think the stone can do?

I didn't bother to tell him that the MacCallister family hadn't been able to answer those questions in the last three hundred years, so I didn't see much hope that he would find the answer either.

"You have to ask yourself, Fiona Knox," Carver said through teeth gritted in pain. "Do you want to know the truth about the garden, or do you just want to spend your time in the garden puttering away? Do you want to understand your legacy, or do you want to be controlled by it?"

I didn't think I puttered away my time. The garden didn't control me, did it? The work I did in the garden was important. Uncle Ian had told me that above all else, the garden at Duncreigan was a real garden and had to be treated as such. All the planting, pruning, trimming, and raking I would have done in a nonmagical garden needed to be done at Duncreigan as well. It was not the burden Carver made it out to be.

"You'll be sorry you did this," I said, but how he would be sorry, I had no idea.

"What are you going to do?" Carver challenged. "Trespassing? Bah, that's a misdemeanor. I have no fear of that."

"Vandalism," I snapped.

He shook his head. "Have me arrested for damaging your garden? The courts would laugh at you." He narrowed his eyes. "You thought you could keep me away from the garden by telling those MacNish brothers about me."

I frowned. "What do you mean?"

"You told them I was the local historian and could help them learn their family history."

"An old man in the pub was the first person who brought you up to them," I corrected. "And I would have thought you'd like someone showing interest in Aberdeenshire history."

"Oh, I am, but they were a little too thirsty for my taste. They would gladly take up all my time. I cannot be distracted from what I really want to know, and that's about the menhir. I told them what I knew and sent them on their way."

I had opened my mouth to ask him another question when Craig put a hand on my shoulder. "Fiona, I have to take him to the hospital. If you want to press charges over the garden, we can discuss that later."

I nodded and stepped back.

Craig closed the back door of the SUV on Carver's complaints.

He turned to me and kissed me in the middle of my forehead. "You will bring the garden back. I believe in you."

Something caught in my throat, and I couldn't speak.

He drove away.

Chapter Thirty-Six

I went back inside the cottage, and Ivanhoe sat by his food bowl looking more than a little put upon.

I looked down at him. "All right, you withstood the chief inspector's bear hug. The least I can do is feed you." I filled his bowl with his favorite tuna-flavored pâté.

He purred, and all was forgiven. I wished it were as easy to appease people as it was my cat.

It was four in the morning, and my eyes were heavy. After feeding Ivanhoe, I stumbled back into the bedroom and lay down.

I must have fallen asleep, because early-morning sunlight was coming through the window when I next opened my eyes. I had pushed the curtains away to see the fox and never set them back. I sat up and grabbed my phone. I needed to check on Craig. Had he made it to Aberdeen okay?

There was a text message from the chief inspector in my inbox. *Carver's leg is broken. Not a bad break. He will be fine. I got checked out too. I'm fine.*

I let out a sigh of relief. I didn't know what to text back, so I simply liked the text on my phone. He would see that I had read it then.

I lay back down. It was still early, and I thought about everything that had happened the day before—my conversation with my parents, the fire, and Carver saying that his leg was so terribly broken that he'd have to graft it back into place.

I shot upright. Ivanhoe, who was on the floor, hissed. The cat really didn't care for sudden movements of any kind.

"Ivanhoe, that's it. Grafting. I can try grafting to save the garden!"

He stared at me, with his flat ears and round eyes, like I had lost my mind. Maybe I had, but I had to try.

I threw on some clothes, my winter coat, and wellies before rushing out the cottage door.

Down the hill, the rocks and grass were still slick with rain and early-morning dew. I took care as I ran toward the garden. I didn't want to end up like Carver Finley.

Inside the garden, there was a small garden shed just to the right of the garden door. It was where Hamish kept all of his tools. I knew he would have grafting tape there. I grabbed the tape from the shelf and a small gardening knife.

All around me the garden was still dead, but I couldn't contain the excitement building inside me. This would work. This had to work. If it didn't, I had no idea what option I had left to bring the garden back.

I hurried around the dead hedgerow to the menhir.

It wasn't very big, as standing stones went. When one thought of a monolith, visions of Stonehenge came to mind, but there were hundreds of standing stones or menhirs across the United Kingdom and Ireland. They had been placed there by long-dead and unknown cultures to honor the dead or track the sun. At least, that was the belief. Their study was ruled by theories, not facts, and some men, like Carver Finley, spent their entire lives studying them, hoping to unlock their secrets.

Thankfully, the yellow rose blossom was still there in its bowl of water. It was as yellow and vibrant as it had been when it grew on the vine.

There were boot prints around the stone. I removed my phone from my pocket and held the photo I had taken of the first boot print next to these. They were a match. Carver had been there. More than once, I realized as I knelt beside the menhir. More proof of that were the black marks on the stone itself and a piece of black graphite I found at the base of the stone. I picked it up. This was what Carver must have used to make his rubbings of the carvings in the stone.

The black graphite stained my hand, and it seemed to disintegrate in my wet palm. I was careful not to move my palm and destroy the piece. I knew it was important, proof I could use against Carver if I decided to press charges. I didn't know if I would. Maybe the broken leg was enough punishment.

Black graphite dripped from some of the engravings on the stone. I looked closer. Someone, Carver I assumed, had written on the stone. I looked at the piece of graphite again in my open palm. My palm was quickly turning black. I tucked the flashlight under my arm and held my hand over the graphite to protect it from the falling rain, not that I thought it would make much of a difference at this point, so much of it had melted away.

Using my phone again, I took a photo of the piece in my hand before it was gone.

I swallowed hard, and when I looked up again, the fox was there. He stood at the end of the hedgerow with his head cocked. Water dripped from his fur and from his pointy ears. He looked cold, wet, and miserable. I wanted to comfort him, but I stopped myself. I knew he was still very much a fox and might bite me, even if he was a form or part of my godfather too.

"I don't know if this will work," I said to the fox. "Will it work?"

As always, he said nothing.

I placed the water bowl with the blossom next to me and picked up the delicate vine that had fallen from the stone. I cut a slice of the stem away. It was only a quarter of the stem. Inside, I was happy to see the stem was green and damp. There was still life there. I did the same with the tiny piece of stem attached to the rose blossom. I pressed the two pieces together with the cut portions touching and wrapped them with the green grafting tape. When I was done, I wound what I could of the withered vine around the stone. I took another tiny piece of grafting tape and taped it into place.

It was only then that I noticed that the rose's tiny thorns were digging themselves into the stone like tiny anchors. As they did, the vine began to slowly turn green. The magic was from the stone, of course; the way the rose seemed to drink the magic in through its thorns had taught me that. Through the rose, the magic could spread to the rest of the garden and the line of owners of the garden, the Keeper, me.

As I touched the stone, I was pulled into a vision.

I was inside the tour bus. Everything was in its place. I felt irritable. When I turned around, I saw my father standing there. "You've done well for yourself, Barley. I didn't expect you to be here in the village when I came to visit my daughters. I wanted to apologize for what happened all those year ago. I know things did not end the way we all had hoped they would."

Was I Barley? I shook the thought away as I realized I was standing right next to Barley, but it seemed my father and Barley couldn't see me. Suddenly, I felt angry. I glanced at Barley, and his face was red with anger. I wasn't Barley, but somehow in this vision, I felt everything he was feeling.

"We both know one of your daughters is not yours." Barley's voice was sharp.

Dad took a step back. "That was a long time ago."

"Does Fiona know? Because I'm thinking she doesn't." Barley crossed his arms. "I was quite surprised when I met her and she said she was your daughter and called Ian her godfather. It was clear to me that you have been keeping the truth from the girl all these years."

I gasped, but neither man heard me. When I'd met Barley, he'd known exactly who I was and who my father was too.

My father frowned. "Don't worry about my Fiona."

"Oh, she's your Fiona, is she? Not Ian's? You and Ian made a pact on that, as I recall."

Dad shook his head. "I didn't come here to argue with you. I just wanted to apologize for what happened. I know there were a lot of hurt feelings, and I'm sorry for that. But time has passed; let's move on. We both ended up in the places we wanted to be in the end. I'm with my wife and family, and you have your music."

Barley sighed. I felt the anger flow out of me like hot air from a balloon.

"Yes," Barley said. "We have both ended up with the life we wanted. I accept your apology, and I should have handled everything differently. I know you all were in a difficult spot. I was only thinking for myself." He paused. "I still think our band could have done great things."

"Maybe," Dad agreed. "But things happened as they were intended to."

The two men shook hands. Relief washed through me, and a sense of peace. It was as if I had been holding on to something for a very long time and had just let it go.

Dad left, and the door opened again. I turned around, but I couldn't see a face.

"If this is about the manor again, I don't want to hear it."

"You're going to have to," a voice said back.

There was a sharp pain around my throat, and everything went black.

I fell back from the stone and had both hands at my throat. I panted, and the fox watched me. A bead of sweat ran down my cheek. I had just seen Barley's murder in a vision, but the most important part had been missing: the killer's face.

I took another big breath and stared at the stone. I blinked and crawled over to it for a better look. There was one tiny green leaf on the vine. It was no bigger than my pinkie nail. It was green, vibrant, and alive. It was the little bit of hope I needed.

Chapter
Thirty-Seven

The vision told me that the manor house was part of the mystery of Barley McFee's death. How that was true, I didn't know. As far as I knew, Barley had known nothing about the manor, but maybe I was wrong. I hadn't known about the manor, but I hadn't grown up in Bellewick like Barley had. Maybe he did know something about it and had a connection to it that I had yet to discover.

The only person I thought might know was Kenda Bay, but would she tell me anything? She still wasn't all that thrilled with me after she thought I lied to her about who my father was. I had a feeling she wouldn't be too excited to see me this morning, but it couldn't be helped. I needed answers. She was my last hope in reaching a conclusion when it came to Barley McFee's death.

After leaving Duncreigan, I went straight to Thistle House. After parking my car in the village lot, I walked over the troll bridge. I smelled cigarette smoke wafting from the back of the guesthouse, so instead of knocking on the front door, I walked around the side of Thistle House to the back garden. Kenda was outside, smoking on the stone garden wall. "You again? Don't you have anything better to do than stalk me?"

"I just have a few questions more about Barley." I stepped through the garden gate.

She blew smoke out the side of her mouth and flipped a braid over her shoulder. "I doubt that's true. One question will lead to two and two to three, and so on. I know what people like you are like."

She was probably right about that, but I forged ahead anyway. "Kenda, did Barley ever talk about a manor near Bellewick?"

She studied me over the butt of her cigarette. "Barley? No. The manor doesn't have much to do with Barley. That's all about the MacNish boys. They are the ones who talk constantly about the manor."

"What do you mean?" I asked.

Kenda rolled her eyes. "I don't even know why they are in the band. They see themselves more as lords of the manor. By the way they talk, you would have thought they were descended from Macbeth himself." She snorted.

"Macbeth was a fictional character." I paused. "At least what everyone knows about him was created by Shakespeare. There was a Scottish king by that name, I think. I'm really not very up on my Scottish history."

She made a face. "You know what I mean," she said. "The MacNish brothers think they have some kind of lineage that makes them better than the rest of us. I know they take one look at me and knew my family doesn't go back in the country for generations. All they talk about is their ancestral home. If I hear one more time about their great legacy, I might throw up."

I knew that my own family went back generations in Scotland, so I didn't say anything. "Lester mentioned to me that he had a lot of interest in their family history. In fact, he's spoken to a few people in the village about it."

She snorted. "That sounds like Lester. I think both brothers are into it, but Lester is definitely one who can go on for hours about the subject, even when it's obvious no one in the room cares."

"Where's their ancestral home?" I asked.

"It's just down the coast. We stopped on the way up here. It was a bit out of the way, but the brothers convinced the driver that they had to stop and see it."

"What is their legacy?"

She shrugged. "I should know it all by heart, with the many times I heard it. Apparently, they are from a long line of wealthy Scots that lived in Aberdeenshire. They were about to lose all their wealth when the English came. They aligned with the English, and the family prospered even more. They built a manor and lived there for over a hundred years until it was lost with mismanagement in the twentieth century. Lester and Jamie grew up with these stories all their lives, and they had a dream of buying the manor again and restoring it to its original glory."

"And they haven't been able to do that?" I asked.

She shook her head. "Not as far as I know. They never had enough money to do it. The brothers have been whispering a lot lately. I've caught pieces of it. I guess they almost had enough money saved up to buy the manor, but then it was too late."

My fingertips started to tingle. I knew whatever Kenda said next was going to be very important.

"And why was it too late?" I asked.

"Someone bought it out from under them. Just when they were about to have all the money they had been saving forever—I knew, because I had heard about it for the last ten years—someone else with a bigger bank account swooped in and bought it out from under them." She dropped what was left of her cigarette on the lawn and stomped on it with the toe of her boot. She removed a pack from her coat pocket, found it was empty, and shoved it back inside her pocket in disgust.

"Do you know who that person was?" I bet I knew, but I wanted her to say the name to confirm it. His boat had been set on fire the night before, I was sure of it.

She shook her head.

"What about the name of the manor?"

"Winthrope Manor," she said. "It's not far from here."

I knew it was not.

"Do you know where the brothers are now?"

She shook her head. "I know they want to leave, but we are all trapped in the village by the police. They won't leave. They are rule followers to a fault. It's so annoying. I wanted them to join me in protesting Barley's treatment, but they would never do it." She shook her head as if this was another major failing on the brothers' part.

I needed to tell Craig what I had learned about the brothers. Was I taking too great a leap to think they might know something about the fire on Ferris Brown's fishing ship? Would they have been angry enough about losing Winthrope Manor to set the *Mourning Star* on fire? Ferris was the person who'd bought the manor out from under them. He was the one who'd stolen their lifelong dream.

I needed to find the brothers too, but I knew Craig wouldn't want me to do that alone. Someone who was crazy enough to set a boat on fire wasn't someone to be messed with. I thanked Kenda and left the garden.

When I was out of earshot of the garden, I called Craig, and he picked up on the first ring. Before he even said hello, I told him what Kenda had told me.

Craig groaned. "It would have been helpful if she'd told someone this a few days ago when Barley died."

"Would it have stopped the boat fire?" I asked.

"I don't know. The two events might not be related." He sighed.

"I think they are," I said.

"I do too."

"Stay in the village, and I will go with some of my officers to check the manor."

I said I would and ended the call. I hurried down the street to the Climbing Rose. I had just reached the door of the flower shop when my phone rang. My sister's lovely face filled my screen.

"Fiona! You have to come and pick me up!" Isla cried in my ear.

"What? What's wrong?" It was still an hour before the flower shop opened, and she had to be at the Climbing Rose.

"It's Seth. He's in trouble. He said his boss has been kidnapped. We need to help him!" She became more hysterical with each sentence.

"Wait! What?"

"You heard me. Two guys broke into the Winthrope Manor and are holding Ferris Brown at gunpoint. Seth barely got out with his life, and he needs a ride. We have to go get him. Now!" She started to cry. "I can't lose him, Fi. He's my life."

"Did Seth call the police?"

"He called me!" she shouted in my ear. I had to hold the phone away from me to avoid hearing loss.

I closed my eyes for a moment. I didn't know what Seth thought my sister could do to help him without a car, and besides, I didn't want my sister to be running into the manor to rescue her boyfriend when there were men there with guns. Was he insane?

"You stay put," I said. "I'll call Craig and the police."

"I have to go to him. He needs me." She was crying harder now.

"I will go and look for Seth. You stay in the village in case he calls," I said. There was no way I was taking my sister to a place where armed men were waiting.

"Fi!" she cried, but I hung up on her so I could call Craig back. He had to know what they were driving into.

Chapter Thirty-Eight

Craig didn't answer my call, so I texted him the message about Ferris and Seth. I ended it with *Please text back, so I know you read this.*

There was no response. I couldn't take it any longer. I knew my sister; if I didn't act, she would. That was something I couldn't allow to happen. I had to go to the manor myself. When I ran back to the community lot, I found Isla in my car.

"What are you doing?" I asked.

"You're going to Winthrope Manor, aren't you?" She folded her arms.

"Isla, get out of my car," I ordered. Not that ordering her to do something had ever worked for me before, but I thought it was worth a shot.

"No way," she said. "If you are going there, I'm going too. My love is in danger." Tears sprang to her eyes. "I love him, Fi. I can't sit back and wait."

It was something Isla and I had in common, the inability to sit back and wait, but I still had to try to leave her behind.

It was too dangerous. It was my duty as her big sister to keep her safe. It had always been my duty.

"You won't help him by putting yourself in danger too," I said.

"I won't put myself in danger. I just have to be there," she said. "I'll stay in the car when we get there, I promise. I just have to know that Seth is okay. I have to see that he's okay with my own eyes. Can't you understand that?"

I could.

"Isla . . ."

"If I don't go, you don't go, because you're not getting me out of this car. Remember that Seth taught me self-defense."

"You would use your self-defense classes on your own sister?"

She showed me her bicep. "If I have to."

I groaned. "Fine, but *do not* get out of the car when we get there, okay? Promise me."

She shrugged. "Sure."

Sure didn't sound like that strong of a promise. It was a very bad idea to take my sister with me. I checked my phone one more time to see if Craig had texted back and I could abandon this mission, but there was nothing. I couldn't wait any longer. He didn't know there were men with guns there.

As I pulled the Astra out of the parking place, I asked Isla, "How did you get in my car. It was locked. I never gave you the spare keys."

She leaned back in her seat. "Oh, I know that. You really should give me the keys in case of emergencies like this."

"So how did you get into the car?" I eyed her.

"Seth taught me how to pick a car lock. I can show you later if you like. There are so many wonderful things that I've learned from him. He's had such an interesting life."

I grimaced and wondered where Seth would have picked up a skill like that. I guessed it was from his former life as a gambler. "That's not something about Seth I would tell Mom and Dad, okay? They are just warming up to the idea of him in your life. I wouldn't want to give them any hint to a shady past, okay?"

She gave me a thumbs-up sign in return.

The drive to the manor was almost twenty minutes, but the village was much closer to it than the city of Aberdeen was. I wasn't surprised that Isla and I beat the police there. I was relieved to see it. That meant I would be able to warn Craig and his officers before they went inside.

I parked the car a little bit away behind a stand of trees at the end of what used to be the driveway. The once gravel drive had almost all been reclaimed by the weeds and thistles that grew alongside it.

"What do we do now?" Isla asked.

"Text Seth and tell him where we are. He should come to us," I said.

She did as I asked, and moments later her phone pinged, indicating a return text. Her mouth fell open as she read it.

"What does it say?" I asked.

She held the phone out to me. *Can't come now. They are going to kill Ferris. Help.*

"Ask him where he is in the house," I said.

Isla did.

Third floor. I went back in to help Ferris. Now I'm trapped too. They don't know I'm here. Can't leave without being seen. Help.

"What can we do?" Isla asked. "We have to go to him. He could be killed."

What we should do was wait there for the police. I was about to tell Isla that when she jumped out of the car. "I can't take it. Seth is in there. I'm going in."

I jumped out too. "Isla! Don't go into that house." I came around the side of the car with the intent to grab her arm. "We're just going to wait here, so we can tell Craig and the other police what's going on before they go inside the manor."

"I can't wait that long. What if something happens to Seth?"

"He's hiding," I said, trying to get close enough to her to grab her arm. I knew my sister, and no amount of rational talk was going to keep her out of the manor as long Seth was in danger. "Please," I went on. "They don't know he's there. Nothing will happen to him. He wouldn't want you to put yourself in danger on his account. Just text him to tell him to stay hidden and the police are on the way."

The crack of a gunshot came from the manor. It was faint, but I heard it. From the look on Isla's face, she'd heard it too. She took off down the driveway and was inside the manor before I even reached the front step.

Isla hated running, but apparently she could run fast with enough motivation.

I went into the house, paused under the great chandelier, and listened. I heard footsteps above me. I peered up the stairs and saw Isla disappear down a corridor. I swore. I knew the last thing Craig would want was for both Isla and me to put ourselves in danger, but I had no choice. I had to go after my sister. Just like she had to go into the house to save Seth, I had to go into the house to save her.

I texted Craig the latest development and received an immediate response. *Do not go into that house.*

"Too late. Isla is in here." I shoved the phone into my coat pocket and felt it vibrate repeatedly against my hip.

Craig was upset. Clearly.

Instead of storming up the stairs like Isla had, I crept up them, taking care not to make a sound. Even so, every other step creaked and whined under my weight. I wondered if I would have made less noise if I had taken the steps at a faster clip.

On the landing to the second floor, I waited and listened. There was the faint rumble of voices above me. That fit with what Seth had said about the men being on the third floor. My muscles tightened.

I should wait for Craig. I knew this.

I wanted to text Isla, but I didn't know where she was, and I didn't know if she would have thought to turn the sound off on her phone. It had been on when we were outside the manor. If she was close to the MacNish brothers, the sound would give her hiding spot away.

I started up to the third floor. On that landing, I saw the disrepair the manor was in. Sunshine poured in through holes in the roof big enough to drive my car through. The walls were crumbling and water-damaged from a decade of being exposed to the elements. The floor felt precarious, as if it could give out any moment and probably would.

"You can have the manor if you will just let me go!" a voice shouted a few rooms over.

I inched in that direction and peeked through the crack in the door.

Ferris Brown stood with his back to the open French doors of the widow's walk. Lester and Jamie stood with their backs to me. Lester held something out in front of him I couldn't see. I assumed it was a gun pointed at Ferris's chest.

The roof over their heads was completely gone. I scanned the area for Seth or my sister, but I didn't see them. I hoped they had found their way out.

"It's too late for that now," Lester said. "We know rich men like you. You say you will do one thing, but do another. Barley was like that. He made promises, but he never kept them."

I shivered. His tone was icy cold. The brothers had killed Barley. I was certain of it.

"If your beef is with Barley McFee, then it has nothing to do with me," Ferris said. "I didn't know the man. I only just met him the day before the concert."

"Our beef is with both of you. It's because of both of you that we lost this manor," Jamie said. "It is rightfully ours. It's been in our family for generations. Our mother told us the stories. She told us how she wanted us to get it back in the family someday, and we promised her we would while she was on her deathbed. We have spent the rest of our lives trying to keep that promise, and you and Barley stole that from us."

"What does Barley have to do with it?" Ferris asked. "I told you I don't know the man."

I noticed that the fishing boat tycoon was wisely making the two younger men talk to buy himself some time. I hoped that it would buy me some time too, so that I could figure out how to get us all out of the manor alive.

"If it hadn't been for him, we would have gotten that record deal and used the money to buy the house. We were offered a deal with Barley's label. It was just for the two of us. It would have been enough money to buy this place and restore it to our ancestral glory, just like we promised our mother we would, but Barley stopped it," Lester said.

"He postponed it," Jamie corrected. "He asked the record company to wait six months until his tour was over to make us an official offer. Barley has a lot of clout with the company. He brings in a lot of money. They did it to keep him happy. His contract with the label was nearing its end, and they didn't want him to go somewhere else. He makes too much money for them."

"Didn't you think about going to another label?" Ferris asked. "Barley's record company wasn't the only one in the world. If you are that good, someone else would pick you up."

"You can't possibly understand," Lester snapped. "You don't know what it's like to work in a creative field. Just to get a label to notice you for your own merit is close to impossible."

"It's the trash they put out there," Jamie agreed. "It's all glossy and prepackaged. Nothing is authentic any longer, but we could bring that to the music. We had authenticity." He frowned. "It was something we learned from Barley."

"But Barley was lazy," Lester said. "He could have let us have the deal and replaced us. Hundreds of bassists and guitarists would kill for our spots in his band, spots we would happily have given up. Barley didn't want to do that. He didn't want to bother to hold auditions for new band members before the tour began. He made us wait, and we lost the manor. No matter if he killed the deal or just postponed it, we had the chance of a lifetime and he stole that from us. He got what he deserved."

"I'm sure he did," Ferris said in a calm voice, as if he was trying to soothe a fussing toddler. "You're right to be upset, but I didn't know any of that when I bought the manor. The real estate agent only told me there was another interested party, and that if I wanted the place I should move fast. They never once told me who else wanted to buy the manor. They never told me you had a personal connection to the manor. Had they done that, I would have gladly stepped back and let you have it."

I wondered if that was true. It was what Ferris said to the MacNish brothers while he was being held at gunpoint, but he was a businessman first. I had a feeling he would have bought the manor out from under the brothers even if he'd known about their mother's dying wish.

"Boys." Ferris forced a laugh. "This is just business and nothing personal. I think we are all wise enough to see that.

310

You can have the manor. I would sign over the deed right now if I could. I can't help you, though, if you kill me. Don't you see that? If you kill me now, I can't give you the manor. It will go into my estate and be tied up for years in probate court. You really don't want to deal with that."

An old phrase came to mind. The hardest part of being at the top wasn't getting there; it was staying there. It had been so true in the case of Barley McFee. He'd been so worried about what would happen if he lost his stranglehold on his band, so he'd held on even more tightly, which had ultimately caused discord and his own death. Perhaps he'd made that choice because of losing his band with Uncle Ian and my father all those many years ago. Even so, Barley might be to blame for many things. Selfishness and ruining musical careers would be at the top of that list. But he hadn't been responsible for his death. That was the choice of the MacNish brothers, one they'd made and carried out.

I saw a small movement, like Lester was lowering his gun. I held my breath. Maybe Ferris's appeal to logic would work. I didn't believe for a second that he would turn the manor over to the brothers, but as long as they believed it, that's all that mattered.

The two brothers whispered to each other, and in the silence there was a sneeze.

"What was that?" Lester asked.

"My allergies," Ferris said. "There is a lot of dust in this house."

There was another sneeze, and it clearly didn't come from Ferris. He gave a half smile. "A ghost with allergies?"

Jamie walked over to a piece of furniture covered with a dirty sheet. He pulled the sheet off and revealed a grand piano in disrepair underneath it. Both Isla and Seth were under the piano, holding on to each other like their lives depended on it. Maybe they did.

"Who the hell are you?" Jamie wanted to know.

Seth and Isla scrambled out from under the piano, and Seth hit his head in the process.

He rubbed the top of his head. "I—I work construction for Mr. Brown and was just doing a walk around."

"Under a piano?" Jamie scoffed. He turned to my sister. "And who are you?"

"I'm Isla Knox, and Seth is my almost-fiancé. We will be leaving now." She grabbed Seth's hand and marched in my direction toward the cracked door. I stepped back.

Jamie grabbed Isla by the hand and pressed her against his body, causing her to drop Seth's hand in the process. "Did you plan this, Brown? Are they here to rescue you?"

"God, no! No one in his right mind would have Seth MacGregor as a rescuer," Ferris said.

Isla kicked at Jamie and glared at Ferris. "Take that back. Seth is very brave!"

"Let her go," Seth shouted.

"We aren't letting any of you go now," Lester said.

"Les," Jamie said. "We can't kill all of them."

"Why not? If you kill one person, what's a few more?"

I had to do something. I looked frantically up and down the moldy hallway for some sort of weapon. The only thing was a weathered piece of beam that had fallen from the ceiling.

It was about the length of a baseball bat and twice as thick. I picked it up. I had to carry it with both hands, it was so heavy.

"Please," Ferris said, trying again. "I'm sorry Barley treated you so poorly, but there is no reason to kill us. I have already told you, the manor is yours."

"It's too late," Lester said, and leveled the gun at Ferris once more.

I took a breath and ran into the room with my wooden beam out in front of me like a saber. "Freeze! Police!"

Lester dropped his gun and held up his hands.

I scanned the room, and Isla wrenched her body away from Jamie. She grabbed Seth's hand and pulled him behind me.

"Let me see your hands," I said in my best cop voice.

The brothers held up their hands.

"Wait, stop! She's not the police!" Jamie cried. "She's that food delivery girl."

"I'm a florist," I snapped. "I was just delivering the food as a favor to my friend. How many times do I have to tell you that?"

"Everyone has a side hustle," Jamie said.

Lester scooped up the gun, and my heart sank.

"Get out, Isla!" I shouted.

"But . . ."

"Now," I said, in my fiercest big-sister voice.

My sister took Seth by the hand and ran with him out of the room. I heard their steps pound down the stairs. "You guys need to give up. Chief Inspector Craig and his constables are on their way here. They know you set fire to the

Mourning Star, and they will know you killed Barley just as soon as my sister tells them."

"I don't think so," Lester said. He turned around and shot Ferris in the shoulder. The man fell.

I screamed and threw my piece of wood at him, but the brothers were standing so close together, I hit Jamie instead. He fell to the ground, holding his leg. I ran around them to Ferris. He moaned and rolled onto his side.

Lester didn't even look at his brother. "Get up!"

I didn't move.

"I said get up." Lester's voice was cold.

I stood slowly. Ferris's blood was on my hands. I felt like Lady Macbeth and remembered how Kenda had compared the brothers to Macbeth. They certainly were the stars of this tragedy playing out around me.

"Ferris needs help or he will bleed out and die," I said.

"That's what we want to happen," Lester said.

"Maybe you. Not me."

"Les." Jamie struggled to his feet. "Everything is screwed up. Let's go. Let's leave."

"Leave the manor?" Lester asked. "Are you insane?"

"No, brother," Jamie said quietly. "You are. You're the one who picked up that fiddle string and killed Barley. If you hadn't done that, we would have found another way to get the manor back. We have no hope of that now. That's your fault, brother. All we can do now is run away."

"How can you say that? I'm the one that really cared about our promise to Mom. I was the one who was willing to go as far as it took to get the manor back. Not you. Me."

"Mom wouldn't have wanted this," Jamie said. "She wouldn't want you to kill anyone."

"I did what had to be done. He had to pay for what he did."

"But you cost us everything," Jamie said.

Lester held his gun up and pointed it at his own brother. "You would turn on me too?"

Jamie picked up the piece of wood I'd had and knocked the gun out of his brother's hand. "Don't make me have to stop you, brother."

"You can't stop me," Lester said. "No one can." He then screamed in rage, turned toward me, and ran. Instinct made me jump out of the way, opening a path through the open French doors and out onto the widow's walk. Lester flew past me out the door. He tried to stop, but it was too late. I watched in horror as his legs pedaled in the air, touching nothing as he plummeted to the ground.

I stared three stories down. Chief Inspector Craig stood next to Lester MacNish's broken body below.

Epilogue

A week later, I hosted a garden party at Duncreigan. The garden was back in its full glory. After the rose took hold of the stone again, it had taken a few days, but the garden had come back little by little. What I had learned from my experience with Carver Finley was that hiding the garden from others put it at more harm. If I let others see it, they would not fear it.

I had invited everyone I could think of from the village. My friends Presha, Raj, and Cally were there, as were the old men from the oil barrels and even Popeye and his cronies from the pub and Maggie and her friends from the tea shop.

My sister and Seth stood with my parents, and the four of them laughed and talked together like they were all old friends. Just as Isla and I had come to terms with our parents' choices when they were young, they had to respect our choices as adults too. I hoped that would remain true when I introduced Chief Inspector Neil Craig to them later, not as a police officer but as my boyfriend.

I strolled through the garden, bending down every few steps to inhale the sweet fragrance of the flowers and touch the waxy leaves and soft petals of the plants. The garden was back, truly back. I'd saved it, but by saving it I had made it different, more open. No longer would it be under lock and key. I had even invited Carver to the party, and he stood on crutches speaking with Raj as the pair of them studied the menhir. I couldn't say I completely trusted the historian, but he was right, the stone deserved to be studied. What it held should not be secret.

Hamish stood a few feet away, watching them carefully and with suspicion. Duncan perched on his shoulder and was on high alert because Ivanhoe was prancing around the garden enjoying having all the people there. He, of course, thought the villagers had come to Duncreigan to admire him, not the garden, and was currently allowing Maggie to scratch his belly while he rolled in the grass.

Hamish was the only one who wasn't thrilled with the idea of making the garden open to the public, but as I'd told him, in the list of rules Uncle Ian had left me, he'd never said the garden should be kept secret. I believed that meant it was the decision of the Keeper—me—whether to share the garden or not, and I wanted to share it.

A large figure came through the garden door and pushed his way through the ivy. It was Chief Inspector Craig, holding a full plate.

I walked over to him. "You brought cookies." I grinned.

"My mother raised me well and told me to never go to a garden party without a tray of sweets. It's simply not done."

His straight white teeth flashed behind his dark beard. "They are chocolate chip, by the way. I thought I would pay homage to my American hostess."

"That was very thoughtful of you. I love chocolate chip. Have you been to a lot of garden parties in your day, Chief Inspector?" I asked.

"A few. I'm Scottish, you know."

"I do know very well."

He glanced around the garden. "You have a nice turnout. Is there anyone from the village that you didn't invite?"

I pretended I had to think about this for a minute. "Not that I know of."

"And you are okay with all these people being in your garden?" He studied my face.

I nodded. "I think it's the right thing to do. It feels right, in any case, and when dealing with the garden, I have learned that going with my gut has always been the best choice."

He nodded. "I see Carver Finley is here." He frowned. Craig wasn't a fan of Carver's after learning what Carver had done to my garden and all the turmoil it had caused me.

"I've chosen to forgive but not forget," I said, and took the cookies from his hands. They smelled just like home, and for the briefest moment I had a pang of homesickness for Tennessee. I glanced around, and the homesickness subsided. This was my home now.

I walked the plate over to the dessert table and set the cookies next to a tray of American brownies Isla had made. Craig followed me.

"You're a wise woman," he said. He was so close to me that I felt his breath on my neck.

"Speaking of forgiving, how is Jamie MacNish?" I asked. After Lester fell to his death from the widow's walk at Winthrope Manor, Jamie had crumbled to the ground in tears. It had been painful to watch. "He has been so heartbroken over Lester's death."

"He's not as heartbroken as he was right after. Now he's blaming his dead brother for everything he can think of, including the murder and the idea to kidnap Ferris Brown. I have no doubt he would also blame Lester for stealing his lunch money when they were lads in school if we would give him the opportunity. Since Lester is gone, he can't refute the murder or anything else his brother says."

"Jamie said Lester killed Barley. Lester never refuted that," I said. "Not did Lester for a moment put that blame on Jamie. I tend to believe Jamie on that point."

Craig nodded. "Even so, Jamie will still be in prison for a long while. He's charged with being an accomplice to murder, kidnapping, threatening bodily harm, and whatever else the prosecutor can think of adding to his docket."

I shivered. "What they did was horrible, but I can sort of understand why they went mad."

"What do you mean?" He cocked his head, reminding me of Duncan the squirrel when he did that, which reminded me to look for the squirrel to make sure Ivanhoe wasn't tormenting him during the party.

"Barley stole their dream. There are too many people in this world without a driving dream. And the brothers wanted that manor house so badly. It was their mother's dying wish that they have it, restore it, and bring her family name back to its former glory. How could they not try to get it back? They were so close to having it, too, before Barley made their record company wait and Ferris bought the manor out from under them."

"They took it too far," Craig said in a low voice.

I nodded. "I know, and I'm not excusing them for what they did. There had to have been a better way to get what they wanted. I'm only saying I can understand it a little. At least I can understand how they must have felt. It doesn't mean what they did was right or should have ever even been on the table as an option."

"There is always another option over murder," Craig said.

I nodded. "And Kenda? What will happen to her? I know she ran from the village as soon as you released her."

He nodded. "I think she will land on her feet. I tried to call her a couple days ago to follow up on what she knew about the MacNish brothers. I got her new agent instead. It took some time for the agent to finally agree to let me speak to her."

"She's going to be a big star," I said.

"Let's hope a different kind of star than Barley."

"Let's hope," I agreed. "What will happen to Winthrope Manor now? A rumor going around the village is that Ferris no longer wants it."

Craig frowned. "From what I hear, Ferris has lost his taste for restoring it. He's considering donating it to the

National Trust. It remains to be seen if he will actually go through with that."

"Fiona! Fiona!" My mother called from across the garden. "Come over here. Your father and I want a family picture with our girls."

I smiled. "Can you take the photo?" I asked Craig.

He waved his mobile phone at me. "I'm armed and ready."

My parents and sister stood in front of a bed of colorful mums in front of the willow tree.

"Squeeze together," Craig said as he was about to take the shot. "Say *Duncreigan*!"

We laughed, said *Duncreigan* in unison, and just as Craig took the picture, the fox stepped into the frame.

Acknowledgments

Special thanks to all my dear readers who have traveled with me on this fictional journey to magical Scotland for the Magic Garden series. Because of you, the series has been able to continue. I hope to share more stories about Fiona and her friends in Bellewick with you in the future.

As always, thanks to my amazing agent Nicole Resciniti, who reads all my books, guides my career, and when the going gets really tough sends me cupcakes to keep me on track. I don't know what I would do without you, Nic.

Thanks too to Matt Martz, Sandra Harding, and the entire team at Crooked Lane Books. Thank you for letting me write a different take on the magical cozies through your publishing house and for creating beautiful books.

Love to my family, Andy, Nicole, Isabella, Andrew, and our two sweet boys. And to David, who feeds me while I'm on deadline and listens to every crazy plot line that bounces into my head. I could not do this without your love and support. Also thanks to my two feline editors, Cheeps and Tummy. My life and my social media would not be the same without you.

Finally, thank you to my father in heaven for gardens, including flowers, bees, and birds that live in them. And thank you for the foxes too.